Newpoint Publishing
Never Say Boring Again

Peter Burley MA, DPhil (born 1947 in Leeds) is a poet and
dramatist whose most recent play, *The Eden Tapes*, has just
completed a successful run at the Grange Theatre in
Oxfordshire. Educated at Jesus College, Oxford, where he read
psychology, he is currently a lecturer in psychology, and also an
Honourary Research Fellow at University College, London. He
is married with four children.

NEVER SAY BORING AGAIN

PETER BURLEY

THE NEWPOINT PUBLISHING COMPANY LIMITED, LONDON

NEVER SAY BORING AGAIN
ISBN: 0 86263 315 X

The Newpoint Publishing Company Limited, Newpoint
House, St James Lane, London N10 3DF

A Reed International Company

On behalf of:
Stoy Hayward, 8 Baker Street, London W1M 1DA

Copyright by Peter Burley © 1990

Typeset by ATSS Ltd, Stowmarket, Suffolk IP14 1RQ
Printed in Denmark by: Nørhaven A/S, Viborg

British Libray Cataloguing in Publication Data
Burley, Peter 1947-
    Never say boring again
    I. Title
    823.914 [F]

ISBN 0-86263-315-X

CONTENTS

1
THE OFFICE

It had been a long hard morning but a successful one. My client had stopped shuffling in his chair and was now relaxed for the first time in three and a half hours.

'How about some lunch, Edward?' he said.

'No thanks, Jim, I've got to call back at Stoy's before my next appointment at the hotel,' I said, though my stomach was groaning in disbelief at my refusal.

'Which hotel is that?' he asked.

'The Royal Stuart.'

'Oh yes, the posh place. Very different to being here I imagine, we're not exactly in that league.'

'Not yet!'

'One day.' He started to shuffle again. 'I know we can grow. It's funny, though, I didn't imagine it could take the direction we've been discussing. I don't know why I hadn't thought along those lines before. You're sure you wouldn't like something to eat?'

'No, I'd better be getting back to Baker Street, thanks all the same.'

'I'd avoid going back through the City if I were you,' he said, 'the traffic was hell there this morning.'

The City and hell were somehow interchangeable.

'I'll just go and round up those papers you asked for,' said he: 'Oh bloody hell! Will you look at that!' He motioned with his head toward the window. 'Those damn kids have got in again and are playing football in the car park — hey you lot!'

He ran out intent on putting the budding Maradonas to

the sword. Jim Wallace wasn't just a man who worried, he was a genetic panicker. His habitual panic reaction to minor irritations was something I could never understand — he couldn't help overreacting first and thinking afterwards. Jim Wallace had spent the best part of two years churning out products costed on old methods and basing jobs on old prices. He wasn't covering the cost of new equipment and was losing money hand over fist. I had managed to establish a good personal relationship with him. Without a strong personal footing, doing a good job technically was not sufficient to retain clients. I was grateful for this strong human element to my profession, but, nevertheless, I was equally thankful that I didn't have to work day in and day out for an employer who was forever letting his thyroid run amok. Panic when confronted with a problem was not a quality over-valued in my line of business.

I got up and moved to the window and looked out on the greying day. The brittle trees in the enclosed gardens across the street stood out against the sky as though sketched by charcoal sticks. They seemed unwilling to survive another winter. I knew they would. They reminded me of the remnant landscapes of war. I had fought a war and won, and could meet the coming seasons the stronger for the fight. Unlike Dai. Poor Dai.

The boys in the car park were behaving coolly under interrogation, they were arguing back, swapping rights and wrongs. How do boys playing in a car park end up like the Kingston brothers, kicking the life out of other men instead of footballs?

Jim Wallace returned flushed, but not with victory. He was a man who needed to perceive regularity and order, but sensed only chaos.

'Those bloody kids get under my skin; it's not the football that they enjoy, it's playing football where they're not supposed to — that's their enjoyment! I bet they also shoplift. I expect they'll bloody well be locked up in time.'

I had become an accountant, a possibility that four years ago was both remote and unexpected, given the kind of person I then considered myself to be. I was an English graduate; words were my domain.

On the way back to the office I tried not to think about Dai and the waste, but he always had a way of crashing through barriers both physical and mental. I recalled my first encounter with him, at the freshers' drinks party. The new intake stood holding their glasses as sedately as Edinburgh spinsters after a funeral but without their composure. Students and staff stood about in clusters trying to look desperately interested in the meaningless flow of polite conversation when the door of the Common Room crashed violently against the wall and Dai charged in like a Welsh bull.

'Right! What's the record for the most glasses of sherry drunk at one of these do's?!' he boomed.

His entrance was received with the same enthusiasm Rome would have shown to a Visigoth chieftain. The President of the Junior Common Room advanced towards him in the manner of a Senator come to discuss terms of surrender.

'How do you do. Ross McGregor, President of the JCR.' His hand shot out like a spear-thrust.

'Hello Bach! Dai Bunch. What's the record?'

'You appear to have had more than enough to drink already,' said McGregor.

'In my case appearances are contraceptive — what's the record?'

'Thirty eight,' shouted someone.

'Righto,' said Dai, turning on the nearest waiter and claiming a tray of twenty amontillados. He did the same with another two trays and sat down with sixty glasses in front of him. It was schoolboy exhibitionism at its worst. A group gathered round and Dai began downing them with the precision of a robotic arm on an assembly line.

'Thirty six! Thirty seven! Thirty eight! — Thirty nine!' A cheer went up but Dai continued his piston-motion without acknowledgement.

'Fifty!' He stood up.

'A pause for relief, finish the rest when I get back.' He then staggered a few steps, was sick all over the Junior Dean, and collapsed to the floor in a coma.

'Stupid berk,' said McGregor, 'what's his room number? We'd better carry him up there to sleep it off.'

'It would make more sense to get him to hospital,' I said. 'He's obviously in a bad way.'

'Yes, he might choke in his sleep,' said someone else. The Junior Dean appeared none too displeased at the prospect.

Dai was bundled into the back of McGregor's car and I accompanied them to the casualty department. While driver and front-seat passenger exchanged niceties, Dai let out loud intermittent grunts and breathy gasps. The volume of some of his emissions startled me, but never having heard a death-rattle I interpreted them as reassuring signs of life.

'At least he's still breathing,' I said.

'Heaven knows what else he'd had before all that sherry,' answered McGregor. 'My only hope is that he isn't sick over the back seat of my car.'

This was the modern Britain where concerns for the welfare of a fuel-injected eighteenth birthday present took precedence over concerns for the welfare of comatose Welshmen. Our charge was admitted to casualty and pumped, or whatever it is they do to arrest the process of death by dry sack.

'There's a friend come to see you,' said the nurse when I called the following day.

Dai looked at me, puzzled, and then suddenly sat bolt upright shouting at the top of his voice. 'Amnesia! I knew it! I knew when I woke I was part brain-dead.'

'What's the matter?' said the nurse, alarmed at the unexpected violence of his outburst. It was fortunate there were no cardiac cases in his ward.

'What's the matter?! What's the matter?! My best friend comes to see me and I don't even recognise him, and you ask me what's the matter! God give me back my past — my glorious past!'

'Stop shouting,' she said. 'I'll fetch matron.'

Off she scurried. Dai looked me up and down for a moment and then extended his hand, his tone quite changed.

'Hello,' he said calmly, 'I'm Dai Bunch.'

'Edward Cartwright.'

'Have we met before?'

'I brought you here last night, though I don't suppose you remember.'

'No, I don't suppose I do.'

'So you see, you haven't got amnesia.'

'I know that, man, but don't tell the matron. I want to see how long they'll keep me in. Besides, the first thing I saw through the glimmering mists when I came round was the fecund outline of that fabulous little nurse. I thought I was in Mahomet's heaven and about to receive my first houri. Another day here and I'll be taking her pulse.'

'You're Welsh, aren't you?'

'As leek soup, boyo.'

'Bunch, it doesn't sound like a Welsh name.'

'Well let's say I'm leek soup with a lot of paprika thrown in.'

'I don't follow.'

'My father is Hungarian, got out in '56. Bunch is a shortened version of our Hungarian name which is unpronounceable even for Hungarians.'

'Dai on the other hand — '

'Born and bred in South Wales, Bargoed.'

I could see the nurse at the far end of the ward with the matron. The nurse looked worried, the matron merely annoyed.

'What are you reading?' Dai asked.

'English.'

'Oh Lord, bloody useless. As long as you can speak it that's enough, reading it will never make you rich.'

'I'm not reading it to make me rich, at least not in the sense you mean.'

'Idealist are we?'

'It's not my favourite word. What are you reading?'

'Economics and pragmatics. You know what my favourite word is?'

'What?'

'Mammonism.'

The matron and the nurse arrived, and took up positions on either side of the bed.

'Well, Mr Bunch, what seems to be the problem?'

'Oh matron,' said Dai in a plaintive voice, his pathetic eyes gazing at the pretty young nurse. 'I've lost my memory, it's terrible.'

'I'm surprised you haven't lost your liver as well,' replied the matron. 'You should be ashamed of yourself.'

'Everything is a blur,' he went on, 'a terrible sand storm, the grains of all past time stinging my eyes and blinding me to myself. I have vague memories of a father — '

'Most people have,' said the matron.

'A sick father — who will look after the estates?' he glanced at the nurse. 'I must get back to Dada and the estates!' he shouted.

'Stop this nonsense at once,' said the matron sternly. 'Are you a friend of this — ' she hesitated, 'patient?'

'Known him all his life,' I replied. 'The present one anyway.'

'Well I think you'd better go now,' she replied, and turned to Dai.

'The doctor will look at you on his round. In the meantime stay quiet and no more nonsense.'

The matron went off. The nurse made to follow her but Dai grabbed her hand.

'Nurse, please stay with me a while. I'm frightened.'

'I've got to — '

'Please,' Dai went on, 'just for a moment, it's like I'm a child again, born all over, it's scary — please, hold my hand, just till I feel I can close my eyes and sleep without fear.'

He was laying it on with a trowel and resembled the Lady of the Camelias on her death bed. He opened one eye and saw me watching him.

'The matron told you to go,' he said.

I got part way to the door and he called out.

'Oh and Bach, thanks for last night.'

'Don't mention it,' I said.

'Last night?' queried the nurse.

Dai looked at her sheepishly.

'It's all starting to come back — you see how good you are for me?'

———————

Thinking about Dai on the way back in the car was like driving in the company of a ghost. I had unwittingly neglected Jim's advice and found myself in the City and going nowhere, which only reinforced the feeling, like a lead sinker dropping into the pit of the stomach. I recalled a time in Paris working from one of our associated offices where, as part of a small team, I was doing an audit for a French company. It was the first opportunity I'd had to be constantly in Caroline's company. And Caroline and Paris were a pretty good combination. A good deal better than the City of London without her anyway. Not that it was easy to associate the City with anything human. A mechanical, metal monstrosity had been transplanted in the place of a living human heart that had pulsed for centuries. The streets had become no more than hollow valves.

I took a detour back to the West End, round Parliament Square, alongside St James Park, past Buckingham Palace to Hyde Park Corner and up Park Lane. It had been a favourite route ever since my first few weeks in the office, when I had been give the fairly mundane task of collecting signatures on a legal document and was ferried around the West End in the back of a taxi. That had been a glorious autumn day, the leaves crisp and golden, spacious avenues bright and clear. Something had changed since then to now make me appreciate the West End even more. But even then I had felt that this area of London matched, at least, anything Paris had to offer — Caroline or no Caroline.

The commissionaire handed me a parcel as I breezed past. 'Wish I could start work at 2.30,' he said, knowing as well as I that he had first wished me "Good morning" at 8.00 when I had come in to prepare for my meeting with Jim.

The office was busier now than it had been then. Still feeling fairly nostalgic after my drive, I remembered how I had once noticed the whirr of the air conditioning each time I entered the building. Someone was watering the tropical plants as I left the lift. I remembered a heated discussion we had had in my first few weeks as to whether they were real or not.

After leaving the lift instead of turning left to the office I shared with Tom and Caroline, two of the other managers in the group, I headed right towards the audit room. As I entered I picked up the usual murmur of conversation: a forecast on a spread-sheet was being set up on the micro in the corner, while a first-year examined with wonder, and no small degree of ridicule, the dusty contents of two cardboard boxes which he and a second-year had been given in order to write up a set of accounts. The second-year student evidently didn't find the boxes quite so amusing, commenting how difficult the job had been last year. I remembered too. I handed her the package I had been given downstairs.

'The bank statements you asked for, I expect.'

'Oh yes,' said Louise. 'I was just about to go and pick them up. But then my time is so much more precious than yours, and anyway Charles said that he'd send a boy up with them.'

I smiled sarcastically. 'By next Friday all finished, OK?'

'We'll try,' Louise said.

I headed back to my office.

Caroline was perched on the corner of her desk, one foot touching the floor, the other swinging playfully as she listened to Bernard Wright, one of the partners in Insolvency. Bernard was a walking encyclopaedia of insolvency law and an historian into the bargain; the Gibbon of insolvency practitioners, though so grandiose a comparison would not, perhaps, have pleased him. On his own admission, being called a 'real market trader' was the highest compliment anyone could pay him. He was strident, entertaining and left one in no doubt as to the exact nature of his feelings. Caroline motioned me in without speaking, Bernard was in full flow.

'Bankrupt is from the Latin — bancus: the tradesman's counter or table, and ruptus: broken — ie broken trade.'

'Well, fancy,' said Caroline.

'If we still had the Law of Twelve Tables there'd be fewer ranting creditors.'

'The Law of Twelve Tables?' I said, intrigued.

'Under this natty little Roman number, creditors could cut a debtor's body into pieces — depending on the amount of the individual's debts, of course.'

'Of course,' I said.

'Usually, though, they got the softer option.'

'What was that?' asked Caroline.

'Lashings, chains, hard labour, wife and kids sold into foreign slavery, that sort of thing. Pretty light considering that other activities merited being hurled from the Tarpeian rock.'

'What other activities?' I asked.

'Talking to Carthaginians, or talking to Vestal Virgins with intent, that sort of thing.'

'Well, I'll be hanged,' I said.

'Funny you should say that, do you know the last person to be hanged in England as a fraudulent debtor was as late as 1761.'

'I bet you can't tell me his name.'

'John Perrott — he concealed part of his effects.'

'Were you involved in that case, Bernard?'

'No, at the time I was compiling a report on tax avoidance schemes for a group of tea traders in Boston. Very successful it was too.' He turned to Caroline. 'Anyway, back to the matter in hand.'

'Shall I go?' I said.

'No, I'm off in a minute,' said Bernard. 'All I wanted to say, Caroline, is if this youngster in your group is thinking about coming into insolvency work, she's got to be able to take the rough with the smooth. You have got to be a bit hard-nosed at times, though I find the older I get the more thin-skinned I become.'

'I can't believe that of you, Bernard.'

'No, I'm being serious now, Edward. Don't forget we are dealing with people too, it's not just the law, but whereas you lot in General Practice have become used to seeing people on the up, we have to deal with people in a trough and it's sometimes very sad. Wives and family often show their true colours when a bankruptcy order is made and it isn't always pretty. When people lose money there's plenty of emotion. When you give unpalatable advice you have to be prepared to be shouted at, or even, if you find evidence of criminal activity, threatened.'

'How often is that?'

'It happens, but most of the time it's lack of business acumen that causes people to go bankrupt. Very often they're relieved to see Stoy Hayward because once we're there they can't be harassed any more by creditors.'

'Well I think this girl can handle it,' said Caroline.

It was generally known in the firm that lack of enthusiasm was a cardinal sin, but it was reinforcing to see an old hand like Bernard still retaining the same mental excitement and pride in his work, the will to be the best. I couldn't countenance a life where one rolled out of an office at 5.30 unstimulated, treating it as a mechanical job, working because it was work, not because it was a challenge. He obviously enjoyed himself as well. That was important to me. I knew I had made the right choice when I first learned of a three-point strategic plan which was written down and passed to all partners, a sort of Stoy's Holy Writ. The first two points, offering a first-class service to clients and being in business to make money, one might expect to be included in any firm's strategy, but the third: to have fun, to enjoy it and let the clients see you are enjoying it was a Stoy Hayward special. For me, business could not have been business without it.

When Bernard left Caroline shut the door. Tom wasn't at his desk, and although almost all the inside walls of the office were made of glass, the venetian blinds had been pulled so, most unusually, we were cut off from the hurly-burly outside.

'Have you had lunch?' she asked.

'No, I'll have to skip lunch, I got held up in the traffic and I'm going out on a job this afternoon.'

'We've made a bit of a mess of everything, haven't we?'

'Not everything. Some things we got right.'

We hadn't been alone together for some time and I could see she was trying to draw me out, choosing her own ground.

'How are things?'

'OK, everything's fine except...' I stopped. I wasn't going to be rail-roaded.

'Except what?'

I was not going to be drawn, I would choose my own time. Whatever the exception was I knew articulating it then would only have turned it into a half truth. She had to realise that I had moved on. My battle with the Kingston brothers had been a kind of sleep and I had become acclimatised to a land of dreams. Like Peter Pan I had lost a shadow; it had been torn off and was wandering where only shapes and shadows wander, looking for me.

'Stephen has asked me to marry him.'

'Oh,' I said.

She slid off the desk and moved to the wall, her arms slightly spread, with her palms pressed flat against it. She appeared to be bracing herself for some revelation, positioned to resist some mighty force that would fell her.

'Is that all?' she said.

'Is what all?'

'Just Oh?'

Stephen Fanshaw was a lawyer. He reminded me of Ross McGregor, everything he did was right. Caroline first met him under cross-examination. She had worked for a time in our legal support department and they had met in court. Fanshaw had pursued her ever since. I started to laugh.

'What's funny?'

'Oh, it just occurred to me that all men should be allowed the privilege of seeing how well a possible future wife stands up under a thorough cross-examination.'

'Am I a future wife?'

'That depends on whether you said yes, doesn't it?'

She then moved from the wall. She cupped her hands to my face and placed her mouth lightly, uncertainly, on mine.

At that moment Danny Liebowitz, one of our new recruits, knocked and entered almost at the same time.

'Blimey!' he said. 'Is this x-certificate or can a trainee watch?'

I liked Danny, nothing ever threw him off balance.

'I've suddenly remembered a very sick grandmother that I should have called last April,' he said. 'If she hasn't passed over to the other side I'll be back. You'll know it's me because of the very loud knock.'

Danny disappeared.

'When can we talk?' she said.

'How about tonight?'

'Where?'

'I'll be at the Royal Stuart Hotel till about seven o'clock.

I could meet you in the cocktail lounge after that.'

'Edward, I've changed too, you know. Let's not hold anything back tonight, let's talk straight leaving nothing out.'

'I've never not talked straight,' I said.

———

My next encounter with the ebullient Dai Bunch occurred a week after the hospital visit. I was sitting contentedly in my rooms in college, basking in the knowledge that I had somehow arrived, when the door swung open — Dai never knocked. He was with the pretty nurse.

'Salutations, Bach — you remember Celia?'

Celia was to remain Dai's faithful attendant and constant companion throughout our university years, though the word companion, in the sense that it implies presence, is misplaced. For three years she was at the wrong end of rendezvous where the other person didn't show; standing for hours in the rain, or drinking coffee alone in railway buffets waiting for the promised weekend away that never came. She would spend whole afternoons dressing to the nines in anticipation of the fairy-tale venue that had been looked forward to for weeks which, at the eleventh hour, would be changed to a night at the dog track or some seedy pub where the beer was always, reputedly, 'the best pint in town'. Wherever they went she was, through no fault of her own, always overdressed and continually being asked to account for it. She was to accept it all with a stoicism that only those who work with the dying can attain, yet there was an appropriateness in the bonding of this tenacious little nurse and her wayward Welsh-Hungarian.

'You know, Bach,' he said to me once, 'I've decided that I do love her. I'll marry her one day, she's passed the test.'

'She's been sorely tried, that's for sure,' I said.

'You see, what she realises, something the others don't...'

'What others?'

'Don't be cheeky, I'm bordering on a romantic revelation which happens rarely and I want to enjoy it while it lasts.

What she realises is that I am the kind of person who will never change. When I was born that was the complete package, it wasn't going to get any better or any worse.'

'The last bit makes me feel better.'

'You probably think I treat her a bit shabbily?'

'There's nothing probable about it, it's an absolute fact. How and why she puts up with you is beyond me.'

'I'll tell you why, I'm lovable, that's why. I've always been lovable, as a child I could be as naughty as I liked and would get away with it because a goodly dollop of lovableness was in my chromosomes. People may not approve of me but they love me. The mystery is, where does it come from? Who knows? You either have it or you don't. Take McGregor for example, he's respected, accomplished, presentable and even likeable every alternate 29 February, but he isn't lovable and it's a certainty he never was. He is as much a victim of circumstance as I am.'

'The only victim of circumstance is Celia, she'd be better off with McGregor.'

'Don't think he wouldn't like to try, I've seen him turning on his Mr Suave act when Celia's about, but you know why he doesn't really give it a go?'

'Go on, surprise me.'

'Because gnawing away at his ego is the possibility that he may not succeed, and to lose out to a disgusting reprobate like myself would be, for him, intolerable. If I were Harrison Ford or Richard Gere he'd give it a go without a second thought.'

'Then you're quite safe.'

'That's where us borderline-repulsive, lesser physical specimens have the advantage — once we find a woman we tend to hold on to her because others think there must be something wrong with her if she's going out with a Dai Bunch and also, to be knocked back on account of a Dai Bunch isn't worth the risk to their pride.'

'You're starting to sound like a cross between Jane Austen and Marjorie Proops.'

'You see, what Celia understands is that basically I'm dependable.'

'What!'

'Personality-wise, I mean she can rely on me to be me, I'm not going to confound her by showing some unexpected side of my character. She doesn't have to understand any more than she already knows and that makes her secure. What is more, she understands that when I disappoint her, or let her down, it is because I have been distracted, that I don't mean to let people down. She trusts my motives which are never malevolent.'

'I'm sure from their own point of view Genghis Khan and Vlad the Impaler were very well-intentioned, but that didn't exactly make them popular.'

'You see how fickle is the order of the universe? For once I try to be profound instead of flippant, and all I am met with is flippancy.'

'If I thought I could save Celia from yet another night at the greyhounds I'd ask her out myself.'

'But you won't.'

'Why not?'

'Because I'm lovable, and because you know I'm right when I say she understands me and I may marry her.'

'Ah, all of a sudden it's "may marry her", a few moments ago you were definitely going to — why the change?'

'Celia is pretty — right?'

'Yes.'

'Good-natured?'

'Yes.'

'Easy to live with?'

'Yes.'

'But *you* wouldn't, would you?'

'What?'

'Live with her.'

He was right, but I made no answer.

'You wouldn't live with her,' he continued, 'because lurking somewhere, unshaped, in that murky psyche of yours is the ill-defined form of some archetypal woman, your own private goddess who will one day descend from Olympus just for you, Edward Cartwright.'

'You're mad,' I said. 'Even I know there are no goddesses; they disappeared with the arrival of mortgage interest rates and the non-stick frying pan.'

'Cynicism worthy of Diogenes. But there are some left who are purchasable through the acquisition of wealth and power, all of which I am resolved to get.'

'Now that's what I call cynicism. Courtesans are bought, goddesses aren't, if you can buy them they don't qualify as goddesses in my book.'

'That is because your goddesses come from reading Milton, whereas my goddesses come from reading the *Financial Times*.'

'So do I.'

'Do you? You surprise me.'

'Well, on Saturdays. It's good on reviewing books no one can afford to buy. Besides, I've always been vaguely interested in business. I could be quite commercially-minded if I chose to be.'

'But Yeats, Dickens — wouldn't they be shocked?'

'You forget that underlying everything else he did Shakespeare was a bloody good businessman, he was entrepreneurial in every sense of the word.'

'But you're not going to get any closer to business than the arts pages of the FT, are you?'

'No, I'm going to try and get a First and an academic post.'

So that was it. Dai was going to hold out till he became rich enough to buy himself a goddess, Celia was going to hold out for the prospect of becoming Mrs Dai Bunch, and I was going to hold on to the hope of getting a First and a university post.

2

CAREERS IN FINANCE

A few months before finals I was working late one night in the college reading room. It was three in the morning and the wind and rain were rattling the leaded windows with a ferocity that made it difficult for me to concentrate. I stopped note-taking and stared at the window. All I could see was the image of my face and the reading lamp on my table. There I was, nearing the culmination of three years working for a First and an academic career when, without any ready explanation, I looked into the dark and knew that it was not for me. It was a sudden, intuitive knowledge and it startled me.

My love of literature wasn't going to go away through not staying in a university. Whether I got a First or not I was going to strike out for change, but change to what? There was only one other person in the reading room, it was McGregor.

'Ross, what are you going to do when you leave?'

'Chartered accountancy,' he said, 'I've already applied for interviews with most of the big six.'

'The big what?'

'The big six. There are small, medium and large-size firms, the big six are the largest firms in the country.'

'Oh,' I said, and returned to my notes.

Over the next couple of weeks I gave the new problem of 'what to do' as much attention as my studies would allow. I was being truthful when I surprised Dai by admitting that I had an interest in business, it seemed the most obvious course now I had abandoned all thoughts of a

lectureship. I actually for the first time in my life felt a
twinge of excitement at the thought of earning good money.
In academia I could work all my life to get to the top of
the tree, a professorship, and still only be on a modest
salary. It seemed unfair, but I wasn't going to wait a lifetime
to earn what I could get in business after only a few years.
But what kind of business? Was I just to apply to a number
of companies and wait till one offered me a job?

What if I didn't like the company or the work when I got
there? What then — apply to another company and start
all over again? It was too much of a trial and error system,
I wanted more direction than that. Although McGregor
going into accountancy was almost enough to put me off
from the start, the more I looked into it the more appeal
it seemed to have. At the time it looked like a rational
starting point for someone, like myself, who was uncom-
mitted to anything in particular. If I had this ill-defined
commercial attitude, why not get a professional qualification
which would allow me to move into industry at a time when
my objectives were clearer. Besides which, it seemed a safe,
high-salaried career even if I didn't hit the top. I knew
several people from college who had gone into accountancy
and, unlike McGregor, hadn't been weaned on starch. We
met up for a drink in London occasionally, next time I
would sound them out. In the meantime I would try to find
out as much as I could from other sources.

The careers officer at the university swamped me with a
list of about thirty companies. I collected as many of the
firms' brochures as I could lay my hands on, and although
they were more informative, they provided no definite basis
for choice. There were differences between them, variations
of the image they were packaging, but all seemed to push
pretty much the same points: good training, interesting
clients and so on. Sure, everyone would want a quality
training, but how to distinguish when every brochure was
telling you they had excellent training facilities? They were
not, after all, going to present an eye-catching, glossy layout
saying 'our training facilities are the pits.'

'You're what?!' Dai said, giving full expression to the
familiar Bunch smirk.

'I'm thinking of going into accountancy' I said.

'You can't be serious?'

'You're the one has difficulty with that,' I retorted, 'and yes, I am very serious.'

'But what about Shakespeare, Milton and the boys, your academic career?'

'I've changed my mind.'

'Why?'

'Well, for a start I've decided that earning a good salary for the rest of my life isn't a bad idea, and academic salaries are pretty pathetic given the time and energy needed to get there. Also movement is restricted and I like the idea of being able to move about.'

'I know what it is,' he said.

'What?'

'Sigmund Bunch will give you a complete analysis of ze problem,' he went on in mock psychotherapeutic tones.

'Don't bother,' I said, 'there isn't a problem.'

'You're beginning to lose confidence, doubt whether you will get your precious First. You are covering yourself in the event that you don't. Rationalisation, I think the shrinks call it.'

I laughed. If anything, I sometimes had to check my over-confidence to make sure I had not overlooked something, left out some vital detail. I instinctively liked to double check things. I had no doubts about my ability to get a First, but I knew that if I didn't, it wouldn't be because I lacked the potential to reach the top. There was a new, different world out there and I wanted to be in it; I didn't know if I would be suited to it or it to me, but I was going to give it everything I had. I didn't bother to explain any of this, Dai had an air of exaggerated truculence about him that day. There was something uncharacteristically aggressive about his tone; it was veiled but perceptible.

'I can understand your ditching the idea of becoming a don, I've always said that's a load of old cobblers, but accountancy for heaven's sake —'

'Do you know anything about it?' I said.

'A bit,' he said knowingly, but his defensiveness told me he knew very little.

'What?' I asked.

'Well I know it's mortifyingly boring for a start —'

'Yes, but apart from that penetrating insight do you know what accountancy is, what accountants actually do?'

'Of course, they add and subtract figures from nine in the morning till five thirty at night when they get up off their pin-striped backsides, pick up their regulation rolled umbrella, and go home — probably to exceedingly dull little houses wherein wait exceedingly dull little women.'

Dai that day was full of bottled-up aggression, he was trying to keep the lid on I could tell, but I had no idea as to the source. I put it down to tension at the approaching exams and tried to steer away from the subject, but Dai persisted.

'Since when has anyone consulted Monty Python for careers advice? It's the people who are in it that matter, not some stereotype knocked up to be knocked down,' I said.

'Well, I could shatter that notion at a stroke,' he said, 'you're quite right, it's people that matter, and who's the only person we know hell bent on a career in chartered accountancy? Ross McGregor. QED — accountancy attracts dullards.'

'OK, so Ross is straight-laced. But what about Toby Brock, Phil Kirkland and Adrian Walker who went down last year? They all became accountants and there's nothing dull about them. It only proves my point, stereotypes are worthless.'

An expression came over Dai's face that was alien to me. Sometimes a momentary turn of the mouth, an inclination of the eye, can suggest that the person before you, no matter how long you have known them, is not that person at all but someone unexpected.

'People matter all right,' he said. 'You can't trust 'em, but by God they're predictable.'

He was hinting, none too subtly, at something.

'Are we talking about anybody in particular?' I asked.

'Not really, but let's take the person we've just been talking about, McGregor, as a case in point. It was so predictable that Mr Upright, Mr Dull-man-McGregor would launch his summer offensive, his big push.'

'On what?'   'On Celia.'

'Ah,' I said. Things were starting to fit, or so I thought.
'That's the predictability of people.'

'And their trustworthiness?'

'He went out with Celia the other night.'

Jealousy, good old solid jealousy. Nothing to do with
accountancy. That was damned by association with McGregor.

'He bedded her of course — the other night.'

'Don't be silly,' I said. I knew Celia's commitment to Dai.

'It's a fact, she enjoyed a bit of good old rolled-brolly
rumpy-pumpy, there's no doubt about it. You think you
know people, but you can't trust 'em.'

'Are you sure?' I asked.

'There's no doubt,' he said.

I was surprised and felt sorry for him. Looking back I feel
dismay at the haste with which I assumed he was deeply
hurt. A few moments before I had warned him of the danger
of making assumptions, and I was now doing precisely that.

Dai was a consummate actor. Some people are so good at
it that standard human emotions become redundant in the
everyday world. Later on my work and the experience of
dealing with people led me to develop a nose for the
half-truth, but at that time I had no reason to doubt Dai's
feelings.

Two days later I met Celia, sad, disconsolate and decidedly
down in the mouth for one so prone to viewing everything,
however negative, with a rosy hue.

I didn't say anything about what Dai had told me.

'Oh Edward, it's awful, just awful! He just won't listen,
there's nothing I can say that will make any difference.
Can't you do something to make him listen?'

'It's difficult for me to say anything. What you do is your
business. If you want to go to bed with Ross that's up to
you, but understandably Dai's got to feel a little hurt.'

'But that's just it, I didn't, but he won't have it any
other way.

About two weeks before this black cloud fell upon the
Dai/Celia house, Dai had talked Celia into making a big
commitment. Not marriage, something far more daring,
quitting her job and coming to London with him after the
exams. She was to rely on his stout arm and dreams of

gold-inlaid streets for support. He put it to her in a moment of drunken euphoria. He hadn't any recollection the next afternoon, but by then Celia had handed in her notice.

Dai had second thoughts about moving to London with Celia in tow. He wanted freedom to respond to the pleasures of the metropolis with an almighty 'Yes Please'. Celia was an encumbrance; she was to be held in reserve. But what could he do, she had quit her job? He needed an out and would not wait. Although not apparent at the time the whole Celia/McGregor episode had been engineered by Dai as a means of escape. All the displays of wounded pride, the jealousy, the insistence that he had been betrayed when clearly he had not, was a sham. Casting doubts on her loyalty would give him the excuse to retract his offer, or so he thought; it didn't work out as he had hoped. His pretext became more insupportable as time went by and he couldn't sustain it without appearing to be a complete fool. Celia got McGregor's help and he confronted Dai telling him that his suspicions were groundless. Ross had a genuine affection for Celia and he behaved very well, but then he always did. He made as much of a show out of behaving correctly as Dai did out of behaving badly. The tempest in the teacup subsided, but it was a pointer to what was to come.

I didn't see much of anybody during my last few weeks at university. I was working all hours and enjoying the sheer quantity of ideas I was devouring. I liked setting targets and imposing a disciplined schedule happy in the knowledge that, whatever the outcome, I was going to play very hard once it was all over. Dai, however, was playing hard in the here and now, not doing an iota of work towards the exams. He was behaving as if finals were over. One lunch time I casually mentioned his show of confidence.

'I don't need to revise,' he said.

'Lucky you' I replied.

'I've already got a job.'

This surprised me, he hadn't mentioned anything to anybody about being interviewed or having been offered a job.

'Where?' I asked.

'In London, the City, my starting salary is £25,000 pa.'

'God! that's tremendous. Who are you working for? What's the job?' I was taken aback by the starting salary and wondered whether it was the result of his tendency to exaggerate, but I was wrong, it was genuine.

'Kingston & Kingston Financial Services Ltd — they're big news and getting bigger. They are the apex of a growing conglomerate — loads of subsidiary companies in all sorts of diverse areas; it's all very exciting.'

'What are you going to do?'

'Become rich, basically.'

'But doing what?'

'Well it's not specific at the moment. The company will train me in a number of their operations and set me on the road to becoming a Bonaparte in the battlefield of commerce.'

'Well congratulations, Napoleon, but if I'd been offered a job with that kind of starting salary I'd be working like crazy to get a good degree to secure it.'

'Like I said, I don't have to.'

'Surely the offer depends on you getting a good degree?'

'It doesn't depend on my getting a degree at all,' he said in a very off-hand way.

'What?! You mean — '

'It's a fact, Kingston & Kingston live in the real world of business, they don't make decisions based on some academic, ivory tower standard of who is intelligent and who is not. They base everything on the interview, or series of inter-views actually. If they think you're the kind of person they want, you're in, unconditionally. They reckon yours truly is their kind of person. Matter of fact your starting salary depends on just how much they rate you.'

'Does Celia know?'

'No, you're the first.'

'When did all this happen?'

'Some weeks ago.'

'Why weren't you shouting it from the roof-tops?'

'The company asked me not to, for a while anyway, it's part of their policy. They prefer to strictly limit graduate applications; they don't advertise.'

'How did you get on to them?'

'Well in a sense they got on to me. My tutor, old Brownlees, recommended me. That's how Kingston & Kingston operate, they have staff contacts at a number of universities who are paid a retainer — that's hush-hush by the way, the university bodies are not to know. These contacts know the kind of personal profiles the company is looking for and put forward the names of those they think will fit.'

'Sounds very clandestine. You haven't been recruited to MI6 have you?'

He gave a sardonic smile and put his finger to his lips.

'Now you understand why the exams are of no consequence to me,' he said.

'Well in one sense, yes, but for your own self-satisfaction don't you want a good degree?'

'Not really, and neither would you in my position.'

'Yes I would, I'm not doing it just to get a job, it's a personal thing with me.'

'And you're still going for accountancy?' he smirked, making it sound like a dicey polar expedition.

'Yes, the more I look into it the more I'm convinced it's what I want.'

'Why's that?'

'Well, frankly, for someone who doesn't really know what they want to do, accountancy seems a pretty good choice. I just think that business might suit me and that an accountancy qualification seems the best way to start. Also I've been down to London to see Toby Brock, Phil Kirkland and some of the others who went into it last year. They were pretty positive.'

'Had any interviews yet?'

'I've got a few coming up soon.'

'All in London?'

'Yes, the City mostly, and one in the West End.'

'What about sharing a flat if you land a job? On my salary I fancy going a bit up-market, be even cheaper to share.'

'What about Celia?' I asked. 'Would she mind?'

'Celia shouldn't be a problem,' he said with an enigmatic look.

'I'll think about it,' I said.

3
THE SECOND INTERVIEW

The summer of my final year was unmercifully hot, dry and hazy. It was a time of strawberries, muscadet and clear running streams for all but those of us locked in mortal combat with past papers and present exam anxieties. Also I missed my cricket. I was a reasonably good fast bowler and sometimes around midday, with the sun at its zenith and my brain sinking below the horizon of hope, I fancied myself coming off a long run-up, Chaucer at the crease, and sending down a succession of bouncers. In these moments of sheer mental exhaustion I started to classify poets and dramatists in terms of their batting ability. Ben Johnson was clearly a compulsive hooker of the ball and could be lured into playing rash strokes to square leg; Milton was a wristy player with a deft leg glance but a blind spot on the off-side; Oscar Wilde couldn't bat at all being a spinner who turned it both ways, but who always came to the crease immaculately dressed in blazer and cravat; Alexander Pope was good at the square cut but his hunch-back made it impossible for him to play other strokes; when he was in with Byron he hardly scored at all because his Lordship's clubbed foot meant calling a quick single was out.

My brain was saturated and all concentration impossible. I would get up, make yet another coffee, and return to the desk only to find myself selecting a rugby side made up of metaphysical poets to play the touring Victorian novelists. The exams themselves were as much a haze as the summer and passed just as quickly. Something must have sunk in other than a vague sense that Dickens would have made a useful centre three-quarter; I got my First.

From the moment I put the last full stop on the final paper to some time after the results were posted, about the only thing I recall is the sound of popping corks. I do remember, however, one or two instances where I stopped and asked 'do I really want to put myself through all this again?'

Taking accountancy exams would be a hard slog. Toby Brock told me when we met in London that it was not possible to cram at the end in order to pass: it needed hard work and at regular intervals. PEI and PEII, as the exams were called, were a great leveller he had said, and getting through university was no guarantee of success. There was also another dimension that baulked some people; accountancy students compete against every other student in the country. This didn't bother me so much, in fact the idea rather appealed, but it did concern me that most of my study would have to be done at the end of a working day, with a necessary curtailment of my social life for the best part of three years. Given the way I felt then, the rewards at the end would have to be pretty substantial to make it worthwhile. Toby, Phil Kirkland and Adrian Walker seemed to suggest they were, though Phil was having a bit of a tough time, having failed at the first attempt, and wasn't very happy about the amount of time his firm allocated for studying for the retake. The time for doubting soon ceased; it had to, for I had a job.

There are moments in any life when it seems as if the Lords of Misrule have singled you out as the victim of their cruel pranks. I had attended several interviews but the one firm I was certain would not offer me a job was Stoy Hayward. I had asked Toby and the others the question 'if you had the chance to work in a firm other than your own, which would it be?'; the name Stoy's kept cropping up. They were seen as being innovative and more aggressive commercially, so naturally I was looking forward to the interview.

My other interviews passed without incident, though on some occasions I got the impression they were more interested in my paper profile than in me personally. There were instances when the message came across, fairly heavily, that I ought to want to work for that firm because of its name. There is something dated about this attitude and it never attracted me to the firms in question. My own prospects within the firm far outweighed, as an inducement, the knowledge that a particular firm was big and its name widely known.

I was still waiting for responses to previous interviews the day I had to attend my second interview with a partner at Stoy's. Dai and Celia had taken a spacious flat off the Fulham Road and I was staying there, more on a trial basis as I wanted to see if it would work out. I valued my privacy but money was short at that time, and everything seemed to be harmonious.

Dai had already started work for Kingston & Kingston. He had scraped an honorable third in his exams and was exuding all the airs of a big-roller. He had purchased, on account, all the fashion accessories he thought were necessary in his new position as City whizz-kid. Expensive broad-chalk-striped suits, that for all their cost accentuated his girth more than his affluence; several pairs of Gucci shoes, spoiled by the loud socks he always wore, and beyond all his other spoils a new Morgan 4 x 4 in midnight blue. Good as his salary was, I couldn't work out just how he was able to afford it. Neither was Celia neglected, she was deluged with evening gowns and tight-fitting cocktail dresses, not one of which could have cost less than £500. Celia was a pretty girl but her figure inclined to what is euphemistically called 'ample', and she wasn't entirely suited to the image Dai was trying to purchase. He was attempting to turn her into some sort of replica of a sophisticated 1930s vamp, she was to become Runcorn's answer to Dietrich. When they stepped out together the overall effect was more Chicago mobster and his moll heading for the nearest speakeasy and a bucketload of cheap bootleg booze. Dai seemed now to have a lot of work-related social engagements and I could tell Celia was nervous and uncomfortable in his new social circle. She sensed that she didn't quite live up to the expensive clothes and luxurious tastes he was imposing. She was an easy prey to that most deadly of predators, the self-confident, taste-conscious, vacuously-educated, well-heeled young woman of an established social set. These lionesses were the pride's hunters and poor uncomplicated Celia was easy meat. She was put down and patronised to her face with a subtlety she was too well-meaning to recognise, and sniggered at behind her back with that crude wit which characterises those whose horizons are limited, and whose aspirations never extended beyond their sense of being one of a 'set'. If Celia didn't have the sophistication to detect all the asides, Dai certainly did and it made him irascible — not with the glittering array of self-styled luminaries with whom he was socialising but with Celia. She in her usual manner tried even harder to please, but a will and a kind heart are often poor weapons in the battle to mollify those we love; cunning more frequently proves to be the effective decider.

I woke in good time to get ready for the interview. I stepped out of the shower feeling fresh and confident and maintained the feeling all the way to number 8 Baker Street.

I arrived early at Stoy's, announced my presence and waited. The place had a light, active feel to it in comparison to a number of the previous places I had attended. I was impressed by the decor and the sense of obvious wealth that went into the layout of the place. The dress-style of some of the employees that passed in and out of the reception area seemed to be self-consciously not in the standard image of the accountant. On the one hand there were none of those corridors smelling of disinfectant that I had got used to at university. And on the other hand there was an absence of the padded leather chairs and smoking jackets that I often associated with the word 'profession'.

I was sufficiently early to realise that I would have to wait a bit and settled back to take in the feel of the place, unconsciously filling my pipe as I did so — a habit I had acquired at university when money was short and I found pipe tobacco, which wasn't taxed like cigarettes, to be better suited to my means. While drinking the coffee provided by the receptionist I had got it to that wonderfully relaxing, cool-smouldering stage known to every practitioner of the art.

'Hello, Edward? I'm James Pearson. I run Graduate Recruitment. If you'd like to come with me.' He seemed scarcely older than me.

I put the pipe in my jacket pocket and then, conscious of its untidy bulge, transferred it to my trouser pocket.

As at most of the big firms, the 'second interview' proved to be a whole day of presentations and meetings arranged for the groups of candidates. We started off with a few tests, given only to those without maths A level — unlike the practice at some of the other firms. The Director of Personnel and a Training Manager gave us presentations about the firm and the training, and preparing for the professional examinations. Two students then took us out to lunch. 'They haven't been wired, so ask them what you want,' James had said when introducing them. 'And if you're offered alcohol, it's not a trick question.'

Lunch was one of the best parts of the day. The students were disarmingly frank about how hard the work was. No sweetening of the pill here. At other firms I had sometimes felt as if I was being sold a second-hand car.

'Lunch' also included a tour of the office. As one of the students taking us round said, 'one office looks much like another' and most tours at other firms missed out the interesting bits. So we started off in the Partners' car park.

'That's the Senior Partner's Aston Martin.' There was also a Ferrari, a few Porsches; 'and it looks as if Johnny Dixon still prefers driving his son's motor,' said one of the students pointing to a 2CV in the corner.

If there was a noticeable difference about the rest of the building it was its lightness and openness. Only partners had their own offices, though the managers shared offices to themselves. Only one door was shut, behind which a very heated discussion appeared to be going on over open green files and an overflowing ash tray. I could see what was going on because most of the offices had glass walls with silver-alloy Venetian blinds for shutting out the world, though no one had exercised that option.

It was into one of the partners' offices that I was ushered.

Howard Blessington greeted me with a firm handshake and cheerful smile. He was a tall, good looking man with a well-tanned complexion which, I was to learn subsequently, scarcely ever faded. It was constantly being renewed via his involvement in the hotel and leisure industries, carrying out feasibility studies to assess the viability of locations for new hotels.

Howard spent the first half hour taking my CV carefully to pieces and putting it back together in a way that gave a more honest, though less flattering, portrait. We then talked about why I had chosen Stoy's.

'Well, I have spoken to friends from university who work for other firms and your name crops up quite a bit in conversation.'

'What are you looking for?'

'Basically, a quality training programme and variety in the type of work I'm doing. What I don't want is to get stuck on mega-audits for months on end.'

'That's the beauty of our client base,' he said, 'you grow with your clients. Companies are not looking just for audit but for business advice.'

'Is that the difference then between yourselves and the big six?' I asked.

'They give a good service but to a different kind of client. If you look at our client list you find a lot of diversification, a big service sector profile for example. I'm not here to put down other firms, all I am saying is that we see ourselves as being different and I think others see it too.'

'I feel somehow, you can get closer to the action if you're not always acting for the big multinationals, that's what I mean.'

'How many people do you think are based in this office?' he asked. I felt myself blush. Of course I didn't know, so I stabbed at numbers between the thousands and the tens — after all, Stoy's was a medium-sized firm.

'Actually, there are over a thousand.' He smiled at having caught yet another smug undergraduate in an often used trap. 'Careers advisers call us medium-sized, but don't jump to too many conclusions. We're a sizeable organisation — with all the perks and problems associated with that.'

I looked out of the wide window to a sky that was clear and a sun that was strong. It was a hot day out there, you could almost smell the heat inside the office.

'How are things structured at Stoy's?' I asked.

'We have five general business groups of between ninety and a hundred people per group. My own group has five partners and twelve managers aged between twenty-five and twenty-nine.'

'That seems quite young,' I said.

'We tend to promote earlier than any other major firm,' said Howard. 'It's possible to become a partner at twenty-eight if you've got what it takes. We like to push responsibility down the line to our people, but you've got to show that you want it.'

No doubt about that strong smell of summer, it certainly was hot. Strange how impressions on the eye translate to the other senses.

'Do the groups specialise?' I asked.

'Not really, but there is the chance to do specialist work. You have the lead partner in the business group which has its own tax staff, audit staff etc. Students move around within it so as to get good general experience. Of course you can call in our specialist departments when needed to service general practice, but they also find outside business.'

'How do people get — '

This was more than a mid-summer fancy. Something was definitely burning.

'How do people get into a particular group?' I continued.

Were we near the staff dining room, I wondered?

There was now no doubting it, something was on fire inside the room. Howard instinctively looked at his waste-paper bin. He needn't have bothered, it was me — I was on fire — indisputably, unmistakenly ablaze. Smoke billowed from my jacket pocket where the loose hot ash, which must have fallen from my pipe earlier, had smouldered away until it ignited my return tube ticket, and the whole lot had burnt through the inner and outer linings. The suit itself was a light-weight summer one only too ready to catch light. I leapt up and started to beat my pocket like a gun fighter practising his quick draws, but with no effect. I flung off my jacket and started to jump up and down on it until I became aware of a searing, burning pain in my groin and let out an agonising cry which brought somebody else into the room: Caroline. My frenzied activity had overturned the pipe and dropped the remaining hot tobacco onto my bare (now barbequeing) flesh. Out of the corner of my eye I caught sight of Howard standing with his mouth slightly agape, as I spun and high-kicked round the room in a manner reminiscent of a demented Dervish. I also caught sight of a very attractive, fair-haired girl directing a pitcher of water at my middle torso. Howard in the meantime had successfully extinguished my jacket and was surveying the scorch marks on his executive carpet. Caroline's dowsing had done the trick as far as my trousers were concerned, but there was a great gaping hole in them where there shouldn't have been, and my groin was still excruciatingly sore. The only thing that could have possibly made this fiasco more dreadful than it was, would have been if my blazing loins had set off the fire alarm, which of course they had — the whoops of my rain dance had merely obscured the fact. That day I encountered many more Stoy's staff than I had anticipated.

'Does it sting?' asked Caroline, dabbing potion from a first-aid kit through the hole in my trousers which vaguely resembled an outline of the continent of Australia.

You bet it stung. My entire ego stung with the tails of a thousand wasps.

'Somewhat,' I said.

'Poor lamb,' she replied in teasing tones, scarcely bothering to hide her amusement. 'Perhaps singing might take your mind off the pain?'

'Singing?' I said.

'Yes, do you know any songs? How about "There's fire down below"? That's a good one.'

'I'm reminded of that old Jerry Lee Lewis number,' said Howard, 'Great something or other. Do you want to go home and get them, I mean it, seen to?'

I was too embarrassed to say anything and just shook my head.

'You should have finished your pipe,' he said, a trifle unkindly, I thought.

Caroline picked up the first-aid kit and made her departure.

'Goodbye,' she said, 'perhaps we'll be seeing more of you.'

'I don't think there's much more of him to see,' spluttered Howard, which sent Caroline off into a final fit of the giggles.

After a while I managed to pull myself together and probed away in the remainder of the interview and gathered a great deal of information.

I knew that I would be happy to work there given the chance — some chance now, I thought! But what impressed me most was not the facts, though they were important, rather it was the general attitude of Howard himself.

But what on earth did he think of me? It was Friday and my weekend would be taken up cursing the Fates and throwing out all my pipes.

'I hope the burn heals soon,' he said when the interview had finished, 'and I'm sorry about your suit.'

'And I'm sorry about your carpet,' I replied, picking up the charred remains of my jacket and covering the map of Australia with it as best I could.

'I'll get a letter out this afternoon regarding the decision. You should have it by Monday.'

No wonder, I thought, a company recruiting potential entrepreneurs doesn't need to deliberate too long about a potential circus act. In reality, however, the prompt reply was no more than a common courtesy.

The letter offering me a place at Stoy's did arrive on the Monday. Handwritten at the bottom of the page was a note which read:

'Offer conditional on (a) the wearing of asbestos underwear until offered a partnership, and (b) generating enough business in your first three weeks to pay for my bloody carpet.

    Kindest regards

    Howard Blessington'

4

ASSISTANT FINANCE DIRECTOR

I sat in the cocktail lounge of the hotel pondering on just what I would say when Caroline arrived.

I was the only person in the lounge and the barman contrived to look bored and business-like at the same time. I ordered my drink but we didn't talk. He found stains on glasses that weren't there and briskly wiped away at nothing, wielding the white, new-laundered cloth as a matador might a cape, with the same meticulous, stylised manner which proclaims — this is my arena, watch me, I am master here. I had seen this before. On each hand he wore a large gold ring with costume stones; they were cheap, cumbersome and got in the way of his fussy twisting and wiping. He was fifty, effete, retentive — replace the costume stones with rubies and I might have been looking at H Desborough Kingston.

Those in the family always addressed him by his first name, Hugo, though he himself always hated it. Within a week of his father's murder — (his father was always referred to as Old Kingston both before and after his death) — Hugo took to signing his name H Desborough Kingston. Old Kingston would have disapproved. In any event it made little difference, for the family still called him Hugo and to the rest of the world he was Mr Kingston. There were no friends or intimates, therefore a first name did not matter.

He was fifty-four years old and as far as possible he isolated himself from both family and employees. He never isolated himself from business where his control was absolute, as Old Kingston's had been, but all communications he passed primarily though his younger brother, Giles. There were personal pleasures though these were few. He had wispy straw-coloured hair which, though genuine, had all the appearance of a toupee, and lips that were inward-turning, like one who is toothless. He was supposed by many to be homosexual, but this was an error. H Desborough Kingston was asexual, the gross concept of bodily drives was alien to him. It was possible for men and women of his generation to reach adulthood utterly ignorant of sexuality; it was reflected in their lives and their literature. Old Kingston fostered this ignorance in his elder son, believing that women in general and marriage into the family in particular were bad for business. Hugo never married and when his contemporaries talked sex he chose not to listen and not to care. He did, however, contemplate marriage once to a third cousin. There were no physical determinants underlying the idea, she was family and he thought marriage might be expected of him. Old Kingston told him firmly that it was not, and Hugo never thought of it again.

He was the elder son of the parable who spent his life in service to his father's house. He had a good brain for anything that was not poetic, was sent to Cambridge and thence to Harvard Business School where he studied successfully, and returned to master his father's business which, though legitimate by that time, had its foundations in the laundering of dirty money. H Desborough would expand the business beyond the Kingston's limited imagination, by means of corporate and personal blackmail, physical and psychological threat, and a succession of broken promises which lead to broken lives. His amoralilty complemented his asexuality in exact proportion; after all, how much more power might Rasputin have exercised had his appetites not intervened?

Giles Kingston might have been looked upon as the archetypal prodigal except that nobody cared that he was, and there is no prodigality without caring. Old Kingston had intermittently found occasions to demonstrate an affection for Giles which he had never shown to Hugo. These occasional shows may have been genuine, but nothing was certain with Old Kingston. Giles was the equal of Hugo, if not his superior in the application of lack of scruple, but he had none of his elder brother's academic intelligence or native cunning. He was sent to a Canadian university where, even if he had applied himself, an unsuccessful outcome was always the most likely result. He found his way to Sandhurst and spent a number of years as an undistinguished Army officer. Although he liked the sensation of giving orders he was always better suited to receiving and carrying out the directions of others. The Army was part of the great playtime of Giles Kingston's young adulthood, but the company was always there beckoning his particular talents; if Hugo was the anaesthetist that put rivals to sleep, Giles was ever at the table prepared to dip his hands in the gore of the body corporate. Giles was cruel and enjoyed it, Hugo's cruelty was strictly business.

Giles was 39, a touch below average height, broad-shouldered, dark-haired, olive-skinned, with a face that was handsome in the regularity of its features, but uninteresting in the limited range of its few well-rehearsed expressions. Like Hugo he always dressed well in the so predictable, unvarying Knightsbridge fashion. He was a clone that reproduced itself in every wine bar in Belgravia.

Unlike Hugo, Giles did not grow up with an indifference to sex, but his sexual development was tinged with a sadistic orientation that betrayed unacknowledged fears of lasting inadequacy.

But there was a more important difference between the brothers. And it was the only difference Hugo was not aware of or in control of, for Giles had kept it a secret, something he kept up his sleeve to prove himself to the world should it ever doubt him. The discovery of that secret all but cost me my life.

Caroline 'phoned to say she would be late and had said, 'Please, please wait — won't you?' Of course I would wait, hadn't I always? I seemed to have done a lot of waiting over the last few years in one way and another. 'You've changed,' I thought to myself. My natural preference was for things to happen fast, but I had learned to dig in, be patient, and hold out for what I wanted.

It wasn't that I had altogether eliminated my desires for immediacy, in my job that would have proved disastrous, for poor work was not getting things done on time. Rather I had learned to monitor it in order to see the widest range of possible options, to maximise effects. This, too, went hand in hand with my working environment. Clients came to Stoy's because we were seen to have a more commercial, interpretational approach to problem solving. I had learned to become just as interpretational in my personal life, very few things could be reduced to being either black or white. We were not there simply to go out and tick a few boxes either professionally or personally.

In my first months at work I learned a number of basics that determined my approach thereafter. I started in Howard Blessington's general business group and the other recruits that started with me all had varied social and academic backgrounds. I found we all mixed pretty well, with the exception of a man called Arkwright whose instant response to everything that came his way was to groan as though his teeth were being pulled. Now Cartwright and Arkwright sound very similiar and I began to realise that I wasn't getting out of the office, which was the kiss of death. I wasn't being picked for jobs. I couldn't understand it, I thought I had acquitted myself well so far, but now even Arkwright was getting out and I wasn't. What had happened was that a manager had confused us and I was taking Arkwright's medicine. Once the penny dropped I went straight to Howard. I know how the mix up had come about but I didn't want to name Arkwright, I wanted to get on but I didn't see it as my place to drag anybody down. Equally, I knew from those ahead of me that a slow start and a poor name early on tends to stick. All I wanted was justice.

'Confused with whom?' Howard asked.

'Well, that doesn't matter, I just know that I'm being overlooked for jobs because one of the managers has mistakenly marked me down as a moaner.'

'Isn't that what you're doing now?' he said.

'No, I'm just seeking fair play.'

'Why have you come to see me and not the manager in question?'

'Well, firstly he is away on a job for the next couple of weeks and I don't intend to wait that long to sort things out, besides I rather think he's made up his mind to write me off. Secondly, I didn't want the same impressions filtering through to your office in a few weeks' time.'

'They've already filtered through, it's my business to know what's going on in my group at all times, as much as it's my business to know everything that's happening with respect to my clients. I must say I was a bit surprised to hear about it.'

It would have been so simple to name Arkwright and to be done with it, but I had never snitched in my life and I wasn't going to start now.

'OK,' he went on, 'I'll get to the bottom of it, and I do hope that a mistake has been made because, you're right, I think we understand each other. But a word of advice, Stoy's is not a social service, if you are to get on you have to get on yourself; once you show you can, then people at Stoy's will bend over backwards to help you.'

This was a piece of advice I never forgot. Fortunately the matter was cleared up fairly quickly. Nevertheless I felt I had some ground to make up and I didn't want to waste time. This meant making some adjustments, for the plain fact was that to succeed one had to get noticed. Though confident in my abilities and dealings with others, I was not naturally inclined to push myself forward. If asked, I never minded admitting to being good at something if I was. I've never seen any real point in shows of false modesty, I find it irksome and unnecessary. The new man who says to the club captain that he 'bats a bit' when he's successfully had a county trial is to my mind just as much a time waster as the man who says he's on a par with Viv Richards when Vivien Leigh would be nearer the mark. Be that as it may, I had never been particularly involved in the business of self-promotion, but it became obvious in those early days that a degree of it was necessary. The question was, how?

That night in the cocktail lounge asking the fussy barman to put some champagne on ice before Caroline arrived, I recalled a night in the flat drinking champagne to celebrate Dai's very rapid rise within Kingston & Kingston. We talked a lot that night about self-promotion.

'This is the life, eh?' said Dai, uncorking another bottle.

His attire was becoming rather more bizarre by the month. That evening he wore an expensive scarlet smoking jacket in velvet and black braid which he had bought in Jermyn Street. 'So what?' one might ask, 'a trifle Noel Coward perhaps but surely not bizarre?' Well no, except for the fact that we were in the middle of the hottest summer on record and it was ninety degrees inside the flat. His face, with the heat, was as red as his jacket and his appearance was less Noel Coward and more demented lion tamer for all the expense.

'You know, I still haven't quite worked out what it is you're doing at Kingston & Kingston,' I said, 'but whatever it is you are obviously doing it well.'

'Learning the ropes, Bach, that's all, and let me tell you there are a lot of ropes at Kingston & Kingston.'

'So this promotion, what exactly is it?'

'I'm moving into another firm for a bit, a sort of secondment. This firm has hit a bit of a sticky patch and have approached Kingston & Kingston for some financial and management advice. I'm joining them as a sort of a troubleshooter.'

'How do you mean, troubleshooter?'

'I can't really say very much about it at the moment, anyway it's only short term. In accordance with the advice of Kingston & Kingston this company has agreed to the appointment of a new finance director of our choosing.'

'And you are the new Finance Director?'

'No, I haven't quite scaled those lofty heights yet, but I'm going in as the assistant to the new Finance Director, he's bringing his own team, it's all part of the package.'

'So really you're no longer working for Kingston & Kingston but this other company.'

'Strictly speaking yes, but Giles assures me I will return to the fold as soon as this company completes its current project and starts to pick up. It's no big deal, it's not a takeover or anything like that, they're just paying us for some management advice and once we've made a few changes in their structure and things are sorted out that will be the end of our involvement.'

I was never to know just how much Dai at that time was telling the truth, whether he believed that this was the extent of Kingston & Kingston's involvement in the new company. What happened later led me to believe that even in the early stages he must have known that Kingston & Kingston had much more of a carnivorous intent than he was suggesting.

'The best part of it,' he went on, 'is that my salary has gone up again.'

'So have your debts,' said Celia with an unusual hint of reproach.

'It's an interesting company?'

'Oh yes. All top secret drugs research, wonder cures — that sort of thing. Company's called Tubelis Ltd.'

'Very top secret, boyo,' I commented.

Even Dai hesitated slightly. 'Why? Have you heard of them?'

'I couldn't be certain, but I have a feeling they were on our Audit Clients list when I joined Stoy's. We went through the client list at second interview.'

'More champagne?' His plump hand held the bottle up from underneath till it was on a level with his head. Holding it like that as he perspired away in his scarlet finery he reminded me of a quack doctor selling the 'elixir of youth'.

'Why not, indeed,' I said and he filled my glass. 'All joking aside, here's to your new job, you've come a long way in a short time, Dai.'

'Thanks to my undeniable talents, and the fact that Giles Kingston is a fantastic man to work for. He's a friend, not a boss. Celia fancies him, don't you, sweetling?'

'He's very good looking,' said Celia, but she didn't look happy.

'And he's number one in the company, is he?'

'No, his elder brother H Desborough Kingston is number one, but nobody gets to see him, he's holed up in an inner sanctum on the top floor. Giles effectively runs the show.'

'But he won't be your boss for much longer, it'll be the new Finance Director and ultimately the MD of Tubelis Research. Have you met either of them yet?'

'No, not yet, but I still regard Giles as my real boss.'

'Like I said, your real boss is now the head of Tubelis Research.'

'But like I said, Tubelis relies on Kingston & Kingston money.'

'But your allegiance has got to be to Tubelis as they'll be paying your salary.'

'It's all one,' he said. 'Let's all go out tonight, somewhere that is likely to melt my Gold Card. Oh how I love the smell of melting plastic.'

Celia looked unresponsive.

'Tubelis — pharmaceuticals you say?'

'That's right, the NHS via the Ministry of Health is, or rather was a big customer; but they've recently been using American companies.'

Dai went to change to go out, and Celia sat silently, cross-legged on the floor, wearing a kimono-style silk dressing gown and peering into her champagne glass. She was like a medium, a side-show fortune teller, waiting for the crystal to clear, apprehending some message that would be ill-received.

'You don't seem quite in the party spirit tonight,' I said.

'No.'

'Anything the matter?'

'It's difficult to get into the party spirit every night of the week,' she pushed her glass away.

'The boyo is living it up a bit, isn't he?'

'He never stops, it's night after night in clubs or some do related to Kingston & Kingston.'

'Well, you must admit he's landed on his feet.'

'Has he? There's something wrong, I feel it; it's all too easy somehow.'

'I wouldn't complain about that, I wish I had a slice of the free and easy at the moment, working for these accountancy exams doesn't leave much time for anything else. But I deserve a break tonight so I'm going to melt a little plastic myself.'

'That's the point, I look at the two of you and things just don't add up.'

'How do you mean?'

'Well you're actually doing something, you work hard I can see that and what you do you can talk about. You enjoy your work don't you, Edward?'

'Well yes, I suppose I do.'

Preparation for the impending exams had tended to obscure the fact of just how much I was enjoying what I was doing. Celia's question brought home to me just how much. Most of all, I liked the different situations in which I found myself, being in places where I could absorb the new environment, to feel the pulse of each business I encountered. That was Howard's phrase — 'You've got to be able to feel the pulse, test its strength,' he said. That's what I had found at Stoy's, it had its own strong pulse where ideas, people and profits circulated ready to display its vitality to the wider world, without confinements. What we had found for ourselves was what we offered to those who sought our advice, our own strength and health was dependent upon making others stronger.

At that time I was doing a job for an art gallery where not too long after I was to become the senior. Looking back I could see a wide range of working environments, all in a short time span, which was denied to many of my contemporaries in other firms. They ranged from my initial, first year investigation for an agency of musicians and conductors analysing expenditure, commissions and income, to looking at the extent of error caused by a computer breakdown in an engineering firm, then to an interim audit for a hotel group and the first feelings of having full responsibility when I was given two of their small hotels to do. I had rapidly moved from work with casinos to royalty work for record companies and my first experience of setting up overseas networks. As well as the kaleidoscope of companies, there had been close involvement with the personal finances of pop stars, script writers, and theatre managers, all of which had become part of Edward Cartwright, extending the scope of my own identity and experience. Yes, I enjoyed my work.

'That's just the point,' said Celia, 'you can say I like this or I don't like that, but you actually have something concrete to talk about. Dai doesn't seem to do any work.'

'He isn't getting all that money to do nothing, some people like to leave their work behind them at the end of the day.'

'No it's not that; there's plenty of people who work at Kingston & Kingston, I've been to their headquarters in the City, but there is a small group of new graduates who cluster around Giles Kingston and who seem to do little more than attend expensive long lunches, and go out partying in the evening. They move as one and they hero-worship Giles Kingston.'

'Sounds like nice work if you can get it, but I'm sure there's a lot more to it than that.'

It was clear to me that Celia didn't understand the nature of business and that nobody, including Dai, was going to get paid for doing nothing. I would soon find out that I was wrong.

'Try not to worry about everything,' I said, 'you never used to.'

She looked at me and said nothing. Looking back I shudder at the thought of how patronising I had been. Especially as she had assessed the situation so much more accurately than I had. I hope that I have changed a bit since then.

She herself had already changed since coming to London, she had lost all that naive optimism which typified the Celia of our university days. But cities harden people, I thought, or was it just time? But then it was incorrect to say that she had become hard, she was just negative and less caring about everything, except her precious Dai. She had also become more slovenly with regard to herself, her appearance. Before coming to London she was always so prim, neat, and fastidious about the way she looked, now in spite of all the expensive clothes Dai had bought her she rarely changed out of that kimono and a pair of tatty old slippers in which she mooched about all day. At nights, of course, she had to become Dietrich again at Dai's insistence. Maybe she was just tired, I thought, the party pace had exhausted her, but this change seemed something other than physical, it was inside.

'Do you miss work?' I asked.

'Oh yes, very much,' she replied, with the first signs of genuine animation I had seen in some time.

'Well, why don't you go back to it, there are so many hospitals in London. I'm sure there'd be no problem in — '

'Oh, Dai doesn't want me to, he's quite insistent, he says his fiancee shouldn't need to work, and that even so nursing is not the kind of work she should be doing.'

'Fiancee?' This was the first I had heard of any engagement.

'Yes, we're engaged, but I shouldn't really have mentioned it, Dai asked me not to tell anybody about it just yet, not even you, he won't even let me tell my parents. I don't see why, but he gets quite angry when I mention it.'

'Does he say why?'

'He says Giles Kingston doesn't like his hand-picked proteges to be married, Giles isn't married, you see. Dai says it's something to do with business and that I wouldn't understand it, and he's probably right; it won't be for long, but it's best we keep it to ourselves for the moment till Dai is established at his work.'

'I don't see what the hell it's got to do with Giles Kingston or anybody else whether you get married.'

'Dai says you can't divorce business from your personal situation, that your employers have a right to ask certain things of you. Aren't your employers interested in your personal life?'

'I'm sure they are.'

'And you don't consider it too private.'

'No, I don't think so. For example, if I presented an image of a heavy-drinking yuppie to the outside world it wouldn't inspire confidence in my company. But if Howard told me I shouldn't marry I'd tell him to find a large hole and bury himself.'

'Does your boss encourage you to spend a lot of money?'

'How do you mean?'

'Well, Giles Kingston encourages Dai to spend an awful lot — buying all sorts of things. And they, the group, go gambling together — casinos and horses — he gets into terrible debt, I get worried sick by all the letters, demands, telephone calls, knocks on the door during the day — then suddenly everything's OK, all's paid up and the next round of big spending starts all over again. I think he covers his debts by any wins he has at gambling. It doesn't seem to bother him, but it's making me sick with worry. Please, Edward will you talk to him? For me, please?'

'Don't start giving yourself ulcers, Dai wouldn't be Dai without all his blustering flamboyance. I think it must be the Hungarian in him. I'm sure there's nothing too much to worry about. It's not unnatural in business to flaunt the trappings of success. You should see the partners' car park at Stoy's, wall-to-wall Ferraris, Aston Martins, Jaguars and why not?'

'Yes, but I'm sure they can afford them.'

'I'm sure they can too.'

'I suppose it's just me, I'm sure everything is all right really. But you will talk to him, won't you, just to put my mind at rest? You see, for all his behaving as if Giles Kingston is a god, I know deep down you're the person that has the most influence on him, what you say matters. I can't influence him at all — sometimes I begin to wonder whether sex is all I mean to him.'

'Come on, I know that's not true, and so do you.'

Neither of us, of course, did know for sure, but Dai had certainly altered. There was a new cruel, cutting edge to his natural humour. At university he often showed, usually with embarrassment, some thoughtfulness and sensitivity, but he had now seemingly eliminated these traits. Mention anything other than surface realities and he would clam up.

'Right, let's hit it,' said Dai when he reappeared. 'Come on, Celia, get a move on.'

'I really don't feel like going out again tonight Dai.'

'Suit yourself,' he said, 'it makes no difference, you wouldn't be much fun in your present mood anyway.'

'No, of course, it makes no difference tonight,' she flashed. 'If it was one of your blessed Kingston & Kingston rave-ups I'd have to go, wouldn't I? Even if I was dropping on my feet! But because it isn't, because it would be just us then it doesn't matter, does it.'

This was the first time I had ever heard her speak to Dai with utter vitriol. Celia too had changed inside.

'I don't know why you should be dropping on your feet,' he retorted coldly. 'You don't do anything all day but slop about the flat.'

'And whose idea is that?!' she shouted.

These little domestic contretemps were happening more frequently, though they had never quite reached the slanging match that this was threatening to become. I could see how Dai's unfeeling attitude got to Celia and how Celia's lack of enthusiasm got to Dai; I liked them both, they had been good friends, but I didn't need this around me when I came home from work. I resolved to get a place of my own as soon as possible, but it would have to be after the PEI exams were over, I couldn't risk any disruption just then.

Dai and I went out that night without Celia to some strobe-lit plastic palace of his choosing, where most drinks were coloured blue, green or pink and had, like the club itself, very little taste. Dai was rarely out of this place, or some other like it.

'Sorry about that bit of unpleasantness back at the flat,' he said. 'I don't know what's got into Celia of late, she's so bloody negative about everything. As soon as I start to enjoy myself she comes down on me like a ton of bricks. I get the full treatment, the mournful expressions, the weepiness — I don't know what's got into her. Her hormones must have gone a bit haywire — well they do, don't they sometimes? The hormones? I mean, she never used to be a sniveller.'

A man of about twenty seven who flung himself around the dance floor without the least suggestion of a rhythmic limb in his body, called across to Dai. He gestured with clenched fists and raised forearms like an old-time, bare-knuckle pugilist, in passing reference to the bleached blonde, short-skirted girl he was dancing with. Dai returned the gesture in acknowledgement of the other's signal, and the girl danced on, oblivious of everything.

'That's Harry Brooks, one of the new hellfire club members as Giles calls us,' he said. 'God does he put it about!'

'The way he dances he couldn't help but put it about,' I said.

'He has the devil's own luck on the roulette wheel as well,' he went on.

'And do you?' I asked.

'I had a bloody good win three weeks ago,' he said, which meant, in fact, that things hadn't been going too well of late.

He started to chuckle.

'Do you know Celia actually believes I finance myself by gambling.'

'Do you?'

'Hell no! I don't need to, not with my salary, you know that.'

'If you say so,' I said, 'but you do seem to spend as though you were on double that.'

'Giles expects it of us, he likes his boys — and girls, I tell you, is he ever good with the women! You should see the women he has, they can't leave him alone — he likes us to go out and live rich, to taste what success buys; he says it makes future executives hungry for it which is good for Kingston & Kingston.'

'Even if it lands you in debt?'

'If we get into trouble we go to Giles and he fixes it.'

'You mean he pays your debts?'

'If we land in real trouble, yes, he's a really great guy, you just wouldn't know how fantastic he is to work for.'

'Sounds a regular fairy godfather.'

'It's numero uno, H Desborough, who's the fairy by all accounts,' he said. All subtlety and incisiveness had somehow evaporated from his attempts to be funny, which was alien, for Dai at university was a genuinely funny man, his humour never obvious. Is this what happens to people, I wondered, when they have to start taking into account the great ranking system that is life in the commercial world?

'You see, you can't understand, can you? What it's like to have a boss like Giles Kingston, he's a one-off. You don't know what it means to have a boss like that do you? Go on, admit it.'

'I have enough trouble getting a drink out of Howard. If

he thought I wanted to buy a Morgan, he'd only be interested if he was selling one.'

'You see, there you are, you don't understand,' he said, drunkenly misinterpreting me and raising another Caribbean blue concoction to his fulsome mouth. 'Giles isn't some philanthropic fool, he's not making a gift, but an investment in the future. He believes in the guaranteed future success of those he knows, by experience, are going to make it. He lends us the money, free of interest, with no fixed date for repayment because he trusts us and he trusts his own judgment.'

He went on to elaborate how Giles Kingston had never been proved wrong in the past about who was going to make it and who wasn't, and that led to talk about getting to the top and how to do it.

'It's an unpalatable fact,' said Dai at one point, 'that to be out in front you have to step over and on a lot of people, but that's business.'

'That may be so in a lot of instances,' I said, 'but I can think of an alternative.'

'What's that?' he asked.

'To be so fast off the mark that there's nobody in front of you to step over. Do you get the feeling we're horribly mixing metaphors as well as mixing horrible drinks?'

'I think you may be right,' he said, 'but stepping over, on, being on top or out in front, it all amounts to one thing, there are a lot of Indians and very few chiefs.'

At that point hellfire Harry and his bleached nymphette joined us and any attempts at intelligibility had to be abandoned for the night. I switched off. After a while their conversation was a buzz in the middle distance. I started to think about work and ways of getting myself noticed.

The resolutions of that night set the pattern for the following months. The first was, indeed, to be first off the blocks in all situations where there was an element of urgency. I made sure that at these times when people looked about for help they wouldn't have to look far, I would be there. I would deliberately seek out jobs that others weren't all that keen on tackling, messy jobs perhaps with a reduced budget, but where a satisfactory result was all the more noticeable because of it. If a senior went on holiday and had a job I knew he or she would not normally put my way I would make sure I got on it and presented him or her with a fait accompli upon their return.

That's how I first came across that job I had given Louise and the new junior the bank statements for that very morning. Poor Louise!

Nothing in my strategies required trampling on anybody else and it started to pay dividends. Everybody at work knew there was a 'high fliers' list circulating around the partners, and I wanted to be on it. Although it was important it was not just for the kudos or the potential financial benefit. Above all else I needed not to stand still, a status quo even if it be in Shangri La would not have suited me.

5

LIQUIDATION

On the last morning of his life Old Kingston allowed himself
an extra hour in bed. He awoke at his usual time, but
stayed under the covers and looked at the ceiling of his
Westminster apartment for a full hour. Every new day was
a clean slate to Old Kingston, nothing would be carried
over from the day before. He dealt only with matters that
required a beginning, continuations and conclusions he left
to his sons. Nor was there any emotional residue to contend
with; he had buried two wives who had each given him a
son, not that he had ever minded much about any dynastic
ambitions. There were brothers and sisters and cousins who
came to pay court when summoned, but the only blood that
mattered was that which turned within his own body. He
had reached that stage, after a lifetime's acquisition of
material wealth, when old men start saying to everybody,
'As long as you have your health that's all that matters'.
And indeed he did have his health, the robust health that
accompanies a lack of conscience.

  Today it would not be business as usual. His chauffeur
would be waiting to drive him to Crewe where he would
take an evening meal before boarding the overnight sleeper
to Inverness. There another car would be waiting to bring
him to his Highland lodge where he would enjoy a week's
fly fishing and perhaps a round of golf at Royal Dornoch.
He had done this once a year for sixteen years. Apart from
the chauffeurs at either end and a woman who did the
cooking in the lodge, he would travel alone, he always did.
He had never taken either his wives or his sons to the

lodge, nor would they have wished to accompany him even if he had thought of asking them. As much as he enjoyed the fishing and the golf, the highlight of the week for him was the overnight sleeper. He loved to travel at night by train, drinking more gin than was usual for him in the evening, and reading his coarse fishing manuals late into the night. He could have flown in luxury anywhere in the world but this was for him.

The drive to Crewe would be strictly business. Hugo would be on the other end of the 'phone to receive his instructions, the real holiday would commence when he boarded the train at eleven that night. Hugo had surprised him, he was always a soppy boy whom he thought would never amount to much business-wise, Giles always seemed the more likely. 'But there you have it,' he thought, Hugo was still a soppy sort of individual personally, but his mind was always one jump ahead, whereas Giles' mind just jumped, in any direction where his own pleasures lay. 'Hugo was always more frightened of everything as a boy,' he thought. 'Apprehension's the key, raise them with a good dose of fear and it makes them better businessmen — there you have it.'

Upon arrival at Crewe he would check into the hotel where he had booked a room. The room would not be slept in, of course, he used it only to wash and it was there as a back up should, for any reason, the overnight to Inverness not run. Once in the room he was tempted to thumb through one of his angling magazines; but no, he would delay the pleasure for the journey. He would take his evening meal, as he did every year, in the hotel restaurant. Old Kingston sat down and was served his first course — the holiday had started.

On the other side of Crewe a man and a woman sat in the darkest corner of a dimly-lit Indian restaurant. The man faced the wall and peered into a book so that his face was obscured as the woman ordered their food. When the waiter returned with the meal the man still had his head in his book where it remained until the dishes were set on the table and the waiter had gone; he then put the book down.

'You've seen the boy?' he said.

'Of course,' replied the woman.

'How is he?'

'That's my business, it's not for you to ask that.'

'Suit yourself,' said the man, 'just being polite. It's a good school, I believe.'

'Yes, it's a good school.'

'He should be very happy there.'

'I told you I will not talk about — '

'OK, OK,' said the man. 'Don't raise your voice, remember my instructions, you're not to draw attention to us in any way.'

'Yes, all right, just don't talk about the boy, that's all. Why all this cloak-and-dagger stuff anyway? Why here in Crewe of all places?'

'Well, I knew you would be across the Pennines visiting the boy. I hope the drive from Yorkshire didn't inconvenience you?'

'No, it didn't inconvenience me,' she said, 'but you still haven't told me why we have to meet here.'

'Oh, but you must remember, we are not meeting here, we have never been here, both of us are miles away from Crewe at this very moment.'

'Yes, all right, get to the point.'

'The point will become obvious when you read tomorrow morning's papers. You will know that I am perfectly capable of doing whatever I decide to do in order to get what I want, and you know what I want above all else.'

'What if I go to the police?'

'And tell them what? No crime would have been committed and it would all sound pretty silly to them, wouldn't it?'

'How do I know that it's not a bluff?'

'After tonight you will know that it's not a bluff, that's why we're in Crewe. Read the papers tomorrow and you will understand that I don't bluff.'

The man paused and then said, 'The school is quite isolated, isn't it? Still its location is part of its attraction. The country air will certainly be good for his lungs.'

'I loathe you,' said the woman.

'That will change, you will come to realise that I only go to such lengths to prove to you that nobody could possibly — '

'You have proved everything you need to prove to me.'

'Not quite everything,' he said, very gently. 'Let's hope it never comes to that.' He took some papers out of his pocket. 'That doesn't make for a bad future, does it? It only awaits my signature.'

'Don't bother, not a penny of it would be used. Everything he wants he'll get from me.'

'Well, we'll see. The main thing is to be there a week on Friday.'

'I won't do it.'

'Read the papers tomorrow.'

He put the book back to his face and told her to signal the waiter for the bill.

'Did you not enjoy your meal, Sir? You haven't eaten very much,' the waiter remarked.

'No, he's just not feeling well,' the woman answered.

The waiter left the bill and went to attend to another table.

'You pay it,' said the man.

'I've left my handbag in the car,' she replied.

With the hand that was not holding the book to his face he felt inside his coat. He placed a credit card on the table, whispered something to the woman and slipped out of the door unnoticed.

'The gentleman suddenly felt that he was going to be sick,' the woman told the waiter. 'If you don't mind, I'll take this outside for him to sign.'

The woman returned to the restaurant with the signed slip and the waiter, enquiring after the gentleman's condition, gave her the card and receipt and she left.

It was dark outside, the woman gave the man his card, they exchanged whispers though there was no one in the street to hear them, and they parted company.

Monsieur Luc Chastaret had been waiting for fifteen minutes under a yellow street light beside a telephone booth. He had taken a Belgian passport from his pocket several times and looked at the photograph; it amused him. Monsieur Chastaret had a sense of humour and he didn't mind laughing at himself. Passport photographs are supposed to be bad, he thought, but this was definitely the worst he had ever had taken, and Monsieur Chastaret had a passport photograph taken at least once a year. Finally, the 'phone rang and he entered the booth.

A few seconds later he came out and walked round the corner to a car parked in an otherwise empty street. He stopped at the door on the driver's side and the darkened, electrically-operated window lowered a fraction of an inch through which was passed an envelope containing a photograph. Monsieur Chastaret took the envelope and the car drove away. He then looked at the photograph, set fire to it and pushed the ashes down the drain with his foot.

Old Kingston settled into his compartment, changed into his pyjamas and dressing gown and spread his fishing magazines out on the bed. The steward knocked, entered and asked if he'd care for a drink.

'I have an ample supply of my own, thank you very much,' said Old Kingston.

And indeed he had. The steward could see an opened drinks case holding a bottle of deluxe whisky and two bottles of gin. Old Kingston was known to enjoy a good tipple from time to time; he was not averse to becoming drunk, though it was not a regular occurrence and was usually confined to holidays or family occasions. Giles was also not averse to becoming drunk and did so often; Hugo rarely touched alcohol. Old Kingston mixed himself a gin and bitters and got into bed with his magazines.

The train stopped at Edinburgh well after midnight and was stationary for approximately forty-five minutes, after which it would not stop again until it reached Inverness the following morning.

Monsieur Chastaret left the train at Edinburgh, walked to the Haymarket, got into a car, drove to Prestwick on the Ayrshire coast, and that morning boarded a flight to Canada.

Shortly before arriving in Inverness the steward let himself into Old Kingston's compartment with coffee and rolls. The whisky bottle was three-quarters empty and one gin bottle completely so. A bottle of sleeping pills also lay empty on the floor. Old Kingston was dead.

6
UNDUE INFLUENCE

George Mischel MP had very little time for constituency work these days. This his constituents and his local party organisation could well understand, for he was, as they say, 'a rising man'. He had chaired an all-party select committee on the drug industry where his knowledge in that area, and the capable manner in which he had handled his chairmanship, was recognised and rewarded. Mischel lived in an apartment below that formerly occupied by Old Kingston, nor was this his only connection with that family, for he had once held a directorship at Kingston & Kingston Financial Services Ltd. H Desborough had been keen to secure the affiliations of 'a rising man', and like a number of select individuals in Hugo's ever expanding empire, Mischel appeared to have to do very little to collect his handsome retainer.

It was Mischel's involvement with Kingston & Kingston that swayed Gordon Campion, head of Tubelis Research, to sacrifice to some degree his total independence in the running of Tubelis, and accept the conditions imposed by the Kingstons in return for their financial backing. At heart, Gordon Campion was a scientist, a highly inventive one, but not a businessman. The project development labs were where he belonged. He freely admitted his limitations and relied heavily on business advisers. Tubelis had prospered beyond all expectations and his tactic of deferring to those 'in the know' had paid off.

He placed particular trust in Alison Lester at Stoy's. Campion was surprised to learn that the firm, initially

employed to do the audit, was able to offer much more by
way of expanding the theatre of operations, and employed
the mechanics of reality to translate what for him had been
merely dreams. Campion was a somewhat insulated, in-
troverted individual, his was a world of ideas and he found
it difficult to talk to people. He had no such difficulties with
Alison Lester, he could talk to her, and talk cost him nothing
because Stoy's was the only substantial firm not to charge
for general partner time.

Alison Lester was in many ways quite different from
Howard, my first boss. Howard, with his Oxbridge background, came to Stoy's from another firm in the City, he
arrived a polished product, communication skills complete,
but then they had always come naturally to Howard. They
had not always come naturally to Alison Lester. She joined
Stoy's at the age of eighteen, straight after taking her A
levels, a shy South London girl from a family that had
been, if not poor, never particularly well off. When she
arrived at Stoy's she had no real notion of her own potential,
and had to develop skills that, initially, she would not have
credited herself with the capacity to develop. All that she
had learned she learned in situ, on the spot. Alison Lester's
emergent talents were the result of what one might call
'learning action', under fire, which gave her a quality that
can best be described as 'street-wise'.

Stoy's had moulded her into a clear communicator to match
her native intellect, but her own developmental history, the
recollection of a time when confidence was less automatic,
gave her a special understanding of reticent men like Gordon
Campion. Alison was able to anticipate the questions that
Campion wanted to ask before he had fully formulated them
in his own mind. When Giles Kingston told him that part
of the deal involved severing past contacts in favour of
Kingston & Kingston men, Campion flatly refused, but
refusal was unknown to the Kingstons. There was a point
at which the deal was so precarious that it appeared it
might not go through. A single light high up in the ugly
glass palace that was Kingston & Kingston's headquarters
signalled that Hugo had summoned Giles to a late night
conference.

The month before his first involvement with Kingston & Kingston was probably the zenith of Gordon Campion's life. He had good reason to feel proud. He was fifty-five years old, wealthy and happily married to Eva who had shared his life for over thirty years. He was now able to repay her for all the frustrations that inevitably result in sharing the life of a researcher, a dreamer. She was always more outgoing than he, and there were many times when she might have wished for a different kind of life and a different kind of husband. She was a social animal, he was not, and if he indulged her now materially (if never entirely emotionally) it was no more than she deserved. They understood and loved one another in their own particular way.

The Campions had two grown-up children of whom they were proud. The boy, who had inherited his mother's more outgoing disposition, was embarking on a political career and had won through his party's pre-selection contest to stand at the next general election. Eva enjoyed organising fund-raising parties for her son, to her it was the sort of activity that constituted life. His daughter had inherited his own scientific orientation, had taken a medical degree and was carving out a reputation for herself as a researcher into neurological disorders. Campion's name and that of his wife, mainly via their association with their son's activities, would appear in the social columns. This amused Gordon, he thought such things were the preserve of social animals which he certainly was not. Eva, of course, brimmed with delight whenever it happened.

George Mischel was wakened out of his sleep very early one morning by hysterical sobbing on the stairs outside. He went to investigate and found a woman in her early fifties sitting, dishevelled, on the bottom step. She was confused, uncomprehending, and abandoned to her own inner agonies at the sudden, shock realisation that something dreadful, unimaginable had taken place. She had obviously been drinking heavily and had found it difficult either to dress herself properly or to move with any kind of stability. When she heard Mischel's door open she cried out instantly:

'Giles? Giles is that you? Where are you, Giles?' and then broke into the staccato sobbing once more.

'Ah,' thought Mischel, understanding the situation. He was quite used to a succession of middle-aged women mournfully haunting the building in search of Giles Kingston, who used his murdered father's flat solely for these trysts. The women would return time after time trying to find the explanation, to make sense out of that one bewildering night. After a while the women would give up and go back to who knows what. Still this one was a bit special, Mischel thought, she was creating a real fuss. The first instinct of the politician told him not to get involved, don't be drawn into anything that commits one to a course of action. It was undesirable that a woman should be behaving like this in the apartment block which housed a 'rising man'. 'Best go back inside,' he thought, 'before you and she are seen on the same landing.' He went inside. The sobbing continued. 'This is intolerable,' he said to himself, 'why can't Giles hang about to mop up his own mess?'

'Giles!' the woman screamed hysterically from the landing. Mischel opened his door and went out again.

'Giles wouldn't want all this,' he thought, 'someone might 'phone the police and then what? Better get her out of the way. Get rid of her, do him a favour. Yes, that's the best thing. He's picked a right one here.'

'Giles!' she called out again.

'Quiet, you'll wake everybody up,' he said.

'Where's Giles?' she moaned.

'Outside,' said Mischel, 'he's waiting outside.'

'I don't understand, who were those men, I don't understand — '

He could smell the drink. 'Got to get rid of the bloody old lush quick,' he thought, 'she's going to feel like death later on'.

He led her to the lift; 'better than the stairs. Soundproof.' They made it outside with difficulty, she needed his support. He hailed a cab and went back to the front door.

'Where's Giles?' she pleaded. 'You said he was outside.'

'Well he isn't, now push off!' Mischel went back inside. Chivalry is of no value to 'a rising man'.

'Where to, madam?' asked the cabby.

Eva Campion found herself involuntarily sitting in the back of the taxi, a few early morning delivery vans just beginning to break the silence on the otherwise empty Westminster streets.

Where to, madam?'

The question stunned her — where to? Where is there to go when one is utterly senseless in the world? The one word she could not possibly have brought herself to say was 'home'. She pulled a card out of her handbag and handed it to the driver.

'Righto,' he said, 'it'll cost a bit, mind, this time in the morning. Been celebrating, have we?'

The Abbey loomed up out of the earth as they passed like some subterranean monster that had broken free of its confines from deep within the world, and thrust a huge gnarled hand through the surface to feel the touch of air for the first time in centuries. To Eva it was man-made and horrible, and would extract a terrible price once it finally heaved its entire frame from deep within to meet the coming dawn; when it would stagger blindly about the world and trample its creators under foot.

He had never met a woman like her he said, so full of life, so positive, she excited him.

He had never felt this kind of excitement before, such rapport; 'it's very physical too,' he had said hesitantly in an embarrassed, boyish sort of way. He was not only handsome, he was sweet. Yes, she could understand that he had known a lot of younger women but that they somehow left him cold, unfulfilled. He was too sensitive, too clever, to be content with unripened, immature preoccupations. They really ought not to be talking like this but she understood his excitement, she felt it too. Had she really had as much champagne as all that? She didn't care, the evening had been exhilarating, and yes she would go back to his flat for a night-cap because she wanted it to go on a bit longer. But that would be it, one last drink and she would go home.

Of course it was inevitable, though unpremeditated by either of them, she told herself, the attraction was too strong. She arched her back on the bed for breath but the weight of Giles and his heavy-handed dragging of her clothes forced her back, and she contented herself with stealing rapid inhalations when she could. She hoped he would not be disappointed when he saw her without her clothes; she wished she had kept to that diet.

'I'm not all that overweight,' she thought, 'just a bit, but not much.'

He was very rough and his face was different somehow from that which had looked at her across the table. She wished him to be a little gentler and to say something, something just right, but wishes wouldn't be voiced and hurt feelings risked. She knew him to be sensitive. He was so different from Gordon. Is this how it is nowadays, the unstoppable ferocity in silence? It didn't matter, it was, after all, inevitable.

Eva, though she didn't want to, fell into that sleep which is the peculiar cocktail of too much alcohol, and not wishing to think about certain things just yet. She saw her son Rory standing on a platform making a speech and then he disappeared; there was the food hall in Harrods and a large cheese cut into segments that she knew were identical, exact in proportion and weight; she saw her own hand resting on Giles' neck but his hair had grown, it was much longer.

And now she was waking. Giles was moving again and her hand was around his neck and his hair was longer. He was being so much more gentle this time and she felt herself being eased forward to meet him. She clung to his neck still but she was being eased upright, her back supported by another arm.

'Get the old sow further up,' someone said.

But what was happening? Was the album being opened again? Where had this other arm come from? There were three men in the room and nothing made sense and a man with long hair was where Giles should have been, and another man, a naked man, was supporting her back. There was someone else also, by the door, whom she couldn't see.

'That's better, keep her there. Make it look like you're all having a great time, boys.'

She saw the flash, and then another, and there were two

men, neither of them Giles, supporting her, moving her with the after-image of the flash in her eyes. Too much drink. Never again. Where was Giles? Who were these men?

She passed out. When she came round she was alone. No Giles, no man with long hair, no man with an arm easing her up from the shoulders, no man with a camera, all was dark and quiet and terrible. It is said that ghosts never appear to those who wish to see them. How such psychic intelligence is derived is uncertain, but if the spectre appears only to the unimaginative nonbelievers, so it is with the unthinkable realities of life. Real life horrors happen only to those oblivious to their existence.

Eva was not sober when she reawoke, she was sick and hungover. Having such a readily available explanation for her nausea only made her mental trauma more incomprehensible.

'Perhaps it was the champagne which made me dream that — '

But no, one knows when one has seen a ghost even if explanations are not to be found.

Gordon Campion arrived home at lunchtime the following day after visiting one of the Tubelis laboratories in Derby. He had promised Eva that he would do so and he expected to find her directing caterers and arranging seating cards. There was to be another fund raising do for Rory's campaign. Several sitting MPs from neighbouring constituencies, and a peer, were to attend and the press would be there to take photographs. This was going to be her biggest do yet and he was surprised not to find her flapping about the house. He was told she was ill in bed. Eva was rarely unwell.

'Probably a bout of nerves, over-excitement,' he thought as he went upstairs.

When he entered the bedroom he was taken aback, she looked terrible, this wasn't nerves. She wasn't in bed, but sitting on a chair.

'Well, what's all this, then?' he said.

'All what, then?' she replied in a startled sort of way.

'You're not feeling well.'

'Oh that, no —' she turned away from him, 'no I'm not feeling well.'

65

'What is it?'

'Probably nerves,' she said.

'I must say, you don't look at all well, it's definitely something.'

'Yes it's definitely something.'

'Why don't you get into bed?' he asked.

The idea of bed repulsed her, but she mustn't give anything away. Behave normally and perhaps nothing would come of last night's nightmare. And maybe after all there was an explanation, perhaps Giles would make it all right. The image of the floodlit Abbey came back to her and she knew that this was nonsense, she had been a fool and was still thinking like one. All she wanted was for Gordon to go so that she could cry undetected.

The guests were arriving and Campion checked on his wife to see if she had revived sufficiently to come down after all. She had not, she couldn't bear the thought of seeing her son — her shame was too overwhelming.

'I shall never be able to face my children again,' she said to herself after Gordon had gone. She did not include Gordon — there was no malice in this, she had simply not thought of him at the time. For Eva Campion this exclusion constituted a habit.

Downstairs Campion did his best to play the sociable host in spite of his inclinations to retreat in company. He found it especially hard going interacting with all the political animals, he was not one himself, and they insisted on drawing him on political topics. She had obviously been crying, why was that, he wondered. It crossed his mind that she might be having a breakdown, but the thought was too painful to contemplate and he shut it out.

He was relieved when a very amicable Dutchman engaged him in conversation and didn't talk about politics. Pieter van Pallandt was very gregarious and talked a lot without seeming to bother that Campion didn't have much by way of response. Van Pallandt was an odd-looking man, he was tall with very long arms which dangled constantly by his side. He had the curious habit of touching the thumbs of each hand with the forefingers and pointed them backwards towards the rear which made his little fingers stick out.

His body was lean and angular except for a very large stomach, which did not spread about him but protruded out of him rather like the belly of a pregnant woman. He had a long, thin head with fulsome lips and very little by way of a chin. Some people are put together in such a way as to make it difficult for other people to look at them and Van Pallandt was such a person. His English was excellent, as is the case with Dutchmen who seem to master it better than any other non-native speaker. Campion was worried because he couldn't seem to find van Pallandt's name on the guest list (though he didn't tell van Pallandt this) and wondered where he was supposed to sit. He wished for Eva to be there to take charge. Campion genuinely admired his wife; she could be irritating at times, but he knew he irritated her far more. It was her way of actively confronting things he admired because he found it so difficult to do himself.

'All this must cost a pretty penny — eh?' said van Pallandt. 'But I forgot, the English think it bad form to talk about money — true?'

'I don't know,' said Campion, 'I seem to have to talk about little else these days,' which was true.

'What's it all in aid of?' asked the Dutchman.

'My son,' said Campion, a bit puzzled. Surely van Pallandt ought to know what it was in aid of.

'It's his birthday or something?'

'No it's a political fundraising dinner, aren't you with the Party?'

'I am with the party, as you can see,' van Pallandt laughed 'because here I am drinking this delightful and refreshing drink that you have so generously provided for me — what is it you call it? Buck's Fizz? that's American I think, yes?'

'Yes, but I meant the political party, you're not — ?'

'Oh no, I don't pretend to understand politics, not even in the Netherlands my own country, and your British politics make no sense to me at all.'

'It doesn't make very much sense to me either,' said Campion, which was the truth but after he had said it he wondered if it hadn't sounded a little disloyal to Rory. He didn't mean it that way.

'No, I'm in business, I told you, but today I'm just a messenger. Very often I'm a messenger. I'm like Mercury, always off somewhere on some errand.'

Campion wanted to ask what he was doing at a political dinner but asking the obvious made him feel awkward. Rory came over to join them.

'It seems to be going quite well, how's Mum?'

'She doesn't look too good.'

'Your lady wife is unwell?' exclaimed van Pallandt, as though the news had caused him great personal distress. 'I'm so sorry to hear it, but it may not be serious because, you know, even though someone does not look too good it doesn't always mean that it's serious. Sometimes people can not look too good even when they are enjoying themselves, it all depends on the circumstances.'

Van Pallandt's tie had blown over his shoulder before he entered the house and he had not bothered to replace it, which emphasised further his protruding stomach. Rory looked enquiringly at his father who returned his look thinking that if anyone knew who this massive, jocular Dutchman was, it should have been his son.

'This is Mr van Pallandt,' said Campion.

'So pleased to make your acquaintance. Who knows, at this moment I may be shaking the hand of a future Prime Minister.' Van Pallandt gripped Rory with his great hand.

'Are you in security by any chance?' asked Rory, thinking by his size that he might be looking after one of the VIPs.

'You might say that,' he replied, 'but today, as I have just been telling your father, I am a messenger, a bearer of good tidings.'

He produced a foolscap size envelope which had been tucked down the back of his trousers and hidden by his suit coat.

'Would you be so kind as to hold this, please?' he said handing the envelope to Rory while he tucked his shirt in. 'In fact, you can open it if you like, it is for you, Mr Campion.'

Rory began to tear open the envelope and van Pallandt waited till he was on the point of taking out its contents.

'Actually, it is for your father, Mr Campion senior,' he said casually.

'Oh, I'm sorry,' said Rory, handing it to his father. 'If you'll excuse me I'd better go and see how his Lordship is getting on.'

'Of course, don't let me interrupt your party, politicians must mingle, I understand. One of my old business colleagues is an MP, George Mischel, have you heard of him?'

'Oh yes, he's a rising man,' said Rory. 'Look, excuse me, will you?' Rory left them.

'Business colleague?' said Campion.

'Yes, he was a director of the company I work for.'

'Kingston & Kingston?' Campion wondered what he was doing at Rory's do.

'I believe our two companies are soon going to become more closely associated.'

'Well that's not certain,' said Campion.

'Oh, I think it is certain.' Van Pallandt put his long arm around Campion's shoulders as he said it.

'You need Kingston & Kingston, I think, Mr Campion, and with our help you cannot go wrong.' He gripped Campion's shoulders even tighter, his face beaming. 'In fact, things will only go wrong if you don't accept the very generous offer made by our company. You see, your son was right in a way, I am a sort of security man, for my company, and because we are soon to be associates I am going to look after you too. That is why I secured the contents of that envelope for you; it was in the possession of some very unpleasant men. Well, I must be going, thank you for the Buck's Fizz — what names they give drinks these days,' he gave a hearty laugh. 'I hope your son has a smooth ride in politics, such a risky occupation. You know what I hate?' His face expressed earnest indignation. 'It is the way some elements of the press are always trying to dig up dirt, even among the families of politicians. Some magazines will pay for anything. Thank you so much again, we will be seeing a lot of each other. I hope your wife is restored to you.'

As van Pallandt left, Campion thought about his last words — 'I hope your wife is restored to you' — it made it sound as though she was dead and waiting for him in some afterworld.

Campion pulled a photograph out of the envelope and looked at a mock headline written on it — 'RAUNCHY MOTHERS, SOME MPS DO HAVE 'EM'. He couldn't at first understand what it was all about. Why had van Pallandt given him this pornographic photo? Who were these two men, and the woman? Although he instantly knew the face he didn't at first recognise it as Eva's because of the impossible context, but eventually he had to believe what he saw. The shock of it rendered him immobile, there was no outlet for an overt response but, internally, his visceral organs raced at an unbearable speed. He placed it back in the envelope and stood like an ancient menhir rooted in the ground. Rory had begun his welcome speech and Gordon Campion had begun his partnership with Kingston & Kingston.

Pieter van Pallandt had not had quite as many passports as Monsieur Chastaret but he had had several. Unlike Chastaret, van Pallandt was his real name and he was Dutch, but he had spent many years moving around all parts of the African continent and he still moved frequently between Europe, Africa and other parts of the world where business was good. He was being truthful when he told Campion he was not political, in the sense that he cared little for ideologies of any kind, but he had many political connections. He supplied his connections with the means of killing one another. With some of his profits he started up an import/export company based in London which was bought by Kingston & Kingston, but Pieter van Pallandt stayed on; H Desborough had researched his purchase as thoroughly as he always did, and the Dutchman he knew to be an even more valuable purchase than his business.

Just before the deal between Tubelis Research and Kingston & Kingston was signed, Giles Kingston suggested van Pallandt as a good man to join the Tubelis board. Campion uncharacteristically exploded and refused even to contemplate it.

'I will not have any dealings with that man,' he said.

'Why?' said Giles. 'He's quite a good businessman, I can't understand your objection.'

'You honestly don't know?' Campion asked. He really did not know the extent to which Giles Kingston was mixed up in the events that had shattered his family life. He had never spoken of the photograph to Eva and she had offered no confessions though there were many times that she felt as if she needed to. Campion simply did not know the extent to which van Pallandt was acting on his own accord or to what extent he was under the direction of the Kingston brothers. Giles Kingston's whole demeanour seemed to indicate that he had no knowledge of the affair and Campion, uncomplicated as he was, was inclined to believe he had none. But then he felt he understood nothing, he had not understood the woman he had lived with all his life. 'Yes,' he thought, 'van Pallandt must have tried to feather his own nest,' but whether it was the truth or not he really didn't care. He couldn't conceive how the loathsome Dutchman had come by the photograph, but what did it matter how he came by it? Nothing really mattered now. He lived in his laboratories and sought refuge in biotechnology as another man might take refuge in drink.

'I've no idea what you could possibly have against the man,' Giles Kingston had said. 'You haven't even met him, have you? Tell you what, how about George Mischel as a compromise? Would he be acceptable to you?'

'Yes, anything you like,' said Campion, and 'the rising man' joined the board of Tubelis.

Mischel, so Campion supposed, would be a useful addition to Tubelis. He had the ear of the Minister and Ministry contracts were vital. Of course, Mischel was obliged to declare his interests which he was scrupulous about doing. After all, Campion thought, it is not Mischel who makes the decision as to who gets contracts and who does not; that was left to others. Any promotion of Tubelis need not tarnish his image at all. Many MPs also held directorships precisely because they had contacts, it was all part of the system. But to Gordon Campion's surprise, far from promoting Tubelis, Mischel appeared to be overly zealous in the opposite direction. Every time a choice had to be made between Tubelis and one of its American or European competitors, Mischel argued forcefully for the competitor. Mischel had been foisted on Campion by Giles Kingston and, even if Mischel did nothing, what he didn't need was an enemy in the camp, especially not at this time.

Campion thought perhaps that Mischel was merely building up credit points, showing his strict and statesmanlike impartiality to the outside world, until such times as the latest and most important Tubelis project was unveiled when hopefully he would push it with all his might. This new project was vital to the survival of Tubelis. Campion was risking just about all on its success and it was for this project that he required the partial support of Kingston & Kingston. Alison Lester at Stoy's had, with the assistance of the specialist departments drawn up an alternative proposal to spread the financing and marketing of the new project without risking the future of the company on an all-or-nothing outcome. Though convinced that he was on the verge of a medical breakthrough that would take its place alongside the discovery of Penicillin, Campion saw the underlying sense of the Lester approach.

'We're in business to take risks as much as you are,' Alison had said. 'But there's no point in taking silly ones when there's more than one way round the problem.'

It appeared he could both have his cake and eat it, but the brief appearance of van Pallandt in his life cancelled out his commercial preferences as well as his faith in just about everything.

The new project was kept very hush-hush and apart from Campion himself the most senior researcher on it was Dr Marcus Pelham, a genetic engineer who had come to Tubelis from a government research institute. He had been with Tubelis for about five years and was one of the country's leading scientists in the development of genetically engineered drugs. The new Tubelis project involved using gene-splicing techniques to produce a drug that would effectively control, and in many cases cure, diabetes. A small batch of the drug had already been produced and was ready to go forward to the elaborate and expensive trialling procedure necessary before licensing and mass production could be achieved. Campion and Pelham had also found an answer to the problem of safe and efficient manufacture of the drug in the quantities that would eventually be required.

Pelham was a scientist pure and simple, and had nothing to do with the business side of Tubelis. Gordon Campion envied Pelham's position and wished that he, himself, did not have to wear so many hats. Campion and Pelham got on well enough as colleagues, though Campion sometimes irritated Pelham by his tendency to bypass or ignore the instrumental, technical difficulties of an issue and focus on the end result. Of the two Campion was the more creative intellectually, but Pelham had the more up-to-date technical skills and practical knowledge, he was much more the problem solver than the originator of ideas. The two men worked well enough together though they were not friends and did not mix socially. They respected each other as organisms that functioned as they should.

Pelham at forty eight was the younger of the two, he was married but had no children. Neither Pelham nor his wife had ever been keen on a family, as organisms children were unreliable and frequently went wrong. Pelham was a small man with a neatly trimmed beard which covered the upper lip and chin only. He was president of his county Bridge association and his wife was the secretary; this constituted their principal social activity. Each year they took a three-week camping holiday, usually in the Perigord noir region of the Dordogne, where Jill Pelham would prepare healthy, uncomplicated lunches to eat in front of their caravan, while Marcus explored the troglodyte dwellings. The caves and their paintings fascinated him. He marvelled at what he regarded as a completely different species from himself, those long extinct inhabitors of caves, their animal minds and animal motives. Pelham did not like the thought of radical change.

Walter Brownlees, Dai's former tutor at university, was used to change. He had moved several times between the academic and commercial worlds. He had been a contemporary of Hugo's at Harvard Business School. They were not what you would call friends, but they tended to move about together because it was circumstantially appropriate to do so, being two of a small number of Britons. Brownlees was an overtly greedy man which manifested itself even in his personal habits. In their Harvard days Hugo could not stand to watch Brownlees eat. Brownlees was a talker and the eating and digesting of large amounts of food did not interrupt his conversation. He thought of himself as a good conversationalist. He thought that the use of slightly antiquated language, meticulous diction, an exact articulatory emphasis, meant that he was both clever and seen to be clever. In reality Brownlees was not a particularly clever man, but he had sufficient ability to fool a sufficient number of people to pass as one. He had never fooled H Desborough Kingston, but Hugo knew Brownlees would have his uses and, in his own way, was as much a worthwhile acquisition as were Mischel and van Pallandt.

Brownlees had been in H Desborough's pocket long before he joined Tubelis Research as Marketing Director. He had held several appointments in this area in the past, and things had become a little hot at university; the rest of the faculty were beginning to take a dim view of the fact that his various outside consultancy jobs meant that he was doing very little by way of actually earning his academic salary. Things were becoming a little hot with the tax man too, for his greed dictated that he declare as little as possible and enquiries were being made. Brownlees always got glowing references whenever he applied for a job, H Desborough saw to that, but he was not averse to indulging in the kinds of dodgy activities that would have interested the Department of Trade and Industry had it known about them. Brownlees had the knack of slipping the net just in time. During his time at Tubelis he had, on several occasions, negotiated contracts then renegotiated them to conceal the fact that he was raking off that little bit extra for himself. He was like the child who, before the party starts, goes round the table and whips off the cream tops on the cakes with his finger. For Brownlees there was always that finger-full to be had.

Mischel, van Pallandt, Pelham and Brownlees would, in time, all lie down and bare their throats before the double-headed hell hound that was Kingston & Kingston.

7

WORKING WEEKEND

Caroline arrived at the hotel, she had been home to change and she had made herself up to look just right. Caroline had a greater sense of balance than any other woman I had known. She had the capacity to look good without betraying that she had obviously spent time doing it. The appearance of time and effort did not intrude on her character, so efficient were her organisational skills that she carried off everything with the lightness of accident or coincidence. She was a much-valued manager in the firm, she left nothing to chance and she was popular with the trainees because under her supervision they were always well-briefed.

'A good day?' she asked.

'Very,' I replied.

'You've been really going hell for leather, haven't you? A partnership looms, perhaps?'

'Perhaps — and as for your partnership with Stephen Fanshaw? May as well get straight to the point.'

She quickly ordered another drink to allow herself time. She was not quite ready to come to it just yet, she wanted a preamble to introduce it in her own time and on her own terms.

'We've known each other for a long time,' she said, taking a sip of her drink. 'Stephen and I, that is. I was going out with him long before we...' She didn't quite know how to finish the sentence.

'Before we what?' I said blankly, enjoying my relative advantage while I had the chance. My time, I knew, was to come and would last longer.

'Before Paris.' She said it as though reading the minutes of a meeting.

The barman stood right in front of us to wipe his glasses, though he could have positioned himself anywhere less intrusive. He had sniffed out a potential conflict and his own frustrations required him to aggravate it. I suddenly got an image of soldier ants ranging in all directions, there is something of the soldier ant in each of us that requires us to get to a fray as quickly as possible.

'I remember you felt very guilty about Stephen, in Paris, I mean.' This I knew to be untrue. At the time, in Paris, she had felt anything but guilty, nobody ever does at the time, it is only afterwards. The soldier ant was coming out in me, we were all of the same colony.

'Yes,' she said, 'I did'. This was a lie and one she knew I wouldn't like. I gave in.

'No you bloody well didn't,' I said with a broad grin.

'Oh yes I did,' she replied, casually returning my smile. 'But I kept it to myself.'

'You certainly didn't do that either,' I was enjoying myself.

'Stop it.' She had picked up my playful mood.

The barman moved away.

'In Paris you were consumed by lust, you didn't give Stephen Fanshaw a second thought.'

'Lust is your domain,' she said, 'not mine.'

'You're right,' I said, which put an end to playfulness, and since I had so suddenly, and unintentionally, ended it I thought it best to press on.

'And is it Fanshaw's domain — lust?' I asked, but wished I hadn't as soon as the words were out, for I knew they would be misconstrued.

'God, that's typical isn't it? First you imply that I am undersexed and then you want to find out how good the competition is. Well the answer is, very good.'

The barman came a bit closer. This was more to his liking.

'Mea culpa,' I said beating my breast in atonement, 'but I wasn't implying you were undersexed. You know I don't think that at all.'

'Then what do you think?' She asked as if she really wasn't bothered one way or another about an answer.

'I think you feel you ought not to enjoy it.'

'I do enjoy it!'

'With Fanshaw perhaps — but the company of a lawyer is always pleasurable when you know he's not writing letters to you or for you. What do they say? — "A barrister in bed's worth two in the chambers" or something like that. Perhaps Stephen could find me a lady solicitor and we could all go out and compare briefs.'

She took another sip of her drink.

'Why do you have to turn everything into a joke?'

'Sex is a joke as well as a whole lot of other things. Why exclude humour from all the other emotions?'

'Why do you think we are here?'

'That's a bit profound, a bit metaphysical for the Royal Stuart Hotel isn't it?'

'Edward, can you just cut it out for a moment? We're here because between you and me there are too many things that have been left unsaid.'

'And perhaps too many things that have been said,' I ventured.

'Yes that too, but the last time I was angry, I had been hurt, that's why we need to talk now.'

'I wasn't referring to that time, but never mind.'

'When were you referring to?'

'The beginning, the in-between perhaps.'

'You don't honestly believe that do you?'

I went back to that beginning in Paris, in the Rue Ancienne Comedie and a restaurant called La Procope where we ate that evening after we had been in bed all afternoon. That afternoon had been the first time. I recalled the woman who took our coats at reception and how attractive she was, petite with short hair and the reddest of red lipstick. She wore a tight suit and had finely shaped strong calves; she seemed so very French, but then she would have seemed so very Italian, so very Greek, so very Irish had it been Rome, Athens or Dublin and not Paris. I was so triumphantly together with Caroline that I recall acknowledging to myself just how attractive the French woman would have been to me once, and how readily I could make that acknowledgement and not care. La Procope was a favourite eating place of Robespierre and perhaps I should have recognised it as a sign not to be quite so indifferent to what went on about me. A head in the clouds one moment may find itself in a basket the next.

Caroline had been going with Stephen Fanshaw for two years prior to Paris. There was no doubting they were close, not only physically, but in the way couples are who have become a habit to one another. The world expected them to move in the manner of the pantomime horse, not always easily or elegantly but eventually in the same direction. Caroline was very committed to her career which sometimes inconvenienced Fanshaw, because, when time needed to be sacrificed, Stoy's came first and himself second. She was not the kind of woman who was going to sacrifice her own interests, mentally and physically, for the sake of someone else merely because there was some vague expectancy that she should. Caroline was a good technician of the kind that every firm needs, and she knew her worth.

Fanshaw too, was a hard worker if not a hard player. This was perhaps the main source of unease experienced by Caroline in their relationship. He was neither humourless nor uninteresting but he was not spontaneous. All things, even enjoyment, had to be ordered and planned in advance. Caroline was more lively and needed to feel she was not excluded from experiences that were spur of the moment; it excited her but it scared her a little too. Fanshaw had no time for spontaneity and I came along when she was feeling most in need of it.

To me, pleasure in all its guises is like the last bus, it won't come back for you, so you'd better get on while you can. I was a complication for Caroline which after Paris, she tried to pass off as a piece of regrettably heady nonsense, an undeniable but passing attraction. It didn't work out that way and her efforts to resume her life with Stephen caused jangled nerves all round which is inevitable in such cases where loyalty is divided. When, finally, she resolved to break with Stephen she very soon recaptured that spring-like vivacity that I will always associate with her. Fanshaw, though mightily miserable, accepted her decision with some dignity; there were no histrionics and I came to respect him much more because of it. I doubt that this respect was reciprocated for she had decided in my favour and I let her down. The reason — A C Winfield.

It is difficult to say which had the most disruptive influence on my life, the Kingston brothers or A C Winfield. I met all three for the first time on the same occasion when I had completed my third year at Stoy's. That year was the best by far, work-wise. I found I was being left alone more to chart my own course and given increasing responsibilities. Clients were 'phoning wanting to speak to me because they felt they didn't need to go any higher. I was being listened to within the firm and without. Over the three years, I had been studiously working my way through other people's portfolios gathering as many contacts of my own as I could and the momentum of my working life increased almost daily; it was now beginning to keep pace with my ambitions. Through the contacts I had made I began to introduce a number of new clients to Howard's business group. Other partners besides Howard made the point, from time to time, to talk to me about my work. I knew they did so because I had made the high-fliers list and it was their responsibility to get to know me and form their own judgements. One of those partners was Alison Lester. I subsequently became good friends with Alison and her husband Dave, whose love of spontaneity surpassed my own. Dave was completely crazy, and his sense of fun made me realise, in the times I most needed to, that I was not alone in the world. I had recourse to seek sanctuary in the Lester household more than once after the guerre a mort with the Kingstons had begun.

The pace had stepped up and things were good all round. I had qualified, my social life was rich, not only because of Caroline but also because those at Stoy's who lasted the course with me were good company as well as good colleagues. This heightened social ambiance that existed in the company stemmed from an awareness of a basic premise that underlined our work for Stoy's. Irrespective of our diverse backgrounds, Stoy's was a total meritocracy and we all knew it. This made us competitive on behalf of ourselves and the company, but it also drew us together in a common purpose — to be the best. There was no 'them and us', there was only us and we knew we were different. I had everything I wanted, or so I thought.

'What are you and Caro doing next weekend?' asked Dai.

'Nothing, as far as I know.'

'Good, then on Friday night you are to pack a bag and drive with Celia and me to the Cotswolds.'

'Sounds good — any particular reason?'

'You are cordially invited, as my guests, to what promises to be one of the best parties of the year. It will last the weekend and no expense will be spared.'

'Don't tell me, one of your horses has come in?'

'Giles Kingston is throwing a party on his country estate, attendance is compulsory for all the hellfire club and we have been given clearance to bring a couple of friends. How about it?'

'Sounds good to me, I'll see if Caroline is free. Celia is coming, you say?'

'Yes.'

'How is she? I haven't seen much of her since I moved out of the flat.'

'She's fine,' he said, but seemed to hurry over it.

'Has she got a job?'

'No, she's become too accustomed to the good life.'

'Last time I saw her she was going to go back to nursing.'

'As an added incentive in coming away this weekend,' he said, totally ignoring any enquiry about Celia, 'I may, if you behave towards me with the deference I deserve — I may introduce you to my boss, A C Winfield.'

'Absolutely thrilling, but one Financial Director is the same as another as far as I'm concerned. What is it about A C Winfield that makes him an event not to be missed?'

'I've fallen in love with my boss,' he said, pressing his hand against his heart in a mock swoon.

'Dedication to work is one thing, but that's carrying it a bit far isn't it?'

'I wish she was at hand, my hands.'

'Who?'

'Augusta C Winfield, my boss.'

'She's a woman?'

'How many men do you know called Augusta? Come to think of it, how many women? Of course she's a woman, but what a woman — I've never seen a woman like her.'

'You say that about every woman you meet who's marginally more attractive than Cinderella's sisters, and even then I'm not so sure.'

'She's not only beautiful, she's got a mind like a razor.'

The four of us travelled up from London on the Friday night and stayed in an hotel that was a monk's hospice in the fourteenth century. In that setting Dai, who had put on two stone, looked very much at home, every time I looked at him I saw Friar Tuck. Celia seemed livelier than I had seen her for some time, I think she was happy to have Caroline and me there as reinforcements against the isolation she felt in Dai's group. Caroline and I slept in a huge four-poster bed that night, its carved wooded supports were so weighted, so heavy that I felt as though I was lying on the floor of some ancient temple with its massive columns rising above me. I had a dream that night in which I was stretched out on an altar as a sacrifice. In my dream the moon shone through the columns onto the floor and there was nobody in the temple, just myself lying on a stone waiting, it seemed for centuries, for a footstep on the floor which heralded some unimaginable end. There were two windows in our room, the small one opposite the bed looked out into the courtyard of the hotel which was lit by an amber light. There was a lily pond in the courtyard, and I pictured it filled with carp by the long-dead monks who would count the fish each morning because sometimes in the night a heron would come and steal away one of their number. The larger window on the other side of the room looked down on a sloping village green, at the end of which the spire of a Norman Church rose to the night under an unbearably white moon, a lucidity that swathed all man-made endeavours with a mocking brilliance.

Caroline's arm coiled around my waist.

'I am —,' she began and then hesitated as though she was uncertain how she should end.

'You are what?' I whispered, expecting some positive declaration that would reflect my own feelings.

'I'm not sorry,' she said, which was not what I expected at all.

'Not sorry for what?'

'Not sorry about how things have worked out, with us I mean, and the business with Stephen.'

This was a much less exalted pronouncement on the state of things as I imagined them to be than I had expected. Not being sorry was something that did not match my present mood.

'Of course I am sorry for Stephen. In the end I behaved cruelly and I know I hurt him a lot. I'll always feel guilty about it but there was no choice.'

Why, I wondered, does guilt mingle so often with sex. Why do we create impossible, tangled rules around an instinct that is no different from any other. We didn't evolve the same illogical do's and don'ts for any of our other instincts. Sexual desire is just as inherent as our desire to eat or drink, satisfying our hunger or thirst gives no cause to regret. Why did she feel it necessary to treat her sexual desire as some unknown transgression against some undefined law?

'There's no easy way to do these things,' she went on, 'I always knew that it would be you in the end. I should have finished it sooner for Stephen's sake.'

'Let's not talk about it,' I said, turning on my side to face her. She moved towards me and I pressed my hand into the small of her back.

'You're very different, you and Stephen.'

'Oh,' I said, indifferent to how alike or otherwise Stephen and I were. We could have been monozygotic twins for all I cared.

'Yes,' she said, 'you somehow seem to expect more of things.'

'What things?'

'I don't know, everything, me.'

She kissed me and after we made love I fell into my dream

where I lay on the altar in the temple. It seemed to last all night, my waiting in the dream. Just before I woke I heard those footsteps on the temple floor and saw a woman, with coal black hair and marble white skin, standing in the moonlight under the columns before my outstretched body.

'Wakey, wakey, rise and shine, the morning's fine, the sun is scorching your eyeballs out!' Dai burst into the room as was his usual fashion. He aspirated the way he said 'eyeballs' so that it sounded like 'high balls' and through my half-open lids I could see that he was dressed in a varied array of pastel colours; pastel-blue summer shoes, pastel-green trousers; pastel-pink shirt, and a jacket that matched his shoes. He stood there looking like a human iced-lolly, leering down at us.

'One day you'll learn how to knock on a door,' I said.

'Morning, Dai,' said Caroline. How could anyone wake up looking so fresh, I thought. She looked as if she hadn't been to bed.

'Good morning delectable creature,' said the iced-lolly.

'Morning,' said Celia poking her head round the door.

'Is there anyone else out there who'd like to come in,' I said. 'The kitchen staff perhaps, or the vicar from the church across the green?'

'I told Dai not to disturb you,' Celia said apologetically. 'We can't hang about, Giles expects everybody to be there by eleven.'

The drive to the Kingston estate didn't take long. It was approached by a long avenue of lime trees through which the sun filtered suggesting an Impressionist canvas. At the end of this avenue I could see some opened wrought-iron gates through which a gravel drive led to the house itself. The gravel drive was bordered by boxed yews and a lawn on either side with laburnums that hung heavily in full-bloom.

'Aren't they beautiful?' said Caroline.

'Yes, but do you know they're very poisonous, laburnums?' said Celia vaguely.

'I wasn't planning on eating them,' replied Caroline.

The house itself was a large Jacobean mansion which Old Kingston had acquired cheaply just after the war when it was run down, and when popular taste inclined more towards cement rendering and aluminum window frames.

The house was never lived in as a family home, it was just another acquisition which had its occasional uses. A sign directed cars to the rear of the house. By the number of cars it was clear that a lot of guests had arrived already. We got out and saw another sign saying 'Thrash' and pointing to some stone steps which led to the formal gardens. Once down the steps the gardens opened out onto three tiers of mixed lawns, trees, rose beds and topiary work. The lower tier had a water garden on one side and a large swimming pool on the other and it was there that the guests were congregated. They seemed a curious mix. I estimated about one hundred and fifty people, some elderly businessmen, accompanied by their wives, standing rigidly in conclaves and dressed as though they had just come from Threadneedle Street. There were young people too, dressed more casually, and there were quite a few people dressed for swimming. I saw Dai's friend hellfire Harry wading about fully clothed; most wore conventional costumes but there were a number of younger women naked in the pool. The whole scene looked like the double booking of a building society meeting and a Roman Bacchanalia. Harry waved to Dai who set off at a sprint and jumped in the water, pastel ensemble and all. Celia, Caroline and I followed more sedately till we reached the pool side.

'In you come,' said Dai.

'I haven't brought a costume,' said Caroline.

'Get 'em off,' said hellfire Harry lurching towards us. It had only just gone twelve and he was half-cut already.

'Perhaps the ladies would prefer a drink first, Harry,' said a voice behind us.

It was Giles Kingston. He was dressed casually all in white, his dark hair was brushed back, and his olive skin stood out against the whiteness of his clothes. He stood smiling at us and he reminded me of some friendly dentist, needle in hand, trying to reassure. He put his arm around Celia's waist and kissed her on the cheek, but his eyes and his interest focussed on Caroline.

'Lovely to see you again, Celia,' he said.

Dai scrambled up onto the pool side, like a whale intent on beaching itself, to do the introductions.

'You're most welcome,' Giles said to Caroline and kissed her hand. He was now less the friendly dentist and more a South American Peon, his blood brimming with machismo, a man prepared to use a knife against another for the sake of a woman.

'And this is my friend Edward Cartwright,' said Dai.

I put out my hand, but as I did so Giles was distracted by a naked girl emerging from the pool. When he turned again he said:

'How do you do, there's plenty to drink over there, so help yourself,' but he didn't offer his hand and I was somehow grateful that he didn't; he had the look of a snake and I imagined his touch to be similar.

'Of course you'll stay for the weekend,' he said, more by way of command than enquiry, and directing it primarily to Caroline and Celia.

'You must have a lot of spare bedrooms,' I said, 'to accommodate this many people?'

'Ah, not everybody will stay overnight, only selected guests. A number of people are here to discuss business, I like to mix business and pleasure. They will stay only for the day and the party this evening. Tomorrow will be given over solely to pleasure.'

'Has A C arrived yet?' Dai asked Giles.

'Not yet.'

'But she is coming, isn't she?'

'Oh yes, she'll be here.' Giles seemed as if he didn't want to be interrogated about the movements of A C Winfield. For the first time he was less self-assured.

'Good,' said Dai, 'I want to prove to Edward that I wasn't making it up when I said she was the best-looking businesswoman in Britain.'

Caroline and I kept pretty much to ourselves for the next couple of hours while Dai frolicked about for all he was worth. Celia contrived to look as if she was enjoying herself, but I did notice a certain tenseness come into her face whenever she was in Giles Kingston's company.

After lunch Dai introduced us to George Mischel who

made conversation in an empty sort of way. Dai left us with Mischel, who talked at length about himself before asking:

'And what do you do, Mr Cartwright?'

'I work for Stoy Hayward, the accountancy firm.'

At the mention of Stoy's a man from a nearby group turned to us.

'Did I hear you say you worked for Stoy Hayward?'

'Yes that's right, I'm Edward Cartwright.'

'How do you do, I'm Gordon Campion. My company, Tubelis Research, used to be one of your clients.'

'Let me introduce Caroline Wheeler, Caroline also works for Stoy's.'

Campion greeted Caroline and asked, 'How's Alison Lester, is she still there?'

'Oh yes,' I said, 'she's still at Stoy's, but she's moved into Corporate Finance. She's doing very well.'

'That doesn't surprise me at all; very clever woman, Alison. I wish we still had her at Tubelis,' he said, almost nostalgically.

Giles Kingston joined us along with a stern-looking little man with a well trimmed beard.

'Ah Gordon, I see you've met Edward and the beautiful Caroline. Let me introduce you to Marcus Pelham who also works for Tubelis. Edward and Caroline are friends of Dai Bunch,' said Giles.

'Who?' asked Pelham.

'Dai Bunch, the new Assistant Finance Director of your own company, don't tell me you haven't met him yet, Marcus?' continued Giles.

'I might have, but finance isn't my line.'

'Marcus is our senior research officer at Tubelis,' said Campion. 'I was just telling Edward and Caroline how I miss the involvement of Stoy Hayward in our business.'

'One firm of accountants is much the same as another,' said Giles, obviously not keen to pursue the matter.

'I beg to differ,' I said, 'it can make a big difference as Mr Campion must know.'

'It certainly can, we wouldn't be in the position we are today without Alison Lester's advice.'

'An audit is an audit,' said Giles still smiling his usual smile, which gave a certain edge to his sarcasm.

'I don't agree at all,' said Campion. 'Now I get nothing more than a cold technical job from this new lot,' he said to Kingston. 'My one reaction now is "Oh God, the auditors are coming". I'm beginning to resent having to pay them. It never used to be like that, I always saw the audit as a chance to ask questions, to review how things were going, to seek advice.'

'That's exactly how it should be,' I said.

Dai by this time had rejoined us and I could see by his florid countenance that he had been drinking a lot.

'The good thing about Alison Lester was she — ' Campion started to say, but before he could finish Pelham butted in.

'I'm glad it's Gordon and not me who has to deal with all this business nonsense — give me pure research anyday; it's science that ultimately determines the future and not business.'

'I don't think that's entirely true Mr Pelham,' Caroline said, 'Non-financial aspects of business — environment, energy, quality of life — all require new services, the development of novel skills.'

'I shall now make a pronouncement,' said Dai who was so sloshed his pronunciation of 'pronouncement' was indistingushable from the gushing sounds made by a burst water main.

'As ashishtant director of finansh of your company,' he cascaded further, 'I hereby advise you Gordon, to get rid of your preshent lot and get my friend Edward here to do it — oh and Caroline too because — becaushe — she's got lovely breasts and he — he —hashn't.'

He was now swaying so much he looked like an inflated rubber dinghy bobbing up and down in a Force Ten.

'Well, if not for those reasons, I certainly would be grateful to get Stoy's help back,' said Campion.

'Fortunately it is not up to you to decide, is it my dear Dai,' said Giles with a tight, disapproving smile.

As they spoke we were approached by a large ungainly man. When he arrived I couldn't make out whether he was smiling or just drooling, his lower jaw seemed permanently detached from the rest of his face.

'Mr Kingston, I am so sorry to be late, but I always have so many errands to run, so many missions to mercy — is that the correct expression? — So many good deeds to do.'

'Hello, van Pallandt,' said Giles, not bothering to introduce him to us.

Van Pallandt turned to Gordon Campion.

'Ah, Mr Campion, how nice to see you again. Are you here alone or is your charming wife here to enjoy herself also? And your son? He is now a member of Parliament I believe.'

I was not prepared for Campion's reaction. He stood as though he had turned to ice, with a wild almost violent look in his eyes. His whole expression was one of uncon-cealed disgust for this Dutchman, who to me appeared to be behaving with nothing other than affability towards him. There was a moment when I half believed Campion was making a move to strike van Pallandt. Giles Kingston broke the silence.

'Go and get yourself a drink, van Pallandt.'

The Dutchman left and Campion spun on his heel almost simultaneously and walked away saying nothing. Giles Kingston then started to say something to Caroline.

I didn't hear the rest of the conversation, all my concen-tration was taken by a woman coming down the stone steps on the upper level of the garden. She wore a deep cherry red suit, had a shock of jet black hair, pale skin and emerald green eyes. She was, even from a distance, impossible to ignore. I saw Giles Kingston looking at her also. She didn't join the party but went to an entrance at the back of the house and disappeared. I immediately recalled my dream of the night before and heard again those footsteps on the marble floor.

'Well, if you will excuse me,' said Giles, 'some of us have business to discuss for the next hour or so. I'm giving a private dinner for a few specially selected guests this evening and I would very much like you to join us.' He was looking at Caroline when he said it.

The group broke up leaving Caroline, myself and Dai alone when, from a little distance off, Giles Kingston stopped and called Dai to him. I saw Giles pat Dai's cheek several times, lightly, and grip it between his thumb and forefinger as one might do to a baby.

'We have been a bit of a naughty boy, haven't we,' said Giles. 'All that drink and all that unnecessary babbling on. We mustn't forget which side our bread is buttered on, must we?' He gave Dai another pat which was imperceptibly but definitely harder. 'We mustn't get too big for our boots, must we? We must learn to control our tongue, eh?'

'I'm sorry, Giles, I didn't mean to cause any bother. I didn't mean to upset anything. I wouldn't want to upset you especially, you've been so good to me. I'll do anything I can — '

'Oh, it's all right.' Giles talked as though to a child, 'I'm not upset, and I'm sure there is something you will be able to do to make up for this little indiscretion. Let me think — I know what, yes you'll like this, it'll be a bit of fun, great sport.'

He whispered in Dai's ear.

'Oh no, Giles, I don't think I could do that,' said Dai when Giles had finished whispering.

'Oh come on, it's a bit of a lark, that's all. Why not? It's only a bit of fun, I'd do the same for you, wouldn't I? I thought we understood each other. I thought you were one of us, the new hellfire club, we stick together, don't we? We share everything? Of course, if you're prudish about the whole thing, forget it.'

'I'm not a prude,' said Dai, 'don't think that, it's just, well — I can't explain but — Giles I'll do anything else, and it wouldn't be much fun for you I know, believe me, not for someone with your experience.'

'I like novelty, dear boy, I like a challenge. Oh, by the way, you know that last lot of money I loaned you, after the latest of your little scrapes? You couldn't see your way to repaying it this coming week, could you? Even people like myself have cash-flow problems from time to time, and you owe me rather a lot; £43,000, I think it was at the last count. Of course I don't want it all back next week, just the last loan, you understand.'

'Giles I... I...' Dai started to stammer. 'I'm sorry I just couldn't get it by next week, I'd have to sell something, if you could give me a bit more time I could save it I know I could and — '

'Oh, never mind, if you can't find the money I shall have to find an alternative. Fancy you letting me down twice in succession. Well it can't be helped.'

'Giles, I'm sorry, I don't know what to say, you've been so good to me — '

'Yes, I have, haven't I, and now you've gone all prudish on me; it's not a good sign, it makes me question my own judgment. There comes a time when everyone must pay their debts, you know.'

'I'll do anything you suggest, there's no need to question your judgment, you're not wrong about me, Giles, I'm still a good investment.'

'Well you're proving a rather costly investment at the moment for very little in return. One disappointment I can accept, but two — that's a different matter. I'd even be willing to write off my last little loan to you - £6000 wasn't it?...if...'

'If what? Anything, Giles, you name it.'

'That's more of the Dai Bunch I know, come and we'll talk about it, you'll see, it's a bit of sport, just a bit of sport, nothing more.'

I saw Giles Kingston leading Dai off with his arm around his shoulder. During the day I couldn't help but notice the deferential, sycophantic tone that all Dai's group adopted in the presence of Giles Kingston and I was disappointed to find that Dai was no different to the rest. I knew this sort of thing happened but I wasn't used to watching it in action. With my superiors I could talk straight. They didn't want people who argued for argument's sake of course, but they liked people to challenge things. Even partners had to be self-critical and questioning, this detailed self-assessment operated at all levels at Stoy's and everybody had to look back over their achievements and wait to be told either 'yes you've done it,' or 'no you haven't'. This was not only how seniority developed in the firm but also how experience was gained. The system was based on honest critical analysis, of oneself and others, toadyism played no part in it. It was necessary to talk straight for the system to remain efficient.

That evening while we were getting ready to go down to dinner I thought about the people I had met that day. It was a bit like going to the zoo, so many different varieties of animal. There was Giles Kingston, sleek, snake-like, with his dark glassy eyes and that half-smile from which one might expect to see a forked tongue dart to collect passing insects. There was van Pallandt with his huge frame, protruding stomach, his lolling tongue and loose lower jaw — he certainly looked to have the strength of a gorilla but he was too ill-proportioned, too ignobly put together to be a gorilla — an orang-utan perhaps. Pelham was a sharp-featured little bird, a woodpecker with his beak rat-a-tat-tatting at the solid trunk of science which was the only thing in his visual field. There was Gordon Campion, who didn't seem like a zoo animal at all, he was more like a domestic pet, a retriever or a labrador with sad eyes, a dog who had been ill-treated, had the spirit all but beaten out of him by a cruel master. Mischel of course was the complete politician, unquestionably a chameleon. During the afternoon Dai had introduced us to Walter Brownlees. I had not met him at university. Brownlees had the appearance of a sea-elephant, crammed full of fish, his skin blotched and peeling. And then there was the woman who had walked down the stone steps. I could not find an animal to fit her, she could only have been a woman.

'I wonder who'll be at this select dinner?' asked Caroline as she sat at the mirror drying her golden hair, with a large bath towel wrapped round her.

'No idea,' I said, watching her tanned shoulders and arms undulate as she worked the hair dryer.

'Why do you suppose we got an invitation?'

'I don't think we did, I think you did and I just happened to be an unwelcome accessory.'

'I couldn't stand the way that man kept looking at me, it gave me the jitters.'

'Which particular man was that? There were a lot of men who kept looking at you — hellfire Harry for one.'

'God, what a wimp, I can't understand how someone as intelligent as Dai can be so friendly with such a brainless overgrown schoolboy. No, I mean Giles Kingston.'

'He didn't appeal to you then?'

'Oh he's quite good-looking in an oily sort of a way, but he's not my type. He's a bit too good-looking if you know what I mean. I prefer men whose features are a little less perfect, rough cast, where you can see the stonemason's chisel has slipped on one or two occasions — like you.'

I went over and pulled out the tuck in the towel so that it fell away from her.

'Stonemason's chisel, is it,' I said, trying to raise her out of the chair.

'Edward!' she said and scrambled for the towel which she managed to retrieve and cover herself with once more.

'Why don't you like me to look at you without your clothes on, except when we're making love?'

'I get embarrassed.'

'Why? I don't think the stonemason made any slip-ups in your case.'

'I just feel uncomfortable, that's all.'

'Were you just as uncomfortable about it with Stephen?'

'Yes, but Stephen didn't make such a big deal out of it, in fact he never mentioned anything about it at all.'

'No, I don't suppose he did.'

'What do you mean by that?'

'I'm not sure; I suppose nothing more than that Stephen wouldn't see it as important.'

'And you see it as important.'

'Yes.'

'You're sounding a little like a voyeur.'

'It's just the opposite of voyeurism.'

'Explain.'

'Wouldn't you rather make love instead?'

'We haven't time.'

'Don't you want to?'

'Of course I want to, but there just isn't time, we've got to get down for the dinner.'

'Forget the dinner, I'm not hungry.'

'Well I am. Hurry up or we'll be late.'

We were slightly late for dinner, most people were seated when we arrived.

'Ah, here they are,' said Giles, 'you look absolutely

wonderful, Caroline, what a beautiful dress, I knew from the moment I saw you this afternoon that you had taste. Please take a seat; Caroline, you here on my left and, Edward, take that one down there if you don't mind.'

He directed me to the other end of the table from himself and Caroline. The other guests were Walter Brownlees and his wife Harriet who was, as I might have expected, the complete female sea-elephant with only marginally fewer blotches than her husband. Marcus Pelham was there with his wife Jill, the perfect lady woodpecker. Van Pallandt thankfully didn't have a wife. Mischel had a wife but she hadn't come with him. Mischel's wife stayed at home in his constituency, but of course as 'a rising man' he had very little occasion to go home; his secretary, a Miss Thomas, had accompanied him that weekend. Celia sat with her head lowered and her eyes those of a frightened doe; she was between Brownlees and George Mischel and there was no Dai. Hellfire Harry was there, much to my regret, with a girl he addressed all night as 'Cynth'.

So there we were, a curious mix. On one side of the table were Giles, Caroline, Marcus Pelham, Mrs Brownlees, hellfire Harry, Cynth, and me in that order. On the other side, from the top, were van Pallandt, Jill Pelham, Walter Brownlees, Celia, Mischel, Miss Thomas, and an empty chair which was opposite me, and which I presumed was reserved for Dai. There was also one other vacant chair at the head of the table where, by rights, Giles as host ought to have been sitting.

'Dai still getting ready, is he, Celia?' I asked.

Celia looked up nervously as though she didn't know what to reply.

'Poor old Dai isn't feeling too well, he won't be joining us this evening. He has an upset stomach; you can probably guess the cause, Edward, knowing him as you do. I told him to go home,' said Giles.

'And has he?' I asked.

'I'm not sure, but never mind Dai, let's begin, shall we?'

'I see there is another place set at the top of the table', said Brownlees, 'might I hope that my friend from my student days will be joining us?'

He couldn't have been more obsequious. Is this what it was like to work for these people? Did the crawling have to go on until retirement age? Why was Brownlees doing it anyway, I wondered.

'You might hope,' said Giles, 'but it's unlikely. Hugo very rarely comes to my little parties. He doesn't like parties.'

'It's a beautiful house,' said Caroline.

'And a beautiful house should be filled with beautiful people,' he replied as a compliment to her.

Looking at van Pailandt and the Brownlees I wasn't so sure about that.

'It's very early Jacobean,' said Jill Pelham with authority.

'I wouldn't know,' said Giles, 'I haven't a clue when "Jacobean" was, I'm not really interested in that sort of thing. It's a heap of stones as far as I'm concerned and damned expensive to keep up. I'd like to turn it into an hotel or a country club but Hugo seems intent on keeping it for some reason.'

'It could even be late Elizabethan,' Jill Pelham went on, blind to Giles' indifference. 'It has the traditional H-shape structure, I'd date it about the 1590s.'

Jill Pelham had married an expert and she considered her marriage vows obliged her to demonstrate her own expertise in relation to just about any topic under discussion. She was a very organised woman; a woman that the world would describe as 'capable'. She gave sound practical advice to other women on how best to organise their lives more efficiently than they were presently doing. That the recipient of her sound instruction might have four children under ten to cope with, which rendered her methods impractical, made no difference to Jill Pelham. A system, if it worked for her, should work for anyone. She never wanted children of her own, but if she had she would have given them

Shakespearean names. There would have been an Ophelia, a Rosalind, a Miranda Pelham to announce to all and sundry that their mother was steeped in the literary arts. Marcus Pelham would have let her call the children anything she wanted, he was steeped only in science, and having a Newton Pelham or a Marconi Pelham was not on his list of priorities. The Pelhams appeared compact and impregnable, two little pigs that sensibly built a house of bricks, but Marcus Pelham hid an untapped seam of vanity which would bring the walls tumbling down.

We had completed the first course of salmon mousse, and van Pallandt was telling us how a certain East African tribe carried out cranial surgery while the patient was fully conscious.

'It's to let out evil spirits that are in the fluids of the brain, which make the head hurt. After they have let them out, these evil spirits, they fold the skin at the top where they have cut a groove, and pack it with leaves and mud, then the patient goes back to work in the fields until it dries. When they take the mud and leaves off,' he broke into his booming laugh, 'they have two big bumps on top of their heads for life. It is so funny to see all these people walking around with big grooves in their heads. But the most fascinating thing,' his voice became even louder for emphasis, 'the most fascinating thing is that they feel no pain, no pain at all.'

'Of course they feel it, but primitive societies have the ability to control its expression much better than people in so-called advanced Western cultures,' said Jill Pelham to indicate that, if pressed, she was no mean anthropologist.

'There's no pain in the brain,' said her husband, as if that should end the matter.

'Oh there must be,' said Harriet Brownlees, 'people get headaches, don't they?'

'That's different, there are pain centres in the brain but — ' Pelham was cut off by Walter Brownlees.

'The biggest brain-pain centres I know are British universities.' He paused to allow us time to appreciate that he was being clever, and to allow himself time to sample his first mouthful of the main course which had just arrived.

'One's time is taken up with nothing but boring and wasteful administration. I am so glad I came back to industry; I shall never go back to academic life again.'

Giles hadn't heard any of this, he was too busy engaging Caroline in a private conversation. I could see him throwing his head back occasionally, in a laugh, he was enjoying her company. He was also being eyed by Miss Thomas who seemed to be weighing up all the males at the table with regard to their possible purchasing power as potential customers; clearly, in her estimation, Giles would have been the ideal client. Miss Thomas was not to know that, as one of his little sidelines, Giles Kingston owned the escort agency for which she worked, which was how George Mischel had come to employ her as his 'secretary' in the first place. Jill Pelham and Walter Brownlees were kept busy trying to out-bid one another in displaying a knowledge of esoteric subjects; van Pallandt had drawn Marcus Pelham into talking about microbiology which Pelham was happy to do as long as the discussion did not touch on the new, and secret, Tubelis project. Harriet Brownlees was trying to extract an explanation for her frequent stomach cramps from the embattled Celia who was too polite to venture the obvious possibility of overeating. Mischel, with a taciturn Miss Thomas beside him, was talking politics at hellfire Harry who received his entire political instruction with his left hand gripping the upper thigh of the impervious Cynth. The talk, which had settled into the usual dinner table rhythms, stopped abruptly when Augusta Winfield walked into the room.

I had not been talking when she entered, but it was certain that something inside me stopped at that moment. Few people have the presence to command an absolute silence by the mere act of appearing. Augusta Winfield did. Having seen her from a distance early in the day, coming down the stone steps, I had been reminded of my dream the night before, but now with her standing opposite me behind the empty chair, so near, I was convinced that this woman had been a perpetual visitor through a lifetime's hours of sleep.

'You're late,' said Giles.

She ignored him and sat down opposite me. Giles

introduced those who didn't already know her and when
he came to me he said:

'Edward is a close friend of your assistant Dai Bunch.'

She looked across at me without any expression in her
eyes and said: 'Assistant is a bit of a euphemism, isn't it?'

Her voice spoiled the initial impact of her looks. It was
not an unpleasant voice in itself, but throughout the evening
everything she said was delivered coldly; she spoke without
expression like an automaton. The only person to whom
she responded with any sort of warmth was Marcus Pelham
which I thought odd as he came across as the coldest fish
in the room. Given my position at the table, my nearest
channels for conversation were either Augusta opposite me
or Cynth to my right. Feeling that it would be improper to
interrupt hellfire Harry's groping for the sake of one or two
'Oh yeahs,' and 'Oh rights,' I said to Augusta after she had
finished speaking to Pelham: 'You seem very interested in
science, did you take a science degree before going into
finance?'

'No, I read English and then did an MBA,' she said. I
estimated her age as being a little over thirty.

'I read English as well,' I said.

'It was a long time ago, I don't remember any of it.'

'You must remember something,' I said, 'there are some
pretty unforgettable — '

'I remember getting a First, that's all' she cut in. 'As I
said, it was a long time ago. I've no time for literature now.
You still read a lot, I take it?'

'As much as I can,' I said.

'You must have more time than I do,' she said.

'I try to make time,' I said, wondering why just being
pleasant proved so difficult for so many people.

'I don't see that it was of any benefit reading all that
poetry. Poetry is an embarrassment to the real world. Poetry
isn't profitable.'

'So you did read a lot of it once, poetry?' I asked.

'Yes, but as I said I've forgotten it all.'

'I don't believe that.'

For the first time that evening she gave just a hint of
being interested in what I was about to say.

'I don't think you're the kind of person who is likely to forget much,' I said.

'What makes you say that?'

'Intuition and something you said.'

'I didn't think accountants could afford to work on the basis of intuition.'

'There are times when it comes in handy.'

'When?'

'When you're not sure whether someone is telling the truth.'

'And you're not sure whether I'm telling the truth, about remembering any poetry?'

'Oh yes I'm sure,' I said smiling. 'I know you're not telling the truth.'

She looked up from her plate and fixed great green eyes on me.

'What was it I said that made you think that — '

'You said that poetry was an embarrassment to the real world, and somebody who remembers no poetry wouldn't have said that.'

'Maybe the real world, as you call it, is more of an embarrassment to poetry.'

The door opened and a man and a woman came into the room. Giles Kingston looked up with genuine surprise.

'Hugo,' he said, 'what on earth are you doing here? Didn't you know I was having a bash here this weekend?'

'A bash?' said H Desborough, sitting down at the top of the table. 'Is that what a party is called these days, Giles? Yes I knew you were entertaining.'

Walter Brownlees stood up.

'Hugo, how delightful to see you,' he said.

'Sit down, Walter,' said Hugo, 'nobody is playing the national anthem.'

Brownlees sat down.

'But you hate my parties, Hugo,' continued Giles, 'I really am surprised.'

'I know how much you like surprises, little brother.'

An elderly but sturdy-looking woman stood beside H Desborough's chair.

'There's nothing further I require for the moment, Miss

Muxloe,' he said, unfolding a napkin and tucking it into his collar. 'You can wait for me in the study.'

Miss Muxloe, Hugo's secretary and formerly secretary to Old Kingston for twenty years, left the room. Giles was about to begin some introductions when Hugo stopped him.

'I know most people here,' he said, 'but as I shall not be here long enough to become acquainted with your other guests introductions are unnecessary. I shall have some-thing light to eat,' he said this looking pointedly at Brownlees, 'and then retire to my study, where I should like a private word, Giles, if you can spare me a little of your valuable playtime.'

He asked the waiter to pass him an orange and sat there silently peeling it with ruby-ringed fingers.

After dinner we rejoined the main group of partygoers in a large conservatory room where there was a jazz band playing to a lot of very drunk people. I left Caroline and Celia and went to look for Dai, for I didn't believe that he would have just left without us. In my search I saw Hugo and Giles Kingston entering a small study room. Everything about them was conspiratorial, even to the manner in which they entered the room and closed the door. I continued searching, unaware that the business they were to discuss would directly affect me.

Inside the room Miss Muxloe had been waiting at her station, stout and true; the loyal service she had given to Old Kingston over many years she had transferred to his eldest son with equal measure.

'Miss Muxloe,' said Hugo, 'my brother and I have some family business to discuss, you will not be needed for the rest of the evening. You may go.'

Miss Muxloe, who had served Old Kingston so faithfully for so long, had come to regard herself almost as family and felt a slight stab at her summary dismissal, but as always, she would do the bidding of the man at the top. Miss Muxloe left the room.

'I want an update on Tubelis, Giles,' said Hugo when she had left.

'Everything seems to be going to plan. Campion will fall when his latest project fails to take off. He's put all his own and the company's resources into the financing of it and any delay puts him deeper in hock to us. If we withdrew our backing the whole of Tubelis would collapse in a week.'

'Yes, but of course it is also costing us, I want to see some returns.'

'Mischel is doing all he can to deflect any Ministry interest, and in that we're helped by Campion who is keeping it very close to his chest till it's ready to present. Furthermore, any interest the Ministry may or may not eventually show will be too late for Campion, we will have gobbled up Tubelis' assets long before that.'

'You understand,' said Hugo, 'that valuable as the assets of Tubelis Research may be to us, they are as nothing to the potential value of the the research project itself. Everything depends on our acquiring the formula and production details before the drug has been trialled and Ministry licences it. Once Tubelis get the licence and start mass production it will be far too late for us to sell the results of their research to the organisations who are willing to pay us so much money for it.'

'Well that's the other bit of good news. Van Pallandt has got all his contacts, primarily those in the Far East, but he's now beginning to tap other organisations as well — he's got them committed to receive and pay on the dot when we give the go ahead and — '

'But, Giles, that is not my point. I know there is a market out there prepared to receive it, and I know that van Pallandt has all his contacts frothing at the mouth, but what I want to know is how close we are to taking possession of what they want to buy?'

'These things take a little time, Hugo.'

'Precisely, but how much time? You see, unlike you I am not prepared to put my faith in Mischel's ability to stall the Ministry indefinitely once wind of the project starts to filter through Whitehall. We know, via Campion, that the Americans are working on a similar drug, but whoever the Ministry goes for it is essential that we are in possession of both Tubelis Research and the formula before it gets that far. So, little brother, let me ask again, how close are we to (a) taking over Tubelis, in which case if the Ministry opts for us it will be an added bonus? And (b) getting the formula to sell to van Pallandt's contacts before the Government licences them?'

Giles was irked by his brother's persistent probing, he had other things on his mind, pleasurable things, and he hadn't expected to have to account to Hugo that weekend.

'Do we have to go through all this now?' he said, pouring a drink. 'Can't you just take my word that we're on course?'

Hugo laughed, which was something he did so rarely that it frightened Giles.

'I am not prepared to take anybody's word,' said Hugo, 'least of all yours, little brother. You have your strengths but reliability is not one of them.'

'Stop calling me little brother, will you. You're an old woman, Hugo, you're not Father. You're much more like Miss Muxloe than Father, so stop trying to behave like him. I won't be patronised.'

'Oh I would never wish to behave like Father, Giles. I hated Father perhaps much more than you know.'

'Hugo, what happened to him was proof of how much you hated him.'

'What happened to him had nothing to do with my feelings, that was strictly business as you know.'

'OK, you've made your point,' said Giles. 'Anyway, if the police didn't exactly buy the suicide or accident theories at least the coroner brought in an open verdict and our alibis hold up, so let's not dwell on it, shall we.'

'Unlike you I didn't need an alibi, but you're right, let's not dwell on it. Back to the matter at hand, where are we at this precise point in time?'

'As far as stitching up Campion is concerned, Mischel, Brownlees and A C are doing a good job, between them they've got him running round in circles and blocking any moves he makes to get Tubelis out of the red or to reduce his dependence on us. Brownlees, of course, is on the fiddle, that's par for the course, but his little perks have only served to further complicate Campion's financial predicament — let's face it, he's no businessman — and Bunch has cleverly covered up everything with a bit of creative accountancy. There is no way he can now free himself from us.'

'And the formula and manufacturing details, how and when do I get them?'

'That's down to AC again, she's already begun to move in on Pelham and it won't be long before he's eating out of her hand and the plans are courtesy of van Pallandt and winging their way to every dubious drug producer and pharmaceuticals pirate on the face of the globe.'

'You depend a lot on the abilities of Augusta Winfield, which worries me somewhat.'

'Don't worry about Augusta, she's already got that over-preened, vain little twerp Pelham flattering himself that she's fascinated by his "brilliant" mind. He's a gonner, make no mistake, she'll have a copy of those documents in no time.'

'Well, go and enjoy yourself, Giles. You must admit I have never interfered in your pleasures. But there is one loose end that will need to be tied once we have the formula and production details and van Pallandt has passed them to his contacts.'

'What's that?'

'Van Pallandt himself, he is a dangerous loose end that is directly traceable to us.'

'He's a handy man to have about,' said Giles.

'Once he has passed the documents to his contacts and we have banked our money in the usual place, he will have served his purpose and be of no further use. I suggest you go back to the source through whom you acquired the services of — what was his name? — yes, Monsieur Chastaret, that was it. Whatever, I want van Pallandt put out of the way.'

'All right, anything else?'

'Yes, George Mischel — '

'Hang on, you don't want him put away too. There could be some nasty repercussions.'

'Oh no, he will be very useful to us in the future precisely because of his influence. What I want is for Mischel to deliver one copy of the documents in person and to receive the money for it. I want him to keep the money for himself and I want us to be able to provide evidence of his transaction should we ever need to — as an insurance policy, you understand?'

'Yes perfectly, that can be arranged.'

'I think that's all for the time being,' said Hugo, 'unless there's anything else you think I should know?'

'No,' said Giles, moving to the door.

'Enjoy your party, little brother.'

I had gone through the public rooms of the house and did a once round the grounds in search of Dai who was not to be found. The car was there so I knew he was still about. I supposed that he had passed out somewhere, a not uncommon eventuality when he drank, and would come round the next morning; probably lying in some rose bush with a raging head. For myself I couldn't really have cared where he was concealing his no doubt prostrate bulk. I had searched at Celia's behest for she was worried. Her concern was, I suppose, understandable, but her company was a strain. She seemed to have acquired a perpetual mournfulness, and I began to understand how her negative attitude had started to get on Dai's nerves. After my search, I resolved not to be so condoling where she was concerned and to get on with enjoying myself with Caroline whose jauntiness contrasted markedly with the doleful Celia. I was relieved when Giles Kingston came out of the study and started to talk to her, giving Caroline and me the opportunity to withdraw.

'Dai and Celia don't seem to make each other happy any more,' said Caroline. 'I'm not sure it's going to last.'

'I don't know,' I said, 'they've gone through some bad patches in the past, but they always seem to go on. I don't think either of them could really manage without the other, they have that Stan and Ollie ability to bungle on in tandem. Celia's continual simpering must put him off though.'

'I'll remember that.'

'What?'

'Not to simper when I'm with you.' She put on a winsome expression and collapsed sideways into my arms, the epitome of frail Victorian womanhood. My desire for her was never stronger than in those moments when her mood was all playfulness.

'Anyway, I don't think it's all Celia's fault,' she said. 'I think she has cause to simper. Dai can be good fun but there's no doubt he can be very selfish when he wants to be.'

'Aren't we all,' I said. 'But I know what you mean. Right at this moment, however, I couldn't care less. I don't think anybody would notice, or care, if we slipped away to our room for the rest of the night, do you?'

'No,' she said, and we went furtively to our room, the venery of adults having all the properties of an impish child.

I heard a clock somewhere chiming two in the morning. Caroline was still awake but she was drowsy. A shower of rain was making a noise on the gravelled courtyard below our window. It seemed to be sanctioning my desire. I slid my hand under her simple white nightdress and moved it along her outer thigh until it rested on her hip. Her body was as still as stone.

'She's very attractive, isn't she?' she said. 'The woman at dinner, Augusta Winfield?'

'I suppose she is, yes,' I said.

She shouldn't have allowed Augusta Winfield to intrude on my thoughts and our loving. That evening I had deliberately blocked any thought of Augusta. There was something too dangerous for me in thinking of those sea-green eyes.

'What's she like — to talk to, I mean? I couldn't hear what she was saying from where I was sitting. Is she as interesting as she looks?'

Somewhere out in the darkness of the country sheep were bleating and the noise they made might have been mistaken for an infant crying in the night. I would answer her question only with overt fact.

'No, she seemed very cold, very dismissive of everything. I got the impression she didn't like people very much.'

'Well I think that's interesting in itself, don't you?'

'I don't know,' I said, wanting to talk about something else. 'I'm not a psychologist.'

'Did you find her attractive?'

'Irresistibly attractive,' I said, trying to make light of the truth.

Caroline sat up in bed and combed her golden hair behind her ears with the fingers of both hands.

'I'm very thirsty,' she said, 'I'd really like a drink.'

'Something soft, I take it?' She didn't recognise the irony in my voice.

'Yes, I don't suppose you feel like popping downstairs and seeing what you can find? An orange juice, lemonade, anything will do.'

The party had not broken up but the noise from downstairs had subsided over the past hour. I had heard one or two doors closing on our landing, including the door to Celia's and Dai's room opposite. I got dressed and went out onto the dimly lit landing, the only light coming from an ugly standard lamp on a table at the far end of the corridor. I heard a cry — a woman's voice — less a cry than the sound of panic being stifled.

'Please, Giles don't!' Celia's voice was quite audible from the corridor. 'I don't want to — please!'

I knocked on the door.

'Celia, are you all right?'

There was silence, an uneasy, unpleasant silence and then a male voice.

'Come on, it's all right, he's gone. Didn't Dai explain to you? Didn't he explain everything? He doesn't mind, he wants you to, and I want you to — very much. What's the matter? Don't you like me? — of course you do, you want it as much as I do, don't you you little trollop — you're dying for it, aren't you?'

'Giles, please don't!'

'You're not being very co-operative. Dai's not going to like that when I tell him, he knows he's got to pay his debts — things won't go too well for you or for him if you don't start being a bit more co-operative. Didn't he explain all that to you?'

'Yes, but — I don't know, I just don't know — oh God I don't know what to do! It's not right, I love Dai!'

'If you love him then do what he's asked you to do. Come on, what's the harm? It's only a bit of fun, a bit of sport, that's all — we all need a change now and then to spice things up. Why so coy? You like to be taken, is that it, you little slut? Is that how you like it?'

There were sounds of a struggle and the noise made by the flat of a hand on flesh.

'You're starting to put me off, you bitch! What are you — frigid? Is that it?!'

I opened the door and saw Giles Kingston clambering all over Celia with his trousers part way down his legs. Her blouse was torn open and one bra cup had been forced up over the exposed breast. Giles, still on top of her, turned his head towards the door with a curious, vacant expression on his face. His mouth was partly agape and his eyes had the uncomprehending blankness of a gaffed fish. With his naked buttocks and that expression he had the appearance of a congenital village idiot caught in some anti-social act of which he has no understanding.

'Cartwright!' he said. 'Dai's not here, try the gardener's lodge out the back. Shut the door when you go.'

'Get up,' I said.

'Can't you see Celia and I are busy right now.'

Celia looked at me with a mixture of shame and fear. I could see that her left cheekbone was red and starting to swell.

'Close the door, will you, Cartwright — there's a good fellow — I told you if you're looking for Dai he's not here.'

I reached out and took hold of one of his ankles, dragging him off Celia and part way along the room.

'What the bloody hell do you think you're doing?!' he cried out. 'Celia, tell him it's all right — tell him Dai knows, that it's all been arranged.'

Celia hurriedly straightened her bra and tried to come up with a reply that would make sense both to me and to herself.

'Dai does know Edward,' she said in a breathless, broken-down voice. 'Please, Edward, go away. I don't want

Dai to get into any trouble.'

'I don't care what Dai does or doesn't know,' I said. 'He's not important right now — do you want this — did he hit you?'

Giles had got up and was struggling to extricate his underwear from the trousers tangled round his feet. He managed to get both his underwear and his trousers on, though the latter were not done up and hung loosely round his hips. He was a man in a hurry to conciliate and advanced towards me with a smile intended to signal a message which I was supposed to read as 'Hey, we're all boys together, aren't we?'

'Look, Cartwright,' he whispered under his breath, 'this is all a bit embarrassing as you can see. Here I am in the middle of giving her a good porking — which she's desperate for — and you come barging in. So be a good little accountant and run along, will you — go and find Dai, your pal, he'll tell you it's all OK.'

Celia could no longer hold back her tears, but whether she cried from anguish or relief, or a mixture of both, it was impossible to tell. I opened the door and motioned with my thumb for Giles to get out. Somehow the thought of even speaking to him seemed to invite a kind of contamination. I was also trying to hold my anger and knew that if I spoke I would risk losing control altogether.

'I think you ought to remember just whose house you're in,' he said, wiping away his 'wink-wink' expression and replacing it with his Latin machismo look.

'Then why don't you come and show it to me,' I said, gripping one of his ears in my fist and twisting it as I led him through the door.

Caroline, wondering where I had got to, had come out onto the landing.

'What's the matter? What's going on?' she asked.

It must have presented an odd sight to her. Me dragging our host by his ear, gripping it with my closed fist and twisting it hard while he shuffled along the corridor, bent over in pain, with his trousers once again falling around his ankles.

'Go and take care of Celia,' I said to Caroline.

'Let go, you bastard,' shouted Giles. I gave his ear another twist for the pure pleasure of it and led him halfway down the stairs until we came into full view of the late-night revellers who had congregated round a table full of drinks in the hall. Everybody went silent and stared up at us. Among the throng I recognised van Pallandt, who towered above the rest, Mischel, Miss Thomas, Harry and Cynth, and Augusta standing provocatively close to a rapt looking Marcus Pelham.

'What's the matter, ladies and gentlemen?' I asked. 'Haven't you seen a true captain of industry in the flesh before?'

'Giles, baby!' hooted a semi-paralytic Harry, 'Hey, Cynth, get a load of Giles, will you!'

I saw van Pallandt put his glass on the table and begin to advance towards the stairs.

'What's going on, Giles?' asked Mischel.

I let go of Giles' ear and he pulled up his trousers, motioning as he did so to van Pallandt, instructing him to stay where he was.

'We're just having a bit of fun, aren't we Giles? A bit of sport?' I said.

'That's right,' he said coolly, 'carry on enjoying yourselves everybody, there's plenty left to drink.'

'What a guy!' garbled hellfire Harry starting to take off his trousers, 'Come on, everybody, let's drop 'em — what's the game, Giles?'

Augusta and I stood staring at one another as Giles descended the stairs. I saw her smile for the first time; it was more a quiet laugh and I realised that hers was a face that was always meant to laugh, that the act of laughing would make what was already beautiful more so. Her eyes showed, equally, that she had long since lost all reasons for laughter.

I started to go back up the stairs when Giles called to me.

'Edward, hold on a minute,' he said, as though we were friends of long standing. 'Can I have a word?'

I watched him ascending with the sleekness of a shark that moves in silence from the sea bed to its victim on the surface.

'You're history,' he said quietly and went back to his guests. I went back upstairs to Celia's room. She poured out a story of how Dai was badly in debt to Giles, how Dai couldn't risk losing his job, how Giles had always, as she put it, 'fancied' her. I felt like saying to her — 'Was that what Kingston was doing when I came in, fancying you?' She continued about how she loved Dai and how Dai really loved her and had hated the idea of her sleeping with Giles but saw no other way out; and how Dai had said that it would be only the one time, and that they would get married almost immediately and forget all about it — out it came in one uncontrollable pathetic torrent.

'Let's pack up and leave,' I said.

'What about Dai?' Celia asked, her voice weak and palliative.

'Oh, to hell with blasted Dai!' exploded Caroline. 'Don't you have any existence of your own — what are you for Christ's sake?'

'Come on, Caro,' I said, 'let's just pack up and — '

'I'm sorry, Edward,' she said, 'but she must realise what she's doing to herself — it's incredible!' She turned to Celia. 'That sleaze box just tried to rape you, don't you understand that?! And that other weak piece of blubber, who you say really loves you, would have been content to let it happen so long as it got him off the hook. We ought to damn well report it to the police now!'

'Oh no,' cried Celia, 'I don't want any more trouble, I've caused everybody enough trouble, please let's go.'

'And what about the next girl he tries to rape, how much trouble is it going to cause her? Edward, I'm right aren't I? We ought to report him to the police?'

'Yes you are right, but I've just got the feeling that there are at least half a dozen people who would be willing to swear blind that Giles Kingston was with them every part of the night. Let's go now, we'll talk over our options on the way home.'

The party guests took little notice of us as we came down the stairs. Giles wasn't with them and we passed quietly through the door. I was carrying the suitcases and Caroline and Celia were some way in front of me. Just as they disappeared round the corner of the house I heard someone calling my name. It was Augusta.

'You will not fully understand what I am going to say, but what you did tonight, humiliating Giles like that, was dangerous in the extreme. It was a foolish thing to do.'

'It was the only thing to do.'

'The Kingstons are not ordinary people — '

'I realised that tonight.'

'I suggest you don't wait until tomorrow, but write a letter of apology — do it tonight. I suggest you fill it with as much regret as you can muster — grovel even but —'

'Why?'

'Because if he receives it now he may not take the action that will naturally spring first to his mind, you — '

'No, I mean why are you telling me this?'

'Because you don't know what it will cost you,' she paused. 'But then, how could you? Suit yourself.' She turned to walk away.

'Augusta.'

'Yes.'

I looked her in the eye for any sign of malice, or emotion. What was she playing at? Was it really a warning? She gave nothing away.

'Thank you,' I said.

Caroline came back round the corner.

'Edward, we're waiting, what are you — ' She stopped when she saw Augusta who turned and walked back to the house.

'What did she want?' asked Caroline.

'Just to see if our rooms were now free.'

'Bloody cheek!'

I loaded the suitcases and we drove back down the avenue of limes. At their end I saw a light; it came from the gardener's lodge. I drove a little way past then stopped the car and got out.

'I'll be back in a minute,' I said. 'Nature calls.'

I walked to the front door of the lodge, it was open. Dai was sunk in a soft, tatty old armchair with his knees together and his back rigid, like a schoolboy who has been told to sit up straight.

'Hello, Bach,' he said.

I noticed, under the lamp, on the table beside his chair, a flattened piece of foil with a pyramid of white powder on it.

'Is that obligatory in your job as well?' I said.

'What are you doing here?'

'We're leaving.'

'Who, you and Caroline?'

'And Celia.'

'Oh,' he said, lowering his head. 'Celia all right, is she? — I've been sick, you see, Bach — too much drink I suppose,' he raised his head again.

'Yes, you've been sick,' I said and went back to the car.

8

CORPORATE VENTURER

'Has Campion arrived?' asked Hugo.

'He's outside,' said Giles. 'How do you want to play it?'

'Play it? This isn't a game Giles, we simply tell him we're pulling the rug out from under his feet, that we will not finance the trialling stage for his drug. You can assure me that the research stage is finally complete?'

'Yes, Campion's been crowing about it for a week.'

'Good, then cutting off his funds now will give van Pallandt the time he needs to negotiate with his foreign contacts. Since it is only the idea that we are selling, and not the finished product, van Pallandt should have no difficulty in completing his operations within the time scale laid down.'

'But suppose Campion somehow raises the money to press ahead with his trials; he might beat us to it before van Pallandt's negotiations have been finalised. Once Campion's got a finished product to show the Ministry it's out in the open and we're sunk.'

'Where's he going to get the money from? He's put in all his own money, and any further borrowing would first have to take into account the money he already owes us, which as you know is considerable. And what's he got left to sell? We've been picking off the only Tubelis subsidiaries that are worthwhile acquiring and made sure the rest are unsaleable.'

'But he has got the idea, which is worth a fortune as we know.'

'Oh my dear Giles,' Hugo breathed on one of his rubies and cleaned it with a handkerchief. 'The research project is only worth something to Campion by the mere fact of its being kept secret until he is ready to proceed to the production stage. If he tries to sell the idea now, he would be merely giving it away to his competitors for a fraction of its real worth — besides which you know how dear the whole thing is to his heart. Can you really see him giving away his baby to someone else, for them to reap the benefit, after all he's put into it?'

'No I suppose not.'

'That is why it's important to make him believe that we are still his best bet in realising his dreams. We dangle the carrot, let him believe that we are likely to come up with the money but that we are simply pausing to consider our position, that we are being no more than prudent.'

'Could we finance it to a conclusion if we wanted to?'

'Not without some risk, which we don't need to take since selling the formula alone to van Pallandt's contacts will make a fortune in undeclared income.'

'I take your point,' said Giles somewhat bored with it all. He was so used to Hugo being right in everything to do with business, and so irked by his brother's perpetual habit of talking down to him, that all he wanted to do was get it over with as quickly as possible. He would enjoy Campion's reaction to the bad news but that was about it as far as he was concerned.

'There is of course one crucial element in all this about which I cannot be absolutely certain,' Hugo said.

'What's that?'

'The drug itself. Will it really work? It's got to be the real McCoy, as they say, or van Pallandt's contacts will turn nasty. I just wish I could get some independent expert opinion without giving the game away.'

'What extra opinion do you need? Pelham is the top geneticist in his field and he says the drug is way ahead of anything else, and that all his tests show, without question, that it will work. What more do you want?'

'That is, of course, what van Pallandt will be telling our foreign buyers and they'll have to purchase it. They couldn't afford not to if it really is a revolutionary breakthrough, but just suppose — '

'Besides which,' interrupted Giles, 'everything that Mischel has been able to find out from inside the Ministry points to the fact that Tubelis have been working along the right lines, that they've come up with answers that others have so far been unable to provide. Look at Harris & Weir, a much bigger outfit than Tubelis. Mischel tells me they've been trying to crack it for the last three years and haven't even come close.'

'That's so.'

'Campion may be a lousy businessman but nobody doubts that he is a brilliant scientist, his track record proves it.'

'Yes, yes little brother, I am aware of all you say. I know it's ninety-nine per cent certain, but you see that other one per cent could very well cost me, us, everything.' Hugo pressed his intercom. 'Miss Muxloe, would you ask Mr Campion to step inside.'

Gordon Campion left the offices of Kingston & Kingston in a state of mental paralysis. His home life had been turned upside down and all he, personally, had left to him was the success of the project. He needed it to succeed, not only financially, but also because it had become for him a symbol of a possible new beginning, a means to put everything right, not just Tubelis but his home life as well. Why were the Kingstons doing this to him? The research was complete, he was almost there — why?

He got into his car and drove in a daze around London for nearly an hour, in tears. He was near to a final breaking point and every bleak feature of his personal circumstances fell in on him like an avalanche of sharp-edged rocks. He became short of breath. He needed to go somewhere, to get out of the car, but where? Returning to Tubelis was out of the question, going home to face Eva, near breaking point herself, was even more so. For want of an alternative Campion drove to his club.

The clientele of Campion's club were high profile members of the scientific community working in business rather than academia. It was not particularly grand as clubs go, in some ways it was a little shabby. Campion went there when he felt depressed. For several months past he had taken to using it a lot. He didn't expect to see many people there at that time of the day and he was right, but he did meet someone that he knew, and that meeting was to have far reaching consequences for his future, and for mine.

Owen Romney, though he had a science background, was not a true scientist in the way that Campion was; he was not in the forefront of research. Romney was, above all else, an extremely astute businessman which again differentiated him from Campion. He had the controlling stake in Harris & Weir and headed the company. Harris & Weir was one of the biggest pharmaceutical research companies in the country, far bigger than Tubelis, though Romney had watched the rapid growth of Tubelis, based on the advice of Stoy's, both with admiration and some degree of alarm. He had also kept an eye on the recent decline in the competitiveness of Tubelis, though he knew nothing of the Kingstons' involvement, and it had set him to thinking acquisitively. Campion was a proven innovator, and Romney had made it his business to find out via the grapevine what Campion was working on currently. Campion's project, if completed, Romney knew would be a winner — Harris & Weir had been trying to develop a similar drug without much success to date. Word had it that Tubelis had solved some of the key problems associated with the concept.

'Gordon, good to see you. Come over and have a drink.' Romney called out when Campion entered the club.

The last thing Campion wanted was any company but he could hardly refuse.

'Hello Owen,' he said, 'I didn't expect to see anybody in here at this time.'

Campion sat down turning over all his problems in his mind while Romney went to buy him a drink.

'Well now, how are things going at Tubelis?' asked Romney when he returned.

'Oh you know — ' Campion was looking into space as he spoke. 'Not too, not too — ' he didn't finish.

'Rumour has it that you're about to make rather a major breakthrough, am I right?'

'What?' Campion said, not really attending.

'Oh come on now Gordon — don't be coy. I realise you wouldn't want to give anything away, especially not to me, and I wouldn't expect you to. But everybody in the industry knows what you've been working on — it's no secret.'

'No secret,' murmured Campion in a vague, not-quite-with-it, way.

'All I wanted to say was congratulations if you've cracked it, I wish to God we had.'

Romney looked at the unresponsive Campion; he didn't look a well man.

'Are you feeling all right Gordon?'

'All right?'

'Yes, you seem a bit — are you feeling OK, you're not sick or anything?'

'Sick! I'm sick to my stomach! Sick of every damn thing!'

This sudden, automatic, outburst of Campion's frustration and disillusion, which he regretted as soon as it was out, took Romney by complete surprise; it was so unlike the rather shy, mild individual he had previously experienced.

'I — I'm sorry Owen,' Campion stuttered, 'I didn't mean to — well it just hasn't been a good day, that's all.'

'I'm sorry to hear it,' said Romney, who could tell that the man in front of him was genuinely at the end of his rope.

'I hope you weren't offended by anything I said,' he continued. 'I mean in asking questions about your project — '

'Oh no, it wasn't anything you said, but it is related to the project I'm afraid — not only that, but it's one of my major problems.'

'Not going so good, eh? I wouldn't be too downhearted; like I said our researchers have been working on the same thing without so far getting anywhere. There still seem to be too many problems — making certain it has no harmful side effects for one; and manufacturing for another. I'm seriously thinking about dropping the whole idea, it's costing too much.'

This wasn't strictly accurate; it was true that Romney was concerned about just how much the research on the concept was costing Harris & Weir, but he wasn't about to drop the idea just yet, he knew there were huge profits to be made and international prestige to be had if a company got it right.

'I've solved them, the problems,' said Campion with, for him, an unusual force.

He was proud of what he had achieved and wanted to talk about it. He knew he shouldn't really say too much, Harris & Weir was, after all, his biggest competitor, along with the Americans, but he had done what they had been unable to do for all their greater resources. 'What does it matter now anyway,' he thought. In that instant, after all he had had to bear, he felt the need to salvage something personal, something for himself, however small and inconsequential. He wanted to hear somebody say 'Well done'. His accomplishment in scientific terms was quite out of the ordinary and he had received not even a passing acknowledgement. Who was there to give it to him — Eva? They hardly spoke to one another now about anything, certainly not anything that mattered, and besides which she wouldn't have understood the extent of it all. His son, Rory, was too wrapped up in his own burgeoning political career to really care very much. His daughter would have cared, but she was away on a sabbatical; and the one person who understood more than anybody else just what he had achieved, Pelham, was too petty, too much the egoist to dole out a 'well done' at the success of others.

'What does it matter now anyway,' he thought again.

It mattered to Owen Romney, it mattered a lot.

'Are you telling me that you've solved all the problems, that you've produced a trial batch?' he asked.

'Yes,' replied Campion.

'Risks eliminated?'

'No side effects we're sure. In the end it was rather simple, the answer I mean. It came from an unexpected source, but still rather simple.'

'You've reached the trial stage?'

Campion drew a deep breath and the merest hint of a bitter smile crossed his face.

'I've reached the trial stage,' he said, 'but — '

'Good God,' said the startled Romney, 'Well what can I say?! Congratulations I suppose, but you'll understand that

as Chairman of Harris & Weir the news doesn't exactly fill
me with delight — losing out hurts.'

'Yes it does,' said Campion, 'but I wouldn't be too concerned
about it, you're still in the running.'

'I don't follow you?'

'Well that's the problem, nobody else is prepared to either,'
said Campion cryptically, thinking only of the icy, factual
monotone with which Hugo Kingston had broken the news
to him that morning.

'You see,' he went on, 'I said that I am ready to press
ahead with trialling but — ' he tailed off again.

'But what?'

Campion was now tired of being quizzed. He didn't even
want to be congratulated any more. What was the point of
qualifications, explanations, if in the end they were all
reducible to the one word — failure?

'Come on Gordon,' said Romney, 'you can't just leave me
dangling in mid air. I don't want to know how you've done
it, just whether — '

'The answers to the problems have proved to have
expensive implications for testing and mass production
and — '

'And what?' Romney said eagerly.

'And! And! And!' Campion could only grind out the words
through clenched teeth, 'I haven't got the money!'

Very little light filtered into the club and what there was
of it had to fight its way through the dark rain clouds
gathering outside. The poor light reinforced the silence that
fell on the room. For some little time neither man spoke,
during which Romney couldn't decide whether the moisture
welling up in Campion's eyes was really tears in restraint,
or merely the accommodations of tiredness to the fading
light. Whichever way, Romney understood that the man in
front of him had reached the threshold of crisis. It was
Campion who broke the silence.

'So you see you're still in the race, along with the
Americans.'

'But if as you say the costs of trialling and mass production
are so prohibitive as to — '

'Oh it will cost but it's not so prohibitive as to prevent

me going ahead if I could. The potential profits, as you know, are enormous and would far outweigh the development expenses.'

'But I really don't understand — ' Romney hesitated. 'Look if you'd rather not talk about it, then — '

'No it's all right,' said Campion. 'It doesn't matter now anyway.'

'Well then, what I don't fully understand is why you can't capitalise on resources from other areas of Tubelis to finance — '

'What other resources?'

'Oh come on now Gordon, I'm not entirely ignorant of the affairs of my competitors. Several years ago I was forced to watch as Tubelis Research embarked on a large scale acquisition programme.'

'Yes.'

'And within a year transform itself from a company with assets of about a £1 million to one with assets in the vicinity of £100 million — am I wrong?'

'No.'

'And you're not saying the cost of production is any way near the total value of Tubelis are you?'

'No they're not anywhere near that.'

'Then I don't see the problem.'

'The problem Owen is that, unlike you, I am not a businessman. I'm a scientist.'

'You haven't done badly for someone who purports not to be a businessman.'

'When Tubelis was first getting off the ground I sought advice from Stoy's, but then I was compelled to seek financial advice from another quarter and things started to go wrong.'

'Why didn't you stick with the advisers who built your success?'

'It's too complicated to explain. I wish I had, but the result is that I've put everything I personally have into the project, and the subsidiaries of Tubelis are no longer strong enough to support the needs of the parent company. In fact, I've lost control of quite a number of them. I'm stuck. I've got nowhere to go.'

Romney's brain cells started to shift into overdrive. Here

perhaps was a chance for Harris & Weir to exploit the breakthrough without spending any more money themselves on research.

'Would you be open to an approach from Harris & Weir?'

'You mean a takeover?' Campion replied.

'No, some corporate venturing on our part,' said Romney. 'A direct equity investment by us to enable you to go ahead.'

'Not a takeover?' Campion asked again still uncertain.

'No.'

Romney genuinely wasn't thinking in terms of a takeover. He couldn't be sure what possible losses might arise in the early stages of the venture and therefore did not want Tubelis to be shown as a subsidiary of Harris & Weir.

'It may be the only way of ensuring that both of us get there ahead of the Americans. What do you say?'

Campion's insides had been knocked about like a tennis ball that day and he found it hard to concentrate, to think. Hugo Kingston had held out a carrot, an ill-defined possibility that they might still continue financing the project at some future date. Campion didn't want to jeopardise a chance if it was a genuine one. Nevertheless it wasn't a firm undertaking and they had let him down before, profited at his expense, whereas here someone who understood the project's potential was offering him a definite lifeline.

'It would be a partnership then?' he said.

'That's right, you'd get capital funding and access to our greater marketing and distribution resources. And we'd both take our share of the profits.'

'And the project, my work, would reach its proper, its rightful conclusion.' A real hope spread inside Campion. Maybe, in the end everything would turn out as he had wished. 'Damn it!' he thought to himself, 'I've worked hard, I deserve a break, I deserve something better than personal and financial ruin.'

'Of course everything would have to be conducted in a formal way. We'd have to carry out an investigation into Tubelis before finally committing ourselves,' said Romney.

'Oh, yes, of course,' replied Campion, not particularly concentrating on anything other than escaping failure.

'And to commit ourselves we'd have to be sole sponsor, the only ones involved.'

'Sole sponsor?'

'I wouldn't intend bringing anyone else in on the deal, syndicating with a venture capital fund or anything like that. By the way, I take from what you've said, that there isn't another party already involved? With a stake in Tubelis?'

'A stake?' said a shaken Campion.

'Yes, there's nobody else, right? Like I said, unless Harris & Weir was the sole sponsor then we wouldn't — '

'Oh no,' said Campion hurriedly, 'there's nobody else involved.'

He wasn't being honest but he couldn't afford to put Romney off from the start, and spoil his chances before they had an opportunity to develop. 'Besides,' he thought, 'I can always sort out my position vis-a-vis the Kingstons later, once I get the ball rolling with Romney. Tubelis still has some subsidiaries left which the Kingstons may accept as a repayment.'

'So it's settled,' said Romney. 'I'll instruct somebody to carry out an investigation on behalf of Harris & Weir tomorrow.'

'Fine,' said Campion.

'Shall we have another drink on it?'

'If you don't mind Owen, I won't. I've a lot of things to do so I'd better get a move on.'

The two shook hands and Romney watched Campion walk to the door. When he had left Romney got up and asked the barman for a telephone book; Owen Romney didn't delay anything to do with business. He found the number he wanted and dialled.

'Good afternoon, Stoy Hayward.'

'Hello, my name is Owen Romney, chairman of Harris & Weir. I wish to make an enquiry; I'd like to speak to one of the partners involved in corporate venturing, acquisition work, that sort of thing.'

'After all,' Romney thought to himself, 'If I have to make an investigation, who better to act for me than the firm that helped build Tubelis in the first place?'

'Hello, Mr Romney, my name is Alison Lester. I am a partner in Corporate Finance and Investigations, can I help you?'

Romney made an appointment to see Alison Lester the following day which would, although no one realised it at the time, officially draw the battle lines between Stoy Hayward and Kingston & Kingston. For me the combat was literally one to be fought to the death.

I was present at the second meeting at Stoy's between Alison Lester and our new client Owen Romney. Our brief at this point seemed relatively straightforward. Romney had asked us as a firm with recognised expertise, to perform an investigation into the business affairs of Tubelis Research. He had insisted on us picking up Tubelis as an audit client as part of his corporate venturing scheme. I was present at this meeting because I was to be the audit manager. Howard was also present in his capacity as partner of the general business group who would have to liaise with Gordon Campion.

'There's one thing I'm not too sure about,' said Romney, 'suppose things aren't going too well and I want you to carry out a further investigation — can we do that?'

'You mean because Tubelis has become an audit client can we still investigate further on your behalf?'

'Yes.'

'The fact that Stoy's have become the auditors of Tubelis is not contrary to any ethical guidelines concerning conflict of interest, indeed it's relatively commonplace,' said Alison.

'Good,' said Romney, 'if I'm going to commit all that Harris & Weir money I want to be able to follow it all the way down the line.'

'You'll be asking for board representation at Tubelis of course?' asked Alison.

'Yes,' said Romney, 'but I don't necessarily need it to be me. I've got far too many other demands on my time to want to be personally involved.'

'Somebody else then, from Harris & Weir?' I asked.

'Yes. Campion can't object, can he?'

'Not if he wants your investment,' I said, 'and we'd recommend that you receive monthly management accounts.'

'I have already spoken to Gordon Campion,' said Alison Lester, 'and he has accepted the condition of board representation.'

'I should mention straightaway,' I said, 'that I have a close friend who is the assistant finance director at Tubelis Research. His name is Dai Bunch.'

'Dai what?' said Howard.

'Bunch.'

'What an odd name.'

'Well he's a bit odd all round,' I said. 'We were at university together.'

'All the better,' said Romney, 'it should make it that much easier to keep track of things if you've already got a good relationship with one of their finance people.'

I wasn't as convinced that it would be such a good thing, I didn't like the idea of working with Dai on a professional basis. I had an uneasy feeling about it but I said nothing.

'Edward's friend is not the only point of known contact with Tubelis,' said Alison Lester. 'As everybody here is aware, Tubelis Research used to be on Stoy's client list. I know Gordon Campion well as I was the partner looking after Tubelis prior to my move into Corporate Finance. It will be of assistance to Mr Romney to outline what I know about Tubelis up to the point of my last contact with the company.'

'I know Campion credits you with supporting the initial growth of Tubelis,' said Romney.

'When they came to us they were worth just under £1 million,' continued Alison, 'but we helped them in an acquisition programme that made them worth over £100 million within a year. When Stoy's left them they were in a strong position with a potential for growth which would have rivalled even Mr Romney's own company Harris & Weir, who are the biggest in the UK in this field. That was the target I had set, but clearly all the indications to date are that Tubelis has been in decline since then.'

'So what happened?' asked Howard. 'Why did Tubelis disappear off our clients list?'

'Well, as we know, Gordon Campion's major concern became the research, development and eventual production of the present project: the project which has caught Mr Romney's attention.'

'Call me Owen,' said Romney. 'Let's all agree on first names.'

'We at Stoy's,' continued Alison, 'did everything in our power to support and to realise Gordon Campion's ambitions in this regard. To say that he was obsessed with his new project above all else would be an understatement. The direction he was wanting to take involved sacrificing many of Tubelis' subsidiaries, but we advised against it; given the overall picture, it was less than viable.'

'Because of the uncertainty surrounding the means to mass produce his new drug — whether in fact Campion could make his research pay off?' interjected Howard.

'Yes,' said Alison, 'but nevertheless we set about arranging the financing of his new venture on terms which did not threaten the long-term independence of the company. Campion seemed to accept it, he saw the sense of our advice, and was genuinely satisfied. But just before we were ready to effect it he suddenly called the whole thing off saying he had made arrangements of his own based on the advice of another party.'

'Why wouldn't he take your advice I wonder?' said Romney. 'After all, he'd profited from it in the past. It's for certain he regrets it now, he admitted as much to me in our club the other day.'

'That's the odd thing,' said Alison. 'If you have the trust of your client he will consult you before he acts, which is what Campion had always done up to that point, and the oddest part was that I knew we still had his trust. Why shouldn't we — we'd built his business. I had this impression that deep down he still wanted to take our advice — but it was almost as if there was some more personal reason, outside straight business, that was stopping him doing it. He kept apologising to me all the time for not doing it. In his last 'phone call to me he actually said he would prefer to continue to do business with Stoy's but that he was too far down the road with his new advisers to back out. By that time Tubelis had changed auditors and that was that.'

'Who was this other party?' asked Howard.

'He wouldn't say,' replied Alison.

'Kingston & Kingston,' I said.

Alison Lester and Owen Romney looked at me with expressions which merely indicated they were waiting for a further qualification, but Howard's expression was of an altogether different kind. He had encountered the name Kingston & Kingston before.

'Kingston & Kingston Financial Services,' I continued, 'I am almost certain they are the other party in question, Campion's current advisers. You see, my friend now at Tubelis came to them from Kingston & Kingston on the recommendation of his former company. He told me they are Campion's advisers.'

'What sort of an outfit are they?' asked Romney.

'Diverse, big and getting bigger — but...' Howard hesitated.

'But what?' the rest of us said almost simultaneously.

'Well it's hard to say, there's nothing definite one can say, it's just that those in the business world who have had any direct contact with them, react to the mention of Kingston & Kingston as though they were listening to the rumblings of distant thunder.'

I felt a strange disquiet coming over me as Howard was speaking, as if the mention of Kingston & Kingston was a prelude to something unpleasant, like the eerie music which precedes the shock event in a horror movie. I had witnessed changes in Dai since he came into contact with them. But were they the result of this contact? Or were they merely changes that would have happened anyway, the cause being in himself, whatever his working environment? Perhaps I was overdramatising Giles Kingston's unwholesome influence, after all he had by all accounts been extraordinarily generous in lending money to Dai. Perhaps my disquiet was unfounded? I would find out soon enough.

'Anyway,' Howard was saying as these thoughts ran through my mind, 'Bernard Wright should be able to tell you more about Kingston & Kingston. He's had some contact with them I believe.'

'Who's Bernard Wright?' asked Romney.

'One of our Insolvency partners,' said Alison. 'He's very experienced, been with Stoy's a long time.'

125

'What else has your friend told you about Kingston & Kingston's role in Tubelis?' Howard asked me.

'Only what I've told you, that they are advising Campion. He did say, however, that the involvement of Kingston & Kingston was only short-term, that it would terminate in a short while.'

'You don't suppose they have any financial stake in Tubelis?' asked a worried looking Romney.

'Well that is one of the things we propose to find out,' said Alison.

'You see I don't want to invest any Harris & Weir money unless we are the sole partner.'

'I quite understand that,' said Alison.

'My friend Dai said, quite specifically, that Kingston & Kingston had no takeover intentions where Tubelis was concerned. They are simply acting in an advisory capacity for a fee.'

'Well that makes me feel better,' said Romney. 'I know Campion's project, if he's cracked it, will be a sure-fire winner. I wouldn't want to share the spoils with anyone else.'

'Let's reserve judgment shall we,' said Alison, 'until the investigation is under way.'

'What's the next step?' asked Romney.

'When I spoke to Gordon on the 'phone, I impressed upon him the necessity of providing us with his business plan as soon as possible.'

Alison Lester spoke in sonorous, measured tones. Her voice carried a sort of quiet, understated gravitas which made one feel that each word chosen was the one she intended. Her husband Dave had told me once that when he first met Alison she had a very slight stammer. There was no trace of it now and anything she said was delivered with a precision that led the listener to understand that here was a woman who would never cut corners.

'I made it clear to Gordon,' she continued, 'that his plan must include the history and activities of Tubelis Research — some of which we are already acquainted with — but I particularly stressed the need for him to detail the company's present management structure and its more recent financial history. We should find out from that the extent of Kingston & Kingston involvement, if any. Howard, I've invited Owen to lunch with us in the partners' dining room, perhaps we could get Bernard to join us if he's available to tell us what he knows about Kingston & Kingston.'

'I'll give him a call,' said Howard, 'but I've got a feeling he's still in New York on the trail of some missing bullion.'

'Well let's have a talk with him as soon as we can,' said Alison, 'when he's taking a rest from being Sam Spade.'

9

SPECIALIST DEPARTMENT

Gordon Campion had many problems but there was one which was uppermost in his mind. He had snatched at the life-line thrown to him by Owen Romney in an attempt to save both his project and his company. His big problem now was holding on to that life-line. Romney's basic condition was sole sponsorship and yet Tubelis owed money to Kingston & Kingston who had helped to finance the research stage. Stoy Hayward had begun the investigation into Tubelis and Campion knew an audit team would soon be arriving. He somehow had to keep the Kingstons' involvement in the affairs of Tubelis secret, until such time as he could pay them off. He couldn't understand the game the Kingstons were playing. 'Why go so far and then stop?' he asked himself. 'How do they expect me to pay them if they won't help me finish it?'

Nevertheless they had intimated that they wanted out — 'consider cutting our losses' were the words Hugo had used. Campion wanted them out too, he had come to despise them, but there was still Hugo's tantalising prevarication that 'perhaps' further finance might be forthcoming. 'Maybe I can play one off against the other, the Kingstons and Romney?' he thought. Another 'perhaps'. Even so he needed a means by which he could pay off the Kingstons quickly and he believed he had a way to do it.

His main priority now was to stall Stoy's, keep them from finding out about Kingston & Kingston, until he could put his plan into effect. Alison Lester had requested that he submit a business plan which Campion had done, hastily, without seeking any advice with regard to its preparation. Naturally he made no reference in it to the Kingstons. He hoped that studying his plan would keep both Stoy's and Romney occupied for a while. He also hoped, and believed, that the acceptance of his plan would be a formality — he knew Romney well understood the worth of the Tubelis project.

'Box clever,' he told himself as he was about to enter the boardroom for a management meeting at Tubelis.

'Play them off, one against the other, Romney and the Kingstons.'

Campion was a clever man but he did not have the cunning for the game he was about to play.

About the same time as Campion was entering his boardroom, I was on my way to a meeting in Stoy's with Alison Lester and Owen Romney to discuss the business plan Campion had submitted. On my way to the meeting I turned over in my mind the many stages I had passed through over the few short years I had been with Stoy's. These thoughts were prompted by the fact that here I was, about to embark on another stage, another facet of business life, a new experience. I'd certainly had the real benefit of the general group structure — the variety of work. How long before they considered me for the ultimate promotion? Making a move out of the general group would be a good idea. Howard had already offered me a secondment to Corporate Finance and Investigations. I had plenty of future options open to me.

My personal future, outside work, seemed to be with Caroline. Neither of us would be rushing into anything, but I don't think there was any doubt in either of our minds at that time that our relationship would be a permanent one. 'Yes' — I thought to myself as I approached Alison Lester's office, where I could see that Owen Romney had already arrived — 'the future looks like it's going to be fun.' I could have no notion that very soon I would step into a nightmare.

'Edward, come in,' said Alison. 'Coffee?'

'Please.'

I greeted Owen Romney and settled into a chair with my coffee and my copy of Gordon Campion's business plan.

'I've asked Bernard Wright to call in later,' Alison said. 'He's back from New York, he may have some information which will prove of interest to us. Well now, perhaps it might be best to begin by asking you, Owen, for your initial reactions to the plan Gordon Campion has given us?'

'Well it seems straightforward to me, I'm quite happy about it,' said Romney, who seemed very perky that morning. I could tell he was concentrating all his thoughts on the anticipated profits he assumed were coming his way.

'I've gone through his financial projections,' he continued, 'upon which he bases the forecast returns. They all look sound to my way of thinking. I know his market because it's my market too. I don't think he's overestimated things.'

'And knowing the industry as you do you still remain convinced that Campion's drug will work and that he has found a way round the mass production problems?' Alison asked.

'I'm certain. He's the only one who's cracked it.'

'If he has cracked it,' I said. 'I mean we really only have his word. It's a tricky situation isn't it? Because the only way to be sure is to get your own scientists at Harris & Weir to verify that he's got the genuine article; they'd have to get a look at the formula. But Campion would be unlikely to allow a competitor to look at the formula and production plans unless you have already committed yourself financially. It's a bit of a catch 22 isn't it?'

'Agreed,' said Alison, 'and there are also a number of other factors to be considered before I could have the degree of certainty that you have Owen. For example, having studied the dispersement of the competition, an obvious question presents itself. In the UK we know that Harris & Weir is Campion's sole competitor and that Harris & Weir hasn't developed the project as yet, but amongst his competitors there are two large American corporations which are working on a similar project. How do we know that they haven't also solved the problems and are ready to go into production?'

'In this business one gets wind of certain goings on. I think I'd have got wind of it if the Americans had cracked it,' said Romney.

'Well perhaps so Owen, but pharmaceuticals research is a secretive business and those in it can't afford to give too much away for all sorts of reasons that are not purely financial. We have to consider what our position is if the Americans are close to producing a trial batch. Hopefully you are right Owen, but in order to protect your investment I can't afford to base the investigation on assumptions. With this in mind I've been on the 'phone to one of our American associates in Horwath International to see if they can sniff out for us any information which might help us determine, more precisely, just how far down the road our American competitors are.'

'Let's now consider your potential market,' she said. 'Initially you are primarily dependent on a particular customer base, namely the Government, as Campion points out in his report.'

'That's right,' said Romney. 'And Campion is, to my mind, correct in his projections as to the likely need for the drug and the profits that would accrue. I've made a similar analysis myself for Harris & Weir.'

'But does he go far enough?' I asked.

'How do you mean?' said Romney.

'Well he only bases his projections on orders from the British Government, but if he really is first past the post with his project could other governments — American, European — be regarded as potential customers?'

'Most certainly,' said Romney.

'Yes I agree,' said Alison who was now on her feet, walking slowly round the room.

'I think,' she went on, 'Campion has underestimated the size of the market primarily because the marketing resources of Tubelis are fairly limited in comparison with a company the size of Harris & Weir. My knowledge, to date, of both companies suggests that the utilisation of the greater resources and marketing strategies of Harris & Weir would substantially increase the potential profits. Harris & Weir are already in the overseas market. Tubelis aren't and that accounts for Campion's limited perspective. I must say, the market side of his proposals looks very positive from our point of view.'

'Exactly,' said Romney whose enthusiasm for the whole deal was clearly obvious.

'The market section of Campion's plan seems to be a definite plus from our point of view, since he has underestimated the combined potential of the two companies.'

'As I said, the plan looks fine to me,' said Romney. 'Diabetes is a widespread disease that produces a whole range of secondary illnesses. If Campion's drug can halt or even cure the disease further development could lead to advances on many other fronts.'

Alison stood still again.

'What are your feelings about Campion's plan, Edward?'

She lowered her eyes to her hands which she rested on her desk, palms touching, as in the position of prayer.

'I have a number of reservations,' I answered. 'I don't think it's a particularly well documented plan at all.'

'My feelings exactly,' Alison said.

'What's wrong with it?' said Romney. 'We've agreed that the product is good and that the market is out there — so?'

'That's true,' said Alison now raising her hands to rest her chin upon them, 'but it's deficient in many respects. It tells us nothing about the management and organisation of the company.'

'People are crucial,' I said. 'Your investment is in their hands.'

'OK,' Romney said.

'We want to know not only who they are but what they have achieved to date, what are their past successes. And other questions like what are their aspirations and ambitions regarding the company?'

'And why these particular people?' interrupted Alison. 'How do their individual skills contribute to the functioning of the company as a whole? Are they committed to the success of the company?'

'These questions are vital,' I said, 'particularly in the light of what we know about the recent history of Tubelis Research. The company fortunes have been in decline of late and it's got to have something to do with the people running it.'

'I take your point,' said Romney. 'I suppose I was getting

a little too carried away with the possibilities of the product itself. Given what you've just pointed out the picture seems a little less rosy.'

'Though Campion's plan is deficient as it stands there is no call for being too pessimistic just yet,' said Alison. 'In order to help you make up your mind Owen, we will carry out a complete investigation of the organisational structure of Tubelis. We shall establish how the various responsibilities are distributed and identify any gaps. We'll have a better idea how things stand once that's done.'

'It may interest you both to know that I've met, quite coincidentally at a social function, a number of the names listed on the Tubelis board,' I said.

'Who?' Alison asked.

'Well Campion himself, Walter Brownlees, George Mischel, and Augusta Winfield.'

As I spoke, those four people were sitting round another table across town. They had concluded the routine business of the meeting which to Campion was no more than a continuing catalogue of failures and frustrations.

'I really can't afford to be here for very much longer,' said George Mischel. 'I have to get back to the House.'

'I sometimes wonder why you bother to turn up to board meetings at all,' said Campion.

'What do you mean by that?'

'Well you're hardly ever here and when you do come you're always watching the clock.'

'I am an MP with responsibility to my constituents.'

'Well you owe a responsibility to this company as well. You're accepting a sizeable salary in case you've forgotten — why take on the directorship if you aren't able to give it any time?'

'I didn't assume that it was my time you are paying for, I thought you were paying for my advice and influence.'

'Well I'd be happy with that if I could just see any results from your so-called influence. From the way you've been carrying on in Parliament one would think you were working for our American competitors and not us.'

'I have to be impartial — ethical questions are involved,' said Mischel.

'I wouldn't mind impartiality,' continued Campion, his voice rising to a higher pitch, the upper registers that affect desperation, 'but what you've been doing is anything but impartial. You've gone out of your way to actively sway opinion towards the Americans in the last three contracts we've tried to win.'

'I think that's an exaggeration,' said Mischel picking off one or two loose hairs that had fallen on the lapel of his suit coat.

'All I'm asking,' Campion continued in pleading tones, 'is just to remember that the project we are now working on is vital not only to the continuation of the company but also to thousands of people who are suffering at the moment. Nothing should be done or said which will prejudice it.'

'If it gets that far,' said Augusta.

'What do you mean?'

'Well we haven't been given any indication where the money will come from to complete it.'

'Never mind that for now,' said Campion, 'the money will be provided when it is needed.'

'But from where?' Augusta insisted. 'The remaining company assets are not in a position to sustain a —'

'I know, I know all that, ' said Campion. 'Just bear with me, the money will be forthcoming.'

Mischel and Brownlees exchanged glances and smiles. It was an amusement to them to watch the pathetic man before them, struggling to maintain his composure, his dignity and his sense of hope. Mischel and Brownlees were thinking the same thought in tandem; 'the money would be forthcoming only if the Kingstons wished it'. They'd seen it all before, companies like Tubelis, men like Campion, whose destinies were under the absolute control of Hugo and Giles Kingston. It never occurred to either Mischel or Brownlees that their own destinies were no less outside their own control, that one day the Kingstons might decide to dispose of them in the same way they had disposed of others down the years. To men with as little scruple as Mischel and Brownlees the constant watching of others being put on the rack was a sufficient distraction to deflect their thoughts from the possibility that they might, one day, end up on it themselves.

'There is one final item that is not on the agenda, which I would like to bring to your attention. It's nothing major,' said Campion. 'I've decided to change our auditors and — '

'You can't do that!' shouted a panicked Brownlees, suddenly fearing that his financial peccadilloes might come under a more rigorous scrutiny.

'Why can't I do that?' said an angry Campion. 'This is my company and I can choose whichever firm I like to do the audit.'

'Does Mr Kingston know?' asked Mischel.

'I really don't see what it's got to do with Mr Kingston — whichever one of them it is you mean. Kingston & Kingston Financial Services, as you know, have had a connection with this company but that connection does not necessitate my consulting them with regard to every decision that has to be made. Giles Kingston recommended all of you, I know, and it is understandable that you feel you owe him some loyalty, but you have got to understand that this is my company and you are working for me! I have never been happy with the services offered to me by our present auditors, and therefore I am re-enlisting the services of Stoy Hayward with whom I had a very successful relationship. As well as — '

Campion stopped himself.

'As well as what?' asked Mischel.

Campion was going to say something to the effect that as well as auditing, Stoy's were also going to be asking questions about the company. He didn't want to come out and tell anybody that Stoy's were investigating on behalf of a corporate venturer, but he did want to prepare the way as best he could.

'Oh nothing really,' he said. 'It's just that you'll find Stoy Hayward have a very different approach to the current lot. Stoy's will be asking a lot more questions about Tubelis as a whole.'

'What sort of questions?' said Brownlees, trying not to betray any anxiety in his voice.

'We'll just have to wait and see,' replied Campion. 'It'll

all be to the good, for the benefit of Tubelis, believe me. Oh, and I don't think there's any need for my decision to go beyond this boardroom; it's nobody else's business.'

'You mean you don't want Giles Kingston to know you've changed auditors?' said Augusta.

'Not just Giles Kingston,' Campion said defensively. 'I don't think it's anybody's business but ours. I know Giles Kingston recommended the current auditors to us and I will be speaking to him on this — and other matters — when the time comes, but for now I should just like everybody in the company to pull together to make this new project a success. Our futures depend on it.'

Back in 8 Baker Street, Alison Lester and myself had been pulling to pieces Campion's business plan in front of Owen Romney, who was beginning to realise that a lot more work needed to be done before he could start banking any profits from an investment in Tubelis. Our meeting was drawing to a conclusion; Alison was summarising the main areas of concern within the plan for Romney's benefit.

'So these then are the three areas that need to be delved into more fully: (a) management and organisation, (b) production and operations and (c) financial information. The questions relating to management I've already made clear. On the manufacturing side we will require a much fuller description of the production process. Also we know nothing about their ability to meet the unexpected, from Campion's point of view, increases in demand in the hoped for eventuality that the drug will be licenced for America and Europe as well as the UK market. I want to find out just how sensitive Tubelis' actual and potential production capacity is to breakdowns, given an unanticipated increase in demand.'

At that moment Bernard Wright came into the room.

'Ah Bernard, I'm glad you could make it,' said Alison. 'Bernard, I'd like you to meet Owen Romney, the Managing Director of Harris & Weir — Bernard is one of Stoy's Insolvency partners, Owen.'

'Pleased to meet you,' said Bernard shaking hands with Romney. 'I had hoped to get here a bit earlier Alison, but —

well I've just received rather a terrible shock which stopped me in my tracks.'

'Oh I'm sorry,' said Alison full of genuine concern. Alison Lester was the kind of person who always took other people's problems to heart and made them her own.

'Serious?' she said.

'Very serious,' replied a very grave-looking Bernard.

'Not family?' I asked anxiously.

'Worse,' said Bernard.

'Oh my God,' said Alison getting up out of her chair. 'Bernard, what's happened?'

'England are forty six for eight in their second innings,' said Bernard without changing his expression.

'Pardon?' said a confused and uncomprehending Alison Lester.

'Forty six for eight — it's bloody disgraceful, in all my years of watching test cricket I've never seen such an irresolute, weak-kneed performance as this shower are putting up.'

'You're talking about the Test Match?' said Alison sinking back into her chair and reaching for the coffee pot. 'I thought you'd lost your wife.'

'That's preferable to losing a Test Match on the morning of only the third day.'

'Can I offer you a cup of hemlock?' said Alison, holding up the coffee pot.

'Please.'

'You'll have to excuse Bernard, Owen,' said Alison pouring out a coffee. 'Working in insolvency for many years has a destabilising effect on people.'

'Are they really forty-six for eight?' asked the unbelieving Romney, totally forgetting about any matters concerned with corporate venturing.

'They're probably all out by now,' came the reply.

'Anyway you've arrived at the right time Bernard,' said Alison. 'We're investigating a company for Owen who's considering a corporate venture. The company concerned is Tubelis Research which, you may remember, used to be on our client list. We're just going through the business plan submitted to us by Tubelis' managing director, and we've reached the point of assessing the financial information in the plan.'

'So what can I do for you?' said Bernard.

'Well you may be able to enlighten us further on a particular matter if you'll just bear with us for a bit. First of all I'd like to ask Edward if there's anything he wants to say regarding the financial information given in the plan — Edward?'

'Well yes, sort of. There's really nothing in the plan, Owen, that helps you to assess the downside risk. I would have liked it to have included some sort of sensitivity analysis, some indication of how results might be affected by changes in the major risk variables — demand, gross margins, limiting factors — that sort of thing.'

'Yes, I see what you mean,' said Romney.

'This is the kind of information we've got to get out of Campion,' said Alison.

'And he's not too specific about the time-scale in which Owen is supposed to realise his investment, let alone indicating whether £3 million will be sufficient to satisfy cash flow requirements in the first place.'

'Anything else?' Alison asked.

'One very important thing,' I said. 'The recent financial history of Tubelis — there's virtually nothing concrete mentioned about it.'

'This is where you may be of assistance Bernard,' Alison said.

'You see,' I went on, 'the recent performance of Tubelis, its fall in the market share and its shedding of subsidiaries that we helped them acquire, casts some grave doubts on the projections in the plan.'

'For your information Bernard,' said Alison, 'Owen is considering an investment of around £3 million for a thirty per cent equity interest in Tubelis.'

'Right,' said Bernard.

'But I agree with Edward, recent Tubelis performance casts some doubt on the project and there is one other matter of some considerable importance. We know, through a friend of Edward's, who works for Tubelis, that a firm called Kingston & Kingston Financial Services were employed by Tubelis in some capacity — '

'Oh,' said Bernard, drawing it out in a deep-voiced, knowing way.

'We'd like to know a little more about them and their role. Campion makes no mention of them in his financial history of Tubelis. Howard said you might be able to tell us a little more about them.'

'Well yes, but only in a very roundabout way. I have had no direct dealings with Kingston & Kingston Financial Services; however, over the last few years there have been a number of occasions where I have been involved in a compulsory liquidation or an administrative receivership where the parties concerned have had some indirect link to Kingston & Kingston.'

'And can I just ask,' I said, 'was it the case on these occasions that the companies involved had no up-to-date financial information?'

'Yes,' answered Bernard.

'Which is the situation we have with Tubelis,' said Alison.

'Another common feature of these companies,' continued Bernard, 'was that they either didn't have a proper accountant on the staff, or that the accountancy services they were receiving were offered by a very small firm with inadequate resources to deal with a company of that size. There was even one instance where the same small firm of accountants were involved in two companies that were subsequently liquidated. Apparently a director in one company recommended the firm to a director friend of his in the other company on the basis that they were inexpensive — can you believe it?'

'What was the name of this small firm?' I asked.

'I can't remember off hand, but it will be somewhere in my records.'

'So where do Kingston & Kingston come in?' said Alison.

'Well they don't exactly walk onto centre stage. They're more like a prompt standing in some dark recess, off to the side. On several occasions when acting as an administrative receiver I've no more than begun drafting an ad to put in the Financial Times to flog off anything saleable when up pops somebody from Kingston & Kingston ready to pay for the particular asset in question. They seem to have a certain clairvoyant capacity to know before anybody else when a company is in trouble, and when the goodies are up for grabs.'

Bernard paused for a moment and gave us all a questioning look as if to say 'draw your own conclusions'.

'Anything else?' asked Romney.

'Yes. In a couple of instances one of the creditors of the company being liquidated was a subsidiary of Kingston & Kingston while at the same time one of those snapping up the assets was somebody who had indirect connections with yet another, different, subsidiary of — guess who?'

'Kingston & Kingston Financial Services,' I said. 'But they themselves were never involved directly?'

'No.'

'But in effect,' said Alison, 'what was happening is that they were getting their money back and acquiring the asset of the liquidated company scot free.'

'Quite possibly,' said Bernard.

'What interests me particularly,' I said, 'is their mediumistic abilities, how they seem to know in advance of everybody else that a particular company is going to go under.'

'Shadow directors,' said Alison.

'Only suspicions, never proof,' said Bernard. 'Whichever way, whether they stand upright and honest in the sunshine, or corrupt and crooked in the shade, they are clearly very clever.'

Unlike the others in the room I had, personally, seen Giles Kingston in action and there was no doubt in my mind as to where he stood, or rather lurked — in the shadows. And as we were concluding our meeting at Stoy's the fortress of steel and glass that housed Kingston & Kingston Financial Services was casting a shadow of its own on the narrow, lightless City streets below.

Inside Hugo had no sooner picked up the 'phone to call Giles when Giles, as though through telepathy, opened the door to Hugo's office. His face flushed with urgency.

'I've just had a call from Mischel,' said Giles.

'And I've just had one from Brownlees,' replied Hugo, who,

unlike Giles, showed no signs of being flustered by the news they had received.

'What's Campion playing at?' asked Giles.

'He's playing at being an entrepreneur, which is a role entirely unsuited to him.'

'Why has he got rid of our auditors?'

'Well it's obvious, since we broke the bad news to him that it was by no means certain that we would finance the trialling and mass production of his wonder-cure, he's panicked. Instead of seeing a triumphant turnaround of Tubelis, he now sees only that his company is in complete disarray and is likely to collapse.'

'So?'

'So quite naturally, in his panic, he has returned to Stoy Hayward. Of course it will be too late for anybody to help him, we will have stolen the formula and killed off Tubelis long before anybody has time to rescue it.'

'Another firm doing the company audit could be very awkward,' said Giles.

'Why?'

'Well, Brownlees and Bunch are on the fiddle with our blessing and together with Mischel they're stitching up Campion and Tubelis, that's why!'

'But then it is only awkward for Brownlees, Bunch and Mischel, not for us, and I don't really care very much what happens to them after we've got the formula. I would like to hang on to Mischel though if at all possible; he will have a future usefulness — Mischel is not fiddling money from Tubelis is he?'

'No, he's just doing everything we tell him to to prevent Tubelis winning any contracts.'

'Good.'

'But that's just the point, they're all working for us. If the new auditors start to ask the wrong sort of questions — '

'Questions are questions,' said Hugo standing up and walking to his office window with his back to Giles. 'Proving the connection is quite another matter.'

'Besides,' Hugo went on, 'if a situation begins to develop that we don't like, we can always make sure that Campion, himself, removes Stoy Hayward.'

'How? He's not likely to do that off his own bat.'

'How did we get him to do business in the first place? Are not the persuasive powers of our Mr van Pallandt utterly irresistible?'

'Point taken, I wasn't thinking straight,' said Giles.

'Thinking straight is not the object of the exercise. Anyway it is my place to think and your place to act.'

Hugo presented a strange figure as he stood there gazing out of his window, his hands held delicately together behind him and resting on his rump. His suit was, of course, of the best material but it did not hang well on him; if one followed its line, from his neck to his feet down the expensive clothing, the eyes would suddenly be arrested by the fact that Hugo wasn't wearing equally expensive shoes but a pair of old carpet slippers. The slippers belonged to Old Kingston and Hugo always wore them in his office. It gave him a warm feeling standing in the same footwear his father had worn on the very night Hugo had had him killed; they seemed to keep out the cold indifference of his childhood years.

'Unless,' said Hugo turning slowly, 'unless — '

He paused and lowered his eyes to Old Kingston's slippers.

'Unless what?' said Giles.

'Unless Stoy Hayward are not working for Campion at all — '

'What do you mean? Of course they're working for Campion, he said as —'

'Unless the silly, deluded man is trying to raise the money to finish his project elsewhere — and trying to hide the fact from us.'

Hugo gave a short stabbing, staccato laugh. 'What fun if he is.'

'Where does he think he's going to raise that kind of money?' said Giles.

'A venture capitalist — oh the poor idiot, he hasn't a hope.'

'Why not?' asked Giles.

'Well apart from the fact that we could kill it stone dead by declaring our involvement — besides which Campion's project is really still in the development stage — no venture capitalist would consider it a good bet until the trials are successfully completed and Campion's scheme for mass production could be shown to work. He hasn't a hope, the stupid man.'

As he finished speaking the voice of Miss Muxloe came through on Hugo's intercom.

'There's a Mr Gordon Campion wishing to see you Mr Kingston, he hasn't got an appointment and I told him you don't usually — '

'Send him up immediately Miss Muxloe. Now my dear Giles, we shall find out exactly which it is, whether Stoy Hayward are working for Campion or for somebody else.'

Campion, clearly a bundle of nerves when he came into Hugo's office, proceeded to put a proposal to the Kingstons that if they were not prepared to finance the trial and mass production stage of his project he, Campion, suggested signing over to them all the other non-project related remaining assets of Tubelis Research in repayment of the money they had advanced. He was prepared to strip the company to its barest essentials and to virtually start all over again, on a wing and a prayer, with the new drug.

'How very interesting,' said Hugo when Campion had finished pouring out his proposal.

'And how very honourable,' said Giles, 'reducing what you have to virtually nothing out of concern for us and our investment.'

'If you're not prepared to see the project through I can see no other way of being able to pay you back.' said Campion.

'But Mr Campion, we are still very much interested in financing the trial and mass production stage,' said a smiling Hugo.

'Then why won't you give me the money to get on with it?'

'As I mentioned at our last meeting, we at Kingston & Kingston financial Services, like everybody else in business, have to stop from time to time to take stock, to consider the overall position of the company, to consider whether we should proceed in some areas or not proceed in others. That is what we are doing and it takes time, but it doesn't mean we definitely will not give you further finance — it all depends.'

If Campion had come into Hugo's office a bundle of nerves, he left it feeling considerably more relaxed and pleased with himself. One thought ran through his mind; 'Romney doesn't know about the Kingstons and the Kingstons don't know about Romney — whichever, one of them is bound to come up trumps.'

'So, now we know,' said Hugo after Campion had left. 'He's trying to interest a venture capital institution, and he wants us out of the picture so he can claim to be offering sole sponsorship.'

The thought of a corporate venturer did not cross Hugo's mind. Campion's line of business was so specialised that it would not have interested most corporations outside pharmaceuticals research, and he couldn't imagine Campion approaching a competitor in the field and offering to pass over his project to someone else.

'I must say,' said Giles, 'his offer was pretty tempting. Why didn't you just accept and take the remaining Tubelis assets in payment.'

'Oh for goodness sake Giles, use your brains. I'm in the business of making money not breaking even. Why accept the assets now when I will get them anyway when Tubelis goes to the wall.'

'So what now?' said Giles, impervious to Hugo's annoyance.

'We have to maintain our involvement until we get hold of the formula which means we have to pretend to go along with Campion, pretend we don't know what he's up to, keep him thinking that we may still come good so he is not forced to pay us off and get rid of our people. But it means we have to be careful — Campion can't afford to let his venture capitalist know about us, and we certainly can't afford for Stoy Hayward to link any of the activities of our people in Tubelis to Kingston & Kingston Financial Services; their actions must not be proven to be directed by us. Tell them to be on their guard and frustrate the investigation until such time as the operation is complete. I can't afford to risk Campion's selling off his remaining assets to somebody else to pay us off before we have what we want. What I don't want is Bernard Wright getting wind of our involvement with Tubelis.'

'Who's Bernard Wright?'

'He's an Insolvency partner at Stoy Hayward. He's had occasion to write some pretty unpleasant things about shadow directors, with Kingston & Kingston connections, to the Department of Trade. He's wound up companies in the past, companies whose demise I have caused, he's hard-nosed and he's picked up the wrong kind of scent where we're concerned.'

10
AUDIT

I very much wanted the deal between Romney and Campion to go through. Now my most immediate task was to marshal an audit team to suit the needs of Tubelis Research, to work in parallel with Alison Lester's Investigations team. It was important to pick staff to fit the personality of the client, the locations, the degree of difficulty of business and their accountancy systems. I needed people who would and could work fast and cope with the time pressures; a manager's biggest frustration is being landed with one or two team members incapable of doing things for themselves. One of the people I did pick was Danny Leibowitz who had only just started with Stoy's. Danny had a quick tongue — which often overtaxed my eardrums — a ready wit, and a tremendous amount of enthusiasm. In only his first few months with Stoy's I knew he was someone to watch; and for me, in his own idiosyncratic way, Danny delivered the goods.

One of my first moves was to set up a meeting with Campion. I needed to get to know him better. Alison Lester was able to fill in a lot of details which saved time because, of course, Campion had previously been her client. The picture I got from Alison was that Campion was a clever man with very little business acumen but full of enthusiasm to succeed and prepared to listen to advice. In my first, and in my many subsequent meetings with Campion I could not believe that this was the same man Alison Lester had described and indeed, in all but physical appearance, he was not the same man.

At our first meeting he remembered me from Giles Kingston's party, and was cordial but guarded. Over the coming weeks I came to recognise that one of the greatest obstacles to the revitalisation of Tubelis Research was the revivification of Gordon Campion himself. Howard, as the partner in charge of our group, had had as many meetings with him as I had and neither of us, at first, could understand his attitude. He would seem to get sudden bursts of renewed vigour which would all too quickly subside into a maudlin bout of capitulation to some hidden, inner anguish. In addition to all the other blows he had taken, he was simply not up to playing the game he was now trying to play, and it was putting a terrible strain on a nature that was not naturally deceitful.

I remember talking it over with Howard late one evening in Stoy's.

'He's simply lost it,' Howard said.

'Lost what?' I asked.

'That one essential element necessary for the survival of any business irrespective of the climate.'

'The entrepreneurial motive?'

'Right. When that motive is lost the business inevitably fails. Do you know why I left the previous firm I was with and came here?'

'Knowing you, I should have thought the money you're now getting had something to do with it.'

'You're fired but correct again — but that wasn't the only reason. I recognised, after years in the business, that Stoy Hayward was best at fostering this motive.'

'Gordon Campion clearly doesn't feel the need to identify with it,' I said.

'That's painfully true.'

'And yet he did once; Alison Lester engendered it in him.'

'Alison's got the patience of a saint, she's very good at engendering things. Look at all those noisy children for a start. Then there's her husband.'

'What's the matter with David? I like David. Apart from being great fun he's a very talented artist.'

'I like David too — he is fun and he is talented — but how many husbands do you know who charge into a Lead

Partners Committee meeting to tell their wife to pick up twelve tubes of 'burnt umber' on their way home, because they haven't time to get to the art shop.'

'Did he really do that?'

'Yes.'

'Good for him — no painter can work without burnt umber. Rembrandt only ever used three colours and that was one of them.'

'Anyway, between burnt umber and her kids, dealing with Campion would have been easy for Alison. Seriously though Edward, how do you go about helping someone who genuinely doesn't want to be helped?'

'I think he does want our help, but he's too frightened to take it.'

'Why?'

'Because he's hiding something he doesn't want us to find out.'

'What?'

'I don't know, but it won't be long before we find out.'

Another problem we encountered very early on involved the previous auditors of Tubelis. It was standard procedure to get professional clearance by writing to the previous auditors to establish if there were any reasons why we should not act for the company concerned (for example if the previous auditors had resigned for any reason, or if there were substantial fees outstanding). Getting a reply from them was like asking Scrooge to lend you a fiver. They weren't obliged to send us a great deal, but the papers they did send were in a terrible mess.

I called Danny Leibowitz into my office one morning. It was quite early, but the hour of day didn't seem to make any difference to Danny's capacity to fire words out at machine gun pace. Virtually before I had time to say 'good morning' he had rattled off the entire plot of a film he had seen the night before. I had intended seeing it myself but there seemed very little point after Danny had finished.

'Danny, I've got a little job for you. I want you to find out anything you can about an accountancy firm called Brookes & Finlay.'

'Find out what?'

'Like I said, anything you can. What their offices are like, how many partners they have, who is on their client list. Here's the address.'

When Danny had left I went up to Bernard Wright's office.

'Bernard,' I said, 'you remember our meeting with Alison Lester and her client Owen Romney from Harris & Weir?'

'Yes.'

'You said that there was an instance where the same small firm of accountants were involved in two companies that were subsequently liquidated — that a director in one company recommended them to a director in the other company on the grounds that they were inexpensive. Yes?'

'Yes.'

'Could you find out the name of that firm for me?'

'If you give me a little time to look at my records.'

'Thanks.' I raced down stairs to Caroline's office to play another hunch.

'What happened to you last night?' she asked closing the door of her office behind me and kissing me very lightly on the lips as she did so. 'I thought you were going to call round to the flat.'

'I was here up to my ears with Tubelis Research.'

'You might have 'phoned.'

'By the time I'd finished what I was doing I knew you'd be asleep.'

'How did you know I'd be asleep?'

'You're always asleep after midnight.'

'Not always, as you should know.'

'Listen,' I said, 'you're experienced with lawyers — '

'I beg your pardon!'

'Well with one certain lawyer anyway — '

She walked back to her chair, treading on my foot on the way past.

'Seriously,' I said. 'I'd like you to find out something for me from Stephen Fanshaw.'

'What makes you think I still see Stephen?'

'Please Caroline, I'm not playing now, this is important — I know you see him for a drink now and then, that you're still good friends.' I was finding it virtually impossible to establish any sort of working relationship, let alone a good one, with Campion's solicitors.

'Could you ask Stephen what he knows, if anything, about this firm of solicitors and in particular whether they have in any way been linked to a company called Kingston & Kingston Financial Services.'

'You mean that bastard Giles Kingston's company?!'

'The very same,' I said. 'Who knows, we may be able to get him back for what he did to poor Celia after all if you can do it for me.'

'With the greatest of pleasure,' she said.

'See you tonight then?'

'No you won't.'

'Why?'

'I shall be out with Stephen, having a drink, doing as you ask,' she smiled.

About five minutes after I got back to my office Bernard 'phoned.

'Edward, the name of that small accountancy firm you asked about, it was — '

'Brookes & Finlay,' I said.

'The very same,' said Bernard. 'Are we winning?'

'Don't we always?'

'Not if you're an England cricketer,' he said, and put the 'phone down before I got a chance to thank him.

Meanwhile Danny had found his way to the offices of Brookes & Finlay. They were in a grubby area of town somewhere between King's Cross and Farringdon, on the ground floor of a small purpose-built block.

He approached a rather fraught looking girl in the reception area, with whom he proceeded to have what turned out to be a rather confusing conversation.

'Good morning,' he said. 'Brookes & Finlay?'

'Yes.'

'Thank goodness. I've been wandering around for the last half hour trying to find — '

'Oh so you're the one,' she said disapprovingly.

'The one?'

'You're over three quarters of an hour late. Mr Brookes keeps ringing me up to see if you've arrived, and then blowing his stack because he cancelled another meeting this morning to make time to interview you — as if it was my fault that you can't be punctual.'

'Interview me?'

'You are the one who's applied to be taken on as a new trainee aren't you?'

'New trainee — um, well um — yes!'

'Well go through there and wait and I'll tell him you've arrived. Mind you, I don't fancy your chances now, not with being so late.'

When Danny got back to Stoy's he bowled into my office and said: 'I've been offered another job.'

'Another job?' I said. 'What you you mean, you've only just started this one! Who with?'

'Brookes & Finlay.'

He then proceeded to tell me the story of his interview with Mr Brookes.

'You mean you actually went in for the job interview?'

'Well it was pretty obvious Mr Nesmith, the real candidate, wasn't going to show up. He probably did turn up, took one look at the place and ran a mile. I should think they'd be happy to take anybody who was brave enough to walk through the front door.'

'That can be the only reason they took you,' I said. 'Anyway what did you find out — let's start with their clients list.'

'Well it's not very impressive except for one very big company — '

'Kingston & Kingston Financial Services.'

'Yes, how did you know? It was all Mr Brookes, one of only six partners, seemed ready to talk about in answer to my queries. It was "Kingston & Kingston this" and "our clients Kingston & Kingston that".'

'OK, that's all I want to know for now. Put everything else you've got in a report for me.'

'I can't understand,' he said, 'how they ever got Tubelis' account. They're an obscure little outfit which seems totally inadequate, in terms of their resources, to handle a company the size of Tubelis.'

I thought to myself that they did have one advantage over

any other firm — a scant regard for independence, the raison d'etre of auditing.

All the senior staff of Brookes & Finlay were financially dependent on Kingston & Kingston and they knew when to turn a blind eye. Having learned what I had so far, it came as no surprise when later on in the week Caroline was able to confirm, via Stephen Fanshaw, that Campion's solicitors had acted for Kingston & Kingston on many occasions in the past.

With each increasing week I came to feel less frustrated by Campion's attitude and more sorry for this man whose every positive move to get out of the morass had been blocked by those he had initially trusted.

The Kingstons were strangling Campion and Tubelis slowly but effectively. Campion found himself in the position of having to sell off various divisions of Tubelis throughout the country; divisions which, previously, Alison Lester had helped him to acquire in order to sustain the financing of his new project. And who was there first to snap them up? Always some subsidiary of Kingston & Kingston. Hugo, of course, could have provided the extra sums required for the untroubled continuation of the research, but his purpose was better suited by pulling the rug out from under Campion's feet at a critical stage by refusing to provide further finance. That way he could pick off Tubelis bit by bit and still achieve his ultimate target of stealing the project plans from under Campion's nose.

This plan of attack also provided the essential ingredient for the realisation of Hugo's ambitions — and that was delay. Apart from having no desire to see a strong, independent Tubelis, with all its debts repaid, the immediate provision of further monies would have speeded up the completion of the new project. He couldn't afford to let it reach the open market, or let the Government get its claws into it, before he was ready. He needed to cause sufficient delay to give van Pallandt time to line up his contacts in the pirate drugs wholesalers who were more interested in the vast profits the diabetes drug would make than in any concern for trials and safe mass production, and to finalise the arrangements for its sale. As far as H

Desborough Kingston was concerned everything was going according to plan.

He had an additional means at his disposal of further delaying the project until such time as he was ready. This was provided by a combination of the burgeoning vanities of Marcus Pelham, and the skill of Augusta Winfield in exploiting them. Pelham's life was ordered on a strict regimen; the personal pleasures he allowed himself were spartan by most people's standards, due primarily to his depleted imagination. Nevertheless, the old proverb about Spartans running riot with indiscipline once away from home, applied in double measure to Pelham in his infatuation with Augusta. She also had the measure of Pelham intellectually and knew how to play on his conceits. She knew when to match him and when to show just the right amount of deference so as to further deepen his infatuation, not only with her but with himself.

Pelham lapped it all up like a thirsty dog and sniffed the dirt like a little terrier recollecting a buried bone, where all he inhaled had the aroma of promise. I watched her going to work on Pelham and saw his besotted responses when he was with her, which he thought he was cleverly hiding from the eyes of the world. It is one of the least difficult things to detect, the infatuation of one person with another, and yet the person enamoured genuinely believes that it is impossible for others to see a difference in his behaviour. I saw his captivation with Augusta over many months and probably I did observe it more readily than others. I had reason to, for I was also captivated with Augusta myself. I made no conscious admissions to myself that such was the case; I glossed over the fact, but it was true. The first thing that came into my mind when I awoke in the morning was the thought that I would see her again that day.

I couldn't understand her apparent fondness for Pelham. To me he was a terse, unlikeable, boring little man. I was to discover later that she had two principal objectives. One was to distract him, as much as possible, from getting on with his work and completing the project until the Kingstons were ready to move, and the other was to manoeuvre herself into the position of being able to get hold of the formula and production plans for the drug, once she had won Pelham's complete confidence. Pelham had signed a legally binding agreement, as part of his contract of employment, not to disclose to anyone information relating to the project. So sensitive was it, that this applied even to other Tubelis employees, apart from those on the research team who were similarly bound.

I had a lot to think about, not least how to put into practice the necessary function forming a good relationship with the client's up and coming management, the next generation leadership. In the case of Tubelis Research this not only included Augusta, which was, though tricky, a minor problem, but it also included Dai, which was a problem of major proportions. Until I started at Tubelis, I had neither seen nor spoken to him since that night in the gardener's lodge on the Kingston estate. I had no wish to. When I next encountered him at Tubelis he behaved with great bonhomie as though nothing had happened, though it was obvious to me that he was feeling guilty and uncomfortable, and wanted to put things right.

'Coming for a drink after work, Bach?' he had said.

I gave him a curt 'no' and got back to talking about business. On this he seemed even more uncomfortable and did a lot of hedging. Both he and Augusta had to provide us with information to carry out an audit under the Companies Act, and both proved tardy in this respect. It was also becoming increasingly clear, as the weeks went by, that the judgments that would have to be made on whether the policies being adopted were in accordance with the standards of accountancy practice would likely prove unfavourable. Dai seemed more directly implicated than Augusta. As far as financial propriety was concerned she was toeing the line, her target was not financial chicanery but to win over Pelham. She left the embezzlement side of things to others, more particularly to Dai and Walter Brownlees who seemed to be the two most directly involved with the day-to-day movement of money. When questioned they seemed to want to change the rules from one moment to the next, and were adamant that things could be done which legitimately could not be done.

People were starting to get edgy. Those with something to hide were starting to feel the pinch of the pincer movement carried out by my audit team on the one side and Alison Lester's investigations team on the other. Poor Campion himself was, of course, included among the number who had something to hide. He was trying his best to conceal from us the fact that he owed money to the Kingstons, to keep Romney from backing out through a lack of guarantee of sole sponsorship. He tried very hard to convince us that his research project to date had been financed solely by the shedding of Tubelis acquisitions, but whatever he did it was clear that the figures just didn't tally. When confronted by the obvious anomalies in what was being presented to us, Campion took refuge in his own lack of business prowess.

'Let me have a think about it,' he would say. 'I've probably explained it badly, I'm not very good at this sort of thing as you've probably guessed, but it's all there, just as I said. Let me go away and think about it for a bit, I'll come back to you.'

And he did come back to us, but each time he had an equally untenable, alternative answer to the question. The kind of questions we were asking, and the information we were uncovering, was making it much more difficult for the Kingstons than they had anticipated. It had been only a matter of hours after I first began work at Tubelis that the Kingstons learned I was the selfsame friend of Dai Bunch's who had attended Giles's party. They cursed their luck that out of a firm of a thousand people I had to be one of those chosen to do the Tubelis audit. Being Dai's friend and being at the party meant that automatically I knew those in Tubelis who had connections with Kingston & Kingston. Giles also cursed Hugo for not letting him act on his primary instinct immediately I had left their country estate.

Unknown to myself, I had had a fortunate escape, albeit a temporary one. The day after the ear-tugging episode, Giles had summoned van Pallandt to him with a view to spattering my person all over the nearest available pavement. Hugo, in his inimitable fashion, got wind of it and prevented his younger brother from deriving the satisfaction he so desperately wanted. I hasten to add that Hugo acted not through any concern for me; he simply did not want to draw attention to Tubelis in any way. His brother's rashness was always likely to upset his plans. Furthermore, after Old Kingston's death the police had their obvious suspicions but could not prove anything. Hugo and Giles had strong alibis, but another death that could be linked to them would have been unwise. Nevertheless I was still a problem to them, and not just me but Stoy's in general. They assumed, however, that since I was the manager on the job, if they could buy me off things would continue the way they wished. They also assumed that since I was a friend of Dai's I could be bought as a matter of course. Their attempt to do so was not long in coming.

After several weeks Alison Lester asked myself and Howard to meet her and Owen Romney. Romney, as had been arranged, had already been with Alison for about an hour before Howard and I arrived. When I came into her room I particularly noticed Romney's expression, which was much more taciturn than usual; he was generally fairly relaxed and wore his disposition on his countenance.

'I have been outlining to Owen,' said Alison, 'some of the central features of my investigations to date. As the Partner and Senior manager of the team doing the audit on Tubelis I thought you would like to hear generally, if not in detail right now, some of our conclusions. It also gives us the chance to pool our respective bits of information.' 'This should be fun,' I said.

'Yes, I'm pretty sure from the patterns that must be emerging from your own work in Tubelis that your conclusions must be very similar to ours. Having gone over Tubelis with a fine-tooth comb, my first reaction was shock at the extent to which the very prosperous company that I had helped to grow had been desiccated beyond all recognition. It has been stripped of most of its stronger subsidiaries that only a short time ago Stoy's helped them to acquire. There has been nothing in the market trends over that period of time to serve as an explanation. My investigations show that it can only be accounted for by appallingly bad management.'

'Bad management from Campion's point of view, but perhaps very good management when viewed from another quarter,' I said.

'I'm just coming to that,' continued Alison. 'I have made far-ranging investigations into the past history of all the senior management of Tubelis, and an analysis of their present functions within the company. I won't go into every case, you can read my report later, but let me just give you one example so you can get the flavour. Let's take Walter Brownlees.'

'Must we?' said Howard. 'I only met him once at Tubelis and his whole manner suggested "look how clever I am".'

'Well in some ways he might consider he has a right to call himself clever. I would call him just plain lucky up to now. He has skipped between the commercial and academic worlds all his life. His business career began in a small company which had ceased trading but had a substantial claim against a supplier. On that basis as a director, Brownlees had paid himself a healthy salary for over two years, but the claim wasn't upheld. Hugo Kingston, who was at Harvard with Brownlees, came to his rescue and, I believe, put him in his pocket at the same time, and Brownlees was saved by the skin of his teeth.'

'But it gave him the taste,' said Howard.

'Yes and he's been taking risks ever since. As a director he's a third or fourth time failure of the kind that the DTI are very interested in, but the Kingstons have always managed to bail him out, while at the same time picking up the assets of the failed company. I believe that what we are dealing with here is a meticulously planned piece of shadow direction. I have advised Owen that under no circumstances would his investment be safe under the present management structure, even if he were to secure a non-executive directorship.'

I then told the others all I had found out about Brookes & Finlay, and Campion's solicitors and the other catalogue of Kingston & Kingston involvement in Tubelis.

'There's no doubt in my mind that Kingston & Kingston have financed part of Campion's research programme and, weighing up the accumulating evidence, I can even roughly estimate the extent to which he is in debt to them. Again this prejudices Owen's condition of sole sponsorship, and is the reason why Campion has kept their role quiet.'

'So obviously the deal is off,' I said.

'Well not quite,' replied Alison. 'Outside my investigations into management, and despite the recent losses suffered by Tubelis, other areas are still potentially palatable. The research team Campion has assembled, including Campion himself, is of the highest calibre. Having looked at the market, the competition, the production process, financial projections — if we were only talking about the new project and nothing else I believe it represents a very good return on investment. But under the present circumstances it is simply not on.'

'You see,' said Romney, 'I would still be willing to go ahead, if we could just get Kingston & Kingston and their minions out of the picture. Alison has shown me how Campion would still be able to pay them off from his remaining assets — he'd be left with nothing but the project, but Alison says with that alone the company has growth potential.'

'What we did for Campion once we can do again,' Alison said.

'What I don't understand,' said Howard, 'is if what you've said about the potential of the project is correct, why don't the Kingstons just continue to finance it?'

'That is a question I just can't answer,' said Alison. 'I only wish I knew. Anyway Owen wants to hold fire and consider my report in all its detail. In the meantime he wants us to press on. If we can draw Campion out into the open we might be able to get him to come across to our way of saving his own skin. Or if we can just hang something definite by way of fraudulent practices on one of Kingston & Kingston's lackeys in Tubelis we might scare them off altogether.'

'What are the chances of that?' asked Romney.

'I think Brownlees would be the obvious one to hone in on,' said Alison. 'Howard, Edward, — I've come up with some pieces of information relating to the three most recent contracts that Tubelis have won. This information is the result of conversations I've had with the buyers. All three contracts were negotiated by Brownlees' department — here are the details. The buyers reported certain hiccups during the negotiations which were common to all three cases. In the end the negotiations were completed to the satisfaction of all parties. There may be nothing in it but I'd like to check. I'd appreciate it if the audit team could follow it up from the inside and we'll compare what we've got.'

The meeting drew to a close, but just before it did I suddenly found myself asking: 'Have you turned up anything that is suspicious with regard to Augusta Winfield?'

'No,' Alison said. 'From all sides she looks pretty clean so far. Why? Have you got something that makes you suspicious?'

'No, nothing,' I said.

'Mind you, her assistant, your friend Bunch, isn't smelling of roses.'

Thinking about it afterwards, it was strange that I should ask about Augusta but not think to ask about Dai. Perhaps even then I instinctively knew the answer in both cases.

Now there are plenty of companies who don't have a proper accountant on the staff, and confusions and difficulties in doing things correctly are always likely to arise. This may happen for a host of reasons, like computer problems, but one very common cause is a genuine lack of ability on the part of a director to fully grasp the situation. Such was the case with Campion, who had a brilliant mind for scientific invention, but an inadequate grasp of correct business procedures. But it was certainly not the case with Brownlees nor, unfortunately, Dai. They knew exactly what they were doing, and through all the evasions and half truths I began to smell fraud, which was exactly what it was. Not only had they failed to produce accounts for their transactions, but they had been misusing company funds on an alarming scale. Dai was a novice at it; it was presented as an option by Giles Kingston as the quickest method of clearing his debts. Dai had initially, with heart-rending reluctance, intended only to filch what was needed to pay what he owed to Giles. Giles, however, sanctioned, and encouraged, the further misappropriation of even larger sums for Dai to keep; it all helped the Kingstons in their attempt to bleed Tubelis to death. They were quite content to take the lion's share of the kill and leave substantial morsels on the bone for the jackals to fight over amongst themselves. There was now no way out for Dai. He had cleared his legally binding debts to Giles, but from the moment he took his first bite from the carcass the Kingstons could blackmail him any time they wanted. In Kingston & Kingston terms he had truly become a company man.

I remembered, after the squalid affair was over, what Dai had said the first time I spoke to him, that day in hospital. He said his favourite word was 'mammonism'. He saw himself, and wished the world to see him, as a kind of latter-day Dylan Thomas, ever present in the bar, breaking all the rules, and a fund of funny anecdotes to toss to an admiring audience. He was also very generous where money was concerned. If I was short then we would both be short together, for he would share what little he had. What Dai wanted most of all was to be noticed; his greatest dread was the thought of existing in obscurity. His parents were hard working, religious people who had raised four sons, of which Dai was the youngest; and they had instilled in each of them the importance of doing the right thing. They were raised to have a conscience. Dai had been indulged more than his elder brothers and was the brightest academically. He watched his brothers go into the hard end of either the coal or the steel industries, and saw them rewarded, for all their years of gruelling labour, by being abandoned as statistical obscurities in the unemployment figures. He was determined that it was not going to happen to him, nor did it; but a different kind of obscurity would overtake him nonetheless. No, Mammon was never his god, but he was never strong enough to resist a pleasure, and never wise enough to know that there are pleasures of a kind that finally have to be paid for.

I followed up Alison's suggestion to take a close look at the last three contracts negotiated by Brownlees' department.

Danny Leibowitz was one of the people I had working on Brownlees' section, trying to trace items back to their documental source. He was the first to draw my attention to the possibility that something was awry, that things either did not add up or were not traceable. Brownlees was being particularly haughty and partronising with Danny — 'that polytechnic boy' he kept calling him — because Danny would not be fobbed off by the kind of vague waffle he was getting. Brownlees' stock answer to everything was 'Go and see Mr Bunch, our assistant financial director, he will be able to explain everything, he has the documents'. Danny, as a consequence, spent a lot of time with Dai.

'He's really quite a fun guy, Dai Bunch, isn't he?' he said. 'He tells me you and he were at university together, that you were good friends.'

'We were, yes,' I said, trying to be as non-committal as possible. I knew Dai's ability to turn on his 'hail fellow, well met' routine, and the favourable impressions he was likely to make on Danny. I would have to make sure that he stuck to the job and wasn't taken in.

It didn't take us long, after delving into the documentation relating to the contract negotiations and after tallying our information with the buyer's side as supplied by Alison Lester, to realise we had Brownlees on the run.

We were getting very, very close to one of his major dodges and he knew it. People in his division would negotiate a contract for Tubelis to supply a piece of expensive scientific equipment and then, believing that all was well, would sit back and wait for their next assignment. Very frequently, however, those same negotiators would be surprised to find that the items they had contracted to sell at a price of £x thousand had been renegotiated by Brownlees for a price of £x thousand plus a bit extra. Much to their chagrin, they were given a mild ticking-off by Brownlees for overlooking certain hidden costs in the supplying of that particular product. The extra amounts paid for those hidden costs never found their way back into the profits of the company, on top of which they were eroding the competitiveness of Tubelis in the market place.

Just before I finished for the day I got a call from Brownlees asking if I would drop in and see him. He said that he had at last tracked down the documents we had been requesting which would prove that everything was above board.

'Ah, Edward,' he said, 'come in, come in — would you like a drink?'

'No, thanks. You said you had found the documents?'

'Yes, in that envelope over there.'

He pointed to a large brown envelope which had 'For the attention of Mr Cartwright' written on it.

'You were a very good scholar, I believe, could have got a lectureship so Dai tells me. Do you miss university life, Edward? I do. I regret ever leaving it, the business world has lost all its attractions for me, it's so cut-throat these days.'

'I seem to recall you saying over dinner in the Kingstons' country house that nothing would ever induce you to go back to academia.'

'Did I say that? Did I really? You must have misheard. No, once a university man, always a university man, eh? In the world of commerce one has to fall at the feet of too many false idols, adorer le veau d'or.'

It surprised me that he had come up with the documents that were needed to disprove the ever-accumulating evidence that he had been cheating the company. I started to question my own objectivity when it came to making judgments about anybody who had had previous associations with Kingston & Kingston. Obviously I had been wrong about Brownlees, after all here were the documents, perhaps he was just incompetent, a bungler. I picked up the envelope.

'I'm sure you will find everything to your complete satisfaction, Edward. After perusing the contents, if there is anything further you require by way of the same, please do not hesitate to come back to me.'

Once outside in the corridor I opened the envelope. I was anxious to allay my obvious suspicions. If I had been wrong about Brownlees there was a possibility that I had been wrong about Dai, that they hadn't been partners in fraud. I stopped counting the money before I had come anywhere near the end, but I estimated there must have been close to £15,000 in the envelope . I pivoted on my heels and went directly back to Brownlees' office.

'Back so soon, Edward?' he said.

'This envelope you gave me, it doesn't contain any documents, it contains — '

'Are you sure?' he interrupted, 'Do look again. The envelope has your name on it. The contents must be for you.'

'It's full of money. Look, see for yourself.' I moved to hand it to him.

'No, don't show it to me,' he said. 'I don't want to see what it contains, I will take your word for whatever you say is in there. If you say it contains documents then it contains documents, and as I said, if you want more I can provide what you need.'

'It's full of money,' I said, tossing it on his desk.

'It is?!' he exclaimed. 'Well my goodness, the secretaries here are so inefficient. That silly girl must have put everything in the wrong envelopes.'

'Mr Brownlees, I am going to see your boss, first thing tomorrow morning and I shall recommend that — ' he stopped me again.

'What you recommend to Campion is of no concern to me. Do you know,' he said, 'I think I can clear up the misunderstanding.'

'Misunderstanding?' I said, thinking he was talking about the attempt to bribe me.

'Yes. When I said I would never go back to a university, it was a British university I was referring to. But a university abroad — now that would make a pleasant change. I would like that.'

The following morning Campion received a letter of resignation from Brownlees who just seemed to have disappeared off the face of the earth. Harriet Brownlees had no idea where her husband had vanished to and was very anxious to know where he was. No less anxious to know his whereabouts was the Fraud Squad.

Alison Lester was delighted when I 'phoned to tell him that Brownlees had made a run for it.

'Fantastic,' she said. 'We've now got the Kingstons on the retreat for the first time. The authorities will catch up with Brownlees eventually, and hopefully he'll drop the Kingstons in it as an excuse to save himself. If one card topples the whole pack could go.'

'At least,' I said, 'Campion will finally see the light and be open with us about owing money to the Kingstons. He'll realise that he's got to decide between their money or Romney's and that it would be better to sell up all but the project, pay off the Kingstons, and throw in with Harris & Weir.'

'With our help,' she said.

'Now Brownlees has done a runner, why don't you give Campion a nudge in the right direction? It must be obvious to him by now anyway. Tell him I'll arrange a meeting with Romney in about a week's time.'

So, without giving too much away, I gave Campion the nudge that Alison suggested.

'Gordon, Alison Lester would like you to meet with Owen Romney next week.'

'What about?' he said almost pathetically. 'I suppose this Brownlees business will have ruined any chance I've got with Romney.'

'Oh the contrary, it may very well have helped it. But I don't know what Romney will have to say so I can't really comment. Do try and make it Gordon: it might not be what you think. Whatever happens, you must be completely open with him to stand any chance at all. You understand, I think, what I'm saying.'

'Yes,' he said.

I thought he wasn't going to say any more and I was about to move on, when in one loud sudden breath he said: 'I will go Edward, I will! And I'll leave out nothing.'

'Good,' I said, 'and when the meeting's over I'll buy you a drink, whichever way it goes.'

'Then you'd sit down and have a drink with me?' he asked incredulously. 'You don't think that I'm corrupt like them.'

'Of course I don't think you're corrupt — let's hope that we'll be drinking to a new beginning for Tubelis.'

'Yes, a new beginning,' he said. I left.

When I next saw Campion a day or two later I expected to find him in the same positive mood in which I had last seen him. I, myself, felt increasingly positive about the business battle with the Kingstons, we were clearly getting on top and I felt that soon Tubelis would see the last of them. Though in the business battle the tide had turned in our favour, my own personal battle with Hugo and Giles was soon to begin in earnest.

Nevertheless I was on a high that day and was consequently ill-prepared to find Gordon Campion pass me without acknowledgement. He stopped, more by reflex than anything else, when I called to him.

Before me was a man whose mind wandered and whose eyes were covered with the film of some private agony. I was not to know that, as he was about to enter the building that morning, the ape-like hand of van Pallandt coming down on his shoulder had stopped him in his tracks.

'You haven't forgotten, have you,' van Pallandt had said, 'how I was able to be of service to you, procuring those nasty photographs from those nasty people?' 'What do you want?' Campion had asked.

'I don't like the way you are talking too much to those Stoy Hayward people instead of listening to the advice we give you. It would be a pity if some similar misfortune, or worse, to that which happened to your wife was to overtake your son, or even perhaps your daughter. You might not be so lucky next time. I might not be able to help.'

'You do anything to hurt my son or my daughter and I'll kill you.'

'That might prove difficult,' van Pallandt grinned. 'I intend to live to a very old age. Anyway, what difference would it make, killing me afterwards, to your son or your daughter?' he said and walked away. After that, Campion had raced to his office to 'phone Giles Kingston. He was determined to sort out van Pallandt once for all.

'Do you know I've just had that bastard of a Dutchman who works for you over here making threats against my son and daughter?!'

'Yes, I know, and he's perfectly capable of carrying them out if you don't do as you're told,' said Giles, who then put down the receiver.

Campion's head started to spin and everything before his eyes went flat, lost some dimension, like a photograph.

'It's starting all over again,' he said to himself, 'all over again.'

About a day later I was in my flat. Caroline had come round for the evening and was curled up on the sofa watching TV, when the 'phone rang. It was Howard.

'John Rose wants to see us both first thing tomorrow morning,' he said.

'OK, what's it about?' I asked. 'You sound very sombre.'

'It's not good,' he said. 'We'll talk in the morning.'

The two top positions in Stoy's were the Senior Partner and the Managing Partner. John Rose was the Managing Partner whose main function was to co-ordinate and oversee the internal operations of the firm and review the performance of individual groups. Howard had sounded very unhappy but I couldn't think of anything that might have gone wrong with any of our group's client list. Nevertheless, it worried me for the rest of the evening.

The next morning when I arrived at work Howard was already up in John's office and his secretary rang through to say they were ready to see me. When I went into John's office I was surprised to find not only Howard but George Mischel, who had stormed into John's office unexpected and unannounced to act the part of the 'outraged' member of Parliament.

'Sit down, Edward,' said John. 'You know Mr Mischel, of course.'

Mischel was puffing himself up in a pose that was calculated to make himself appear to be at his most magisterial.

'What's the problem, John?' I asked.

John lit a cigarette and then exhaled the smoke slowly before he spoke.

'I'm very sorry to have to tell you,' he said, 'that Gordon Campion attempted to commit suicide yesterday.'

'Oh my God,' I said.

'Your concern is so touching,' said Mischel, tartly and sarcastically.

John Rose appeared to ignore his remark.

'Fortunately,' John went on, 'he did not succeed and is now in a stable condition in hospital.'

'I'm so sorry,' I said. 'He is a very likeable man. I must go and see him as soon as the doctors think he —'

'What and finish off the job?!' said Mischel.

'Mr Mischel claims,' said John, 'that Mr Campion's suicide attempt was caused by your handling of his business affairs and the pressures that resulted from your inefficiency. Mr Mischel also claims that not only have you been inefficient but that you have been rude and badgering in your attitude.'

'Round two,' I thought.

'You were ruining the poor man's company before his very eyes,' said Mischel snidely, 'causing him impossible distress, he told me so himself. Your bungling brought him to the end of his tether. His whole life was in Tubelis Research and you were dismantling it beyond all hope of redemption. Poor Campion simply couldn't take any more, and neither can the rest of us. I have already informed Mr Rose of the fact that one of our most senior directors, Mr Brownlees, resigned from the company because he could not longer take your — '

I'd had enough.

'Brownlees left the company, and probably the country, because he knew he was about to be exposed for fraud.'

'That is a scandalous suggestion,' said Mischel.

'You are a director of Tubelis Research, correct?' I said. 'But you don't take your orders from Gordon Campion, do you?'

'What do you mean?' he said, puffing his chest out again like Cock Robin.

'You take your orders from Hugo and Giles Kingston. Gordon Campion wants to be free of them.'

'In my position as Senior Director I have taken over sole responsibility for the running of Tubelis Research until such time as Gordon recovers sufficiently to take back the reins. I will not have you interfering in my affairs.'

'Don't you mean Hugo Kingston's affairs? Go back and tell Hugo and Giles, whichever one you will be reporting to as soon as you leave this room, that they've got a real war on their hands and that I intend to win it.'

Mischel stormed off. John, Howard and I sat there blankly staring at one another.

'What's it all about, Edward?' said John.

'What I've been doing is what the firm and the client expect me to do.'

'Did Campion seem depressed at all to you?' asked John.

'Yes, of course,' I said.

'To me as well,' said Howard.

'And the underlying cause of his depression is his involvement with the Kingstons, of that I'm certain. They don't take prisoners, believe me. I've seen what they do to the people who work for them,' I said.

'I've got to remember that my first responsibility is to the good name of the firm and to the well-being of our clients. This is a very tricky situation. Stoy's are supposed to promote the health of our clients, not bump them off. This man Mischel is in a position to stir up quite a bit of trouble,' said John.

'So what do you think?' I asked.

Very shortly after, I visited Gordon in hospital. He looked a worn and lonely man. The world to him seemed no more than a big horse that kept kicking him in the teeth. He had bottled up inside himself all the heartbreak he had felt since van Pallandt had first handed him those photographs. Eva and he inhabited the same house as two jellyfish might inhabit the same wide ocean, the distance between them was almost unmeasurable. Each longed to reach out to the other but found it impossible to do so for fear of exacerbating the hurt. He saw his scientific and business achievements being swept aside by the Kingston brothers along with his personal home life. And then, finally, the threat to his children, the only two things left in his life. That was the last straw. He asked himself how he could have caused all this, how he could have brought so much pain into the lives of those he loved. And in the illogic of true depression, he had decided that he was the cause of it all, and that those he loved would be safer if he did not exist.

He poured it all out for the first time to me. He told me about van Pallandt, Giles Kingston, the lot; because I was not family. I was outside it all, a third person that could listen, like a therapist, and not be hurt by what he heard. He needed to do it, to let it out, and when he had finished he said, 'So you see, Edward, I'm finished. I haven't the courage to take them on.'

'You don't need to take them on,' I said. 'I'll do all that if you want me to. All you need to do is to rest and get yourself well again.'

'What's the point?'

'The point is that unless someone takes on the Kingstons and wipes them out, then you and a lot of other people will be trapped for the rest of your lives.'

'They're too big,' he said.

I said my goodbyes and left him to sleep.

I waited and wondered what their next move would be; what tactics they would adopt in round three. I didn't have to wait long. I got home to my flat about ten o'clock one night and threw myself into a chair. No sooner had I done so then the door bell rang. I wondered if it might be Caroline, but I wasn't expecting her that evening; anyway she had my spare key and would have let herself in. I opened the door, to find the last person I expected. Augusta.

'May I come in?' she said. 'I think we need to talk.'

She walked into my living room, without bothering to wait for an answer, took off the raincoat she was wearing and threw it casually over the chair I had been sitting in.

'What did you want to talk to me about?' I asked.

'All in good time,' she said. 'Aren't you going to offer me a drink?

'What would you like?'

'Dry white wine if you have any,' she said, wandering casually around the room and stopping at my bookshelves.

'You do like poetry, don't you? What a lot of books.'

'Who's your favourite?' she asked.

'I've got lots of favourites depending on my state of mind at the time. I do like Byron though.'

'You like sharp changes of mood, do you?'

'What is it that you want Augusta?'

'Right now, a glass of wine.'

I went into my kitchen and looked around, wondering why it is that of all utensils corkscrews are the ones that go missing most frequently. I eventually found it, got the wine and the glasses, and went back to the living room where astonishment rendered me immobile. Augusta had got undressed and was on the sofa, her elbow resting on its arm and her body curled along it. All she wore was a pair of ivory silk stockings and a short silk slip, expensively embroidered with lace around the bust.

The bell had gone for round three.

'Giles Kingston sent you here, didn't he?' I said, struggling to keep my composure and probably only succeeding in looking foolish.

'Yes,' she said, with a truth that was almost brazen in its confidence. 'But what does it matter who sent me? I'm here.'

'Who do you think you are?' I shouted. 'You strut into my flat under orders from Giles Kingston and strip down to the regulation seduction kit. Save it for Marcus Pelham.'

She laughed; a genuine laugh this time. I was right in what I had noticed the night I dragged Giles Kingston down the stairs; hers was a face that was always meant to laugh.

'At least that means you have been watching me.'

'I've been watching everybody,' I said.

'Well you must admit I'm being more honest with you than I am with Marcus Pelham.'

'That's true, at least you're not pretending that you have any feeling for me like you do to Pelham. Why treat me differently though? Why the sudden taste for honesty?'

'You're not as stupid or as vain as Pelham. I told Giles that, but I was told to try anyway. So I did.

There was a pause. She had a strange, almost expectant look on her face.

'Please sit down here,' she said indicating the sofa, 'and show me your hand.'

I did as she asked without thinking.

'Perhaps you're uncertain about sampling the merchandise before you've inspected it properly; make sure it's in good working order,' she said, pulling her slip over her head and letting it drop on the floor.

She was now completely naked except for her stockings. She took hold of my hand and put it on her breast just where the curve began at the top.

'That is reality,' she said, holding my hand in its place. 'It works, nothing much else does.'

There was a turning of a key, and before I knew it Caroline was standing in the living room. She went red, pivoted on her heels without saying anything and left, slamming the door behind her. It all happened so quickly and took me so much by surprise that I didn't even have time to say anything, or move. It was all over and I was still sitting there with my hand resting on Augusta's breast. Giving the key to one's flat to someone, (man, woman or deaf, dumb and blind pet monkey), is a foolish thing to do; something is always likely to go wrong.

'Oh dear,' said Augusta. 'I'd better get dressed before any more of your women start coming through the door.'

I rushed out into the hall but it was too late, Caroline was gone. When I got back Augusta was dressed.

'I'm sorry,' she said. 'That wasn't supposed to happen; it wasn't in the plan. I hope you will be able to explain.'

'Oh, of course,' I said, exaggerating the irony, 'it's the easiest thing in the world for any self respecting accountant to explain to his girlfriend why he's sitting with a naked woman on a sofa, one hand on her breast and the other on a bottle of chilled plonk — we learn that before we do the conversion course in the first year!' I was angry at the attempts to manipulate me, but I couldn't help a comical sense of the absurdity of it all mingling with my anger.

She laughed that beautiful laugh for a second time.

'You know, I can't quite figure out why you're still alive,' she said.

'I probably won't be after I try to explain to Caroline.'

'No, I mean why Giles has left you untouched after what you did to him.' She moved to the door. 'Anyway, I shall go back now and tell him this particular little tactic didn't work. I told him it wouldn't.'

'No, you can call in on Pelham on your way there.'

'I've never had to sleep with Pelham, for which I thank God. The whole point about Pelham is precisely not to sleep with him, but to hold out the promise until he would do anything to — but now I'm talking too much.'

My head was still buzzing, partly with the shell shock of what Augusta had done in the first instance and then with Caroline's arrival in the middle of it all. But my attention was caught by her discussion of Pelham.

'Get him to do what?' I asked.

'It's safer for you not to know that. In fact it would be safer for you all round to fall in line with whatever Giles Kingston wants. He always gets what he wants in the end. I don't think you understand quite what he is capable of.'

'Oh yes I do. I know all about van Pallandt, and what Kingston has done to Eva and Gordon Campion, what he's done to Dai and what he tried to do to Celia.'

'There are things you don't know. He's capable of doing much worse.'

'There isn't anything I can think of that's much worse than what he's already done,' I said.

'Like I said, he always gets what he wants. Still, I'm glad you didn't fall into line with his little plan for this evening.'

'I'm sure you are. I'm sure it's saved you a lot of unnecessary inconvenience and bother.'

'I didn't mean it that way.' Her voice seemed suddenly to waver, just ever so slightly. 'But then what does it matter what I mean.'

'And what has he done to you, Augusta? What hold has he got on you? Or is it just money?'

It was she who found herself unable to reply.

'No. It's not just money,' she said at length. 'I have no choice.'

And then, I suppose, I knew her for the first time.

11
DEADLINES

I was going to have dinner at Alison and Dave's Chelsea house. It was about a mile away from my flat and I decided to walk. Colossal flakes of snow had started to fall before I left and, like a child, I couldn't resist being out in them. Each season had its special associations but the hush of falling snow in winter was the time I prized the most. My mind always seemed sharper, more alive, in winter. I took a slight detour along the way, past Augusta's flat. I had looked up her address in the telephone book the day before. I don't know what made me do it; it was a spontaneous action and I had felt stupid afterwards. Nevertheless I experienced a schoolboyish kind of excitement at finding that she didn't live too far away.

Danny Leibowitz opened the door when I got to the Lesters'. I hadn't expected to see him but it was a nice surprise. I liked his company.

'Hello,' I said, 'I didn't know you'd be here.'

'Your head's all wet,' he said.

'I know, I walked.'

'In this? You must be mad.'

'Very likely,' I said.

When I got inside Alison was halfway up the stairs shouting at the children and telling them to go to sleep. Dave was sitting impassively in a chair holding a large Scotch, he was one of those fathers who secretly loved to hear his children making a racket and misbehaving slightly while Alison laid down the law. He pretended of course, to Alison, that she was absolutely right and their behaviour reprehensible, but he liked them best of all when they were naughty.

'Edward, hi,' he said. 'What would you like to drink?'

'Same as yourself will be fine.'

'I'll get it since I'm up,' said Danny.

'I didn't know you knew one another socially,' I said to Alison who had returned from looking after the children.

'He's Dave's cousin's son — from Newcastle,' she told me.

'Things must have come to a sorry state in the business world if Stoy's have to rely on employing the likes of him for their bread and butter,' Dave added.

'Thank you, Uncle,' said Danny.

'And stop calling me Uncle. We're cousins, a good distance removed, thank God. He's all right really,' he said, turning to me, 'but he talks too much.'

'It's a family trait, Uncle, you ought to know that,' said Danny.

'I'm sorry Caroline couldn't make it,' said Dave when we had sat down to dinner. 'When are you going to make an honest woman out of that gorgeous girl?'

'That's a bit unfair,' said Alison.

'Rubbish,' he said. 'If he doesn't marry her someone else will and he'll regret it for the rest of his life. They're perfect together.'

The fact was we weren't together at all. I had gone to her flat after Augusta had left, but Caroline hadn't been there. I had left a note under the door asking her to call me when she got home but she hadn't. I saw her the following day at work but it wasn't the place to sort out our personal life. 'We've got to talk,' was all I had a chance to say in passing out of Baker Street on my way to Tubelis. The next opportunity I had to see her was at a party given by a mutual friend. I hoped that I could explain everything then, but when I arrived there she had already gone. I went home and put everything in a letter. That had been a week before the Lesters' dinner and I was still waiting for some sort of a response.

'How's Gordon?' asked Alison, changing the subject. Campion was about to return to work at Tubelis.

'Not too bad. The thought of completing the project has

helped him keep his head above water. All the simulations and tests are complete and the final production blueprints were on the boards in the lab yesterday.'

After Gordon's suicide attempt, Romney and Alison had agreed between them to put the corporate venture offer on ice until Campion was ready to think about business. The suicide attempt had benefitted Hugo and Giles; if it had not happened when it did, Campion would probably have clinched the deal with Owen Romney weeks ago. But Gordon Campion was still far too brittle to care about business. He did care about his project, though — as a matter of pride and because of his belief that it would eventually stop much preventable suffering.

'I wonder why Dai Bunch resigned?' asked Danny. 'I can't believe it was for the same reason as Brownlees. He's too nice a bloke to be on the fiddle.'

Dai had taken his opportunity. He had gone back to Kingston & Kingston, perhaps feeling that Campion's suicide attempt had left him too concerned about the larger issues in life to bother pursuing a 'small time' thief into the courts. 'Small time' thief was how Dai would have thought of it; though the sums were anything but small, he had come to regard a thousand pounds as mere tissue paper, and now he was back in the City with his mentor.

Mischel was still in Tubelis, and so too Augusta; so until Campion recovered there was a position of stalemate. Stoy's did their best to keep Tubelis going and growing once more, while the Kingstons via Mischel and, I assumed, Augusta were doing their best to kill it stone dead, though I still couldn't understand fully what they were aiming to do.

'Funnily enough, I saw him the other night,' said Danny, 'in this wine bar I go to. He was with a crowd of people.'

'He usually is,' I said.

'I went over to speak to him, but he didn't seem as chatty as he normally is. In fact he didn't look very well.'

'Perhaps he had a lot on his mind,' I said. I didn't really want to talk about Dai; we had shared good times, and it depressed me to think about what had happened since.

'One of the people who stayed on in the wine bar after his crowd had gone told me Dai Bunch was into hard drugs, but I can't believe that, can you? He doesn't seem the type.'

'I don't think there is a type when it comes to that sort of thing,' said Alison.

I wanted Dave to launch into one of his monologues to cheer me up. I looked at the clock. It was a quarter past ten.

———

At precisely a quarter past ten the previous night, Pelham and Augusta had quietly entered the laboratories of Tubelis Research.

'Well, here you are at last,' Pelham said. 'This is where it all happens, where your little genius lets his brain run riot.'

Pelham had ideas of letting more than his brain run riot that particular night. He knew he was taking a big risk letting anyone other than authorised personnel into the labs, but it had occurred to the 'little genius' that it was perhaps the one place where he and Augusta could be completely alone. He knew from all the late nights he had spent there that the security guard was not due on his rounds for at least another hour. And, after all, hadn't she once said: 'I've got to be sure that we can trust each other completely.'

What was this if it wasn't showing his trust? Surely this would demonstrate just how much she could trust his love, if he was willing to take such risks?

'Now this,' he said, unfolding a massive sheet full of cell structures, DNA paths and equations, 'this is how things stood before I came to Tubelis — you see it's marked Formula A? I don't expect you to understand any of it, but it simply wasn't workable. All the basic conceptual requirements are there, but they could only be safely produced in minute amounts. Now wait a minute,' he unfolded another seemingly identical sheet on the table except that it was marked Formula B, 'this is the real McCoy — '

'The final formula and production details?' said Augusta.
'Yes,' he said, 'and what I'm going to do is try and explain
to you as simply as possible how we, or rather I, went from
Formula A, the dud, to this, Formula B, which works.'

Whereupon he guided her to all points in the laboratory
showing her charts, bits of equipment, computer print-outs
of statistical analyses, from time to time going back to either
Formula A or Formula B, and all the while keeping up a
totally incomprehensible commentary. By the time he had
finished there were only ten minutes left before the security
guard was due, and all time for dalliance in the laboratory
had elapsed. Pelham hadn't got what he wanted but Augusta
had; she now knew that Formula B was the one to deliver
to the Kingstons.

It was about two in the morning when I left Alison Lester's
house. Walking back after one of her dinners would have
been impossible, so I took a cab. When I got out I took a
few deep breaths of frosty night air and started fiddling in
my pockets looking for my key. I took another deep breath
and the very next sensation I had was lying face down in
the snow with a horrible pain between my shoulder blades
from the force that had been used to knock me down. I
know I said something when I was on the ground but can't
remember what it was. Then I was being turned over on
my back and two balaclava-clad figures were standing above
me. One of them loomed like the giant in the fairy tale, he
was huge.

'Not here,' a voice said, 'too many taxis go up and down,
get him round the corner.'

I let out a cry for help which was cut short by the giant
seizing my jaws and holding them open, while the other
one packed great handfuls of snow into my mouth until
I was choking. As the snow was being heaped into my
mouth I knew that I recognised the voice. Round four had
begun. It seemed likely that it wouldn't last very long. I
was hauled up under the armpits and dragged round the

corner. I couldn't get my hands to my mouth, as I so desperately wanted to, to pull out the snow. I tried to spit it out but there was too much of it and it was packed so tight. The inside of my mouth and tongue were being scalded by a brick of ice. I could see, in my mind, van Pallandt's grinning, lolling lips under his balaclava. My ordeal would be another, future, source of amusement to him — like the African tribesmen who had had their craniums ripped open by blunt stones. We were now round the corner and I was punched on the side of my face. This actually dislodged some of the snow in my mouth and I was able to spit most of the rest out. I saw the small figure pull out a knife and thought of bleeding to death in the snow. Then something happened that, in other circumstances, would have been absurdly comic. The punch to my face sent me back against the wall and the two figures were in front of me blocking any escape. Van Pallandt advanced, intent on pinning me against the wall to allow the smaller man to plunge the knife in at will. But in his haste to get to me his feet he slipped in the snow. Instead of falling down immediately, he automatically tried to compensate to keep his balance, with the effect that the balls of his feet kept sliding backwards alternately, while the rest of his body leaned forward at an angle of forty five degrees to the ground. His arms were pointed straight out from his shoulders and he looked like a vaudeville comic finishing his routine with a 'that's all folks' dance. The smaller man grabbed van Pallandt's arm to help him stay upright, but the vectors were all wrong and the bulk of van Pallandt brought them both down.

I raced round the corner and up the main road itself where the snow had cleared. They gave chase for about fifty yards and then gave up. I glanced over my shoulder and saw them running to a parked car. Thereafter it was a game of cat and mouse that seemed to go on interminably, me running, stopping, hiding, watching from the shadows as they went kerb crawling past me. I had originally intended to make for Alison Lester's but I realised it would be too far and I would need more luck than I was likely to get.

Nor could I risk standing exposed on some stranger's doorstep trying to explain through an intercom that they ought to let me in. There seemed only one viable option.

I knew I was very near Augusta's flat. Would she give me sanctuary? It hardly mattered anyway, given that I had no choice. There was no time to think about it, there would be no 'maybe' if van Pallandt caught up with me again. I scrambled through gardens, held my breath on steps to basements, froze at the sound of a distant engine, and cursed the light of street lamps. It felt so exposed, it seemed to me that I was obvious to anybody who cared to look. The night gave me no protection and I wondered how burglars ever got away with it. The more cautious I became, the more aware I was of the pain from the beating.

I pressed Augusta's intercom and said something, I can't remember what. All I remember was the buzzing as I pushed the door and the flood of relief at the thought of having got there. I had a vague image of Augusta coming down stairs and helping me to a bed — my head was splitting and I passed out. When I came round Augusta was dressed and packing clothes in a suitcase.

'Hello,' I said.

She came and sat on the bed next to me.

'What happened?' she asked.

'Van Pallandt and a friend.'

'Giles,' she said. 'I knew he would have to come after you. He wouldn't let you get away with having humiliated him.'

I told her what had happened.

'I don't think they would have killed you,' she said.

'Oh no?' I said. 'Well it looked very like it — that chum of van Pallandt's had a knife.'

'They were probably ordered just to beat you up and cut you a bit, that's all.'

'That's all?! That's enough! Anyway, what makes you so sure that they didn't intend to kill me?'

'Because I've seen it all before. Giles likes his victims to suffer for what they have done. Anyway I know he was under orders from Hugo not to kill you and Giles is too much of a coward to ever cross Hugo.'

'Why are you packing?'

'I'm going to take you somewhere I know you'll be safe.'

'But I thought you just said I was safe, that they weren't going to kill me.'

'That's right, but they'll be back with the knife to finish the carving-up operation, believe me. Giles won't be satisfied with just giving you a beating, he'll want to leave his mark on you. He's a psychopath; I learned that a long time ago and you had better learn it too. You're not safe. I know of a man in Sunderland who crossed Giles and his face and chest was so badly scarred that he became unrecognisable.'

'I don't understand, Augusta. Why do you work for him, why do you do what he wants?'

'Because I have no choice.'

'You said that before. Everybody has a choice, I told Dai that just before he left Tubelis. He shouldn't have gone back to Kingston & Kingston. I told him the only thing to do was to break with them, make a clean start.'

'You're being naive if you think it's as simple as that. Do you know Giles has made him a drug addict? He relies on Giles for the money to feed his addiction.'

A searing pain went through me as she said it.

'What are you going to do?' I asked.

'Did they see you come in?'

'No.'

'Good, they won't think I'm sheltering you. But I've got to get you out of London. I know a place where they'll never think of looking for you.'

'I can't just disappear, I've got my work to do.'

'It'll only be for a few days. I'm going to bargain with Giles for your safety.'

'How?'

'Never mind, I know what to do to stop him.'

'Why are you doing this for me, Augusta?'

'Because I don't want you to end up like the man in Sunderland.'

'Yes, but why are you risking upsetting the Kingstons?'

I got up but started to stagger when I was on my feet. My body hurt all over. Augusta helped me into her living room and sat me in a chair. I was surprised to find that her flat was not richly furnished, in fact it was quite ordinary. I had supposed that she had been paid well for her services to the Kingstons and expected her to live in more sumptuous surroundings.

'You haven't answered my question,' I said.

'I'm thirty three years old. I've had, let us say, an unusual life; things haven't exactly been easy. I have had to do some things that nobody should have to do. I don't like the world and I don't like the people in it. Any emotions I once had have been knocked out of me. I don't like being this way but I can't help it, I can't summon up feelings inside anymore. I'd like to be able to react, to feel something real, but however hard I try I'm left with the same blank. I know in my head that I will probably regret doing what I am about to do, hiding you from Giles, but I haven't quite yet abandoned all attempts to get things right.'

'Don't you care for anyone?'

'There is one person I care about very much.'

'A man?'

'Yes, his name is Julian. He doesn't live in London so I don't see him as often as I would like. But when I do I feel human again.'

'Known him long?' I said.

'Eleven years,' she said.

It was about four in the morning and the snow was falling again as we drove along the motorway.

'Where are we going?'

'The Dales.'

'The Dales?'

'Yes, Yorkshire. I have a cottage there, it is the only place where I ever feel happy.'

'Is Julian a Yorkshireman?'

'You may as well close your eyes and get some sleep,' she said, not answering my question. 'I'll wake you when we get there.'

When I awoke dawn was breaking and the whole of the countryside was covered in snow. The sky was cloudless and the light of the winter sun was slowly edging along the glorious valley of Coverdale.

'Do you think we could stop a moment?' I said.

She pulled over to the side of the road, and when I got

out I could hardly move I was so sore. We were very high up and the view looking down on the valley was one of calm magnificence which made me think 'this would be a good place to be buried'. And then I remembered van Pallandt and thought that nowhere is a good place to be buried.

'Have we got far to go?' I asked.

'We're almost there,' she said. 'It's beautiful here, isn't it?'

'Yes, it makes me feel like not wanting to leave, and that the rest of the world should just vanish.'

'But it won't,' she said.

We got back into the car and drove to her cottage. It was on the side of a large hill, completely isolated from anywhere, and reached by a narrow, winding track which was difficult to follow because of the cover of snow. The cottage inside was small and cold.

'Do you think you're up to lighting a fire?' she said. 'There are plenty of logs out in the shed, and some coal too. I'm going to drive into town, I've got to do something which could take a while. There isn't any food in the house, I'll pick some up while I'm there; there should be some coffee in the kitchen, though.'

I wandered out to the woodshed, and watched her driving back up the narrow track. 'She's going to her lover,' I thought to myself and started to stack the logs into my arm; it hurt. I lay down on the sofa in front of the fire and fell into a deep, dreamless sleep.

I must have been asleep for about three hours when I was awakened by the key turning in the door. It was Augusta but she wasn't alone, I could hear her talking to someone. I wondered if she had betrayed me. She came in with a young boy.

'This is Julian,' she said. 'He's big for eleven, isn't he? Julian, I'd like you to meet Edward.'

Julian stepped forward and shook my hand very formally.

'Julian, I want you to come outside and help me get some more wood. The fire's getting a bit low.'

On their way out I heard him ask:

'Is Edward your boyfriend, Mum?'

After lunch the three of us went for a long walk through

the snow. Julian was at a boarding school about twenty miles away.

'Being Saturday they didn't mind me taking him,' she said, 'but they won't let me have you tomorrow, will they?'

'No, we've got a rugby match against Arlington under-twelves,' he said.

'And they couldn't do without their star winger, could they?' she said.

'Mum,' he said, dragging out the word in a tone of amiable exasperation, 'how many times have I told you, my position is wing forward not winger.'

'There's a difference?' she said.

'Of course there is,' I said, 'one's a forward and the other's a back.'

'How very interesting,' she said. 'But to me there's no difference — all their limbs end up getting bruised or broken. My heart is in my mouth every time I know he's got a match coming up — which is once a week. You don't forget to wear that gum shield, do you?'

'Of course I wear it,' he said.

'Thank God, I don't mind bruises or even the occasional plaster cast, but I want you to keep your teeth.'

'Did you used to play rugby at school, Edward?' he asked.

'I still play it now,' I said.

'Oh not you too!' said Augusta. 'Then I haven't a hope.'

'What position?' asked Julian.

'Outside half,' I said. 'You wing forwards make life pretty difficult for me.'

He and I talked about who should or who should not be picked for the coming Lions tour and he spoke about his heroes with the earnest passion of boys of his age. The sporting heroes of my own past came back to me and I told him about them with an enthusiasm that was no different from his. When night started to draw in Augusta drove him back to the school.

After they had gone, I sat in front of the fire and stared into it. I had seen an Augusta that day who was so far removed from the clever businesswoman involved in the dirty work of Kingston & Kingston. Today she had been just another mother, albeit a very beautiful one, walking the hills with her rather ungainly wing-forward of a son. I wondered who his father was, and then for no logical reason at all it crossed my mind that he might be Giles Kingston's son and the thought made me feel sick. I was still staring into the fire trying to make sense of it all when Augusta came back.

'It's snowing again, very heavily,' she said, shaking out her coat and moving to the fire to warm herself. Her face and hair glistened with the melting snow.

'Well, what do you think of Julian? Are you still jealous of him?'

'No.'

'I can't, in fact, understand why you should —' she stopped, too reticent to finish.

'Be jealous where you're concerned?'

'Yes,' she said. 'I haven't exactly done much to make you feel anything for me, quite the contrary. What you do know about me isn't very attractive.'

'I know what I saw today. I know what risks you're taking for me now.'

I looked up and saw that her eyes were moist, that she was fighting back tears.

'I'm sorry, I didn't mean to — ' she beckoned me to her and when I moved to her she held onto me and cried quietly, her head on my chest, for what must have been a full five minutes. I stood feeling the heat from the fire on the back of my hands and the warmth of her strong back on my palms.

'I'm sorry,' she said without moving her head from my chest.

'Who is Julian's father?' I asked.

She gave a little laugh and stepped back.

'Just after I finished my first degree, I was twenty two. I went on vacation to the Cote Basque and one evening had a nonsensical, uncharacteristic and not particularly enjoyable fling. Julian was conceived in the foothills of the Pyranees. Of course I didn't discover it until I was back in England. I wrote several letters to his father and eventually got a reply but basically all he was saying in a very polite way was that it was my problem not his. That was OK, I wasn't writing to him for any reason other than I thought he should know.'

'Were your parents able to — '

'There was no one. I was the youngest child of elderly parents. My father died when I was too young to remember him, and my mother when I was sixteen. One of my elder brothers helped out a bit looking after Julian while I studied for my MBA, but basically I was left with my brains, a baby and not much else.'

'It must have been hard.'

'I don't regret having Julian, everything I've done since has been for him. I'm not a good mother in the conventional sense, but he's happy and that's all that matters.'

'Is it,' I asked.

I stood facing her with the silent snow falling outside and only the light of the fire burning inside with the same silence. The naked flame cast shadows over our bodies, as I moved to her and rested my hands on her shoulders. Her eyes were cast in the fire as I traced the line of the blades of her back with my fingers.

We closed together on the floor before the fire. She and I were equals, two distinct, very different people, meeting each other in the equality of silence between the fire and the snow.

We lay there for most of the night making love, then talking, then making love, with the stark realities of the world outside coming ever closer as the hours passed.

'What the hell are we going to do?' I said.

'About what?'

'About the Kingstons, about the horrible mess that you and I are in, along with everybody else that comes into contact with them.'

'They can't be beaten, but at least, if we're lucky, I should be able to prevent them from doing further physical damage.'

'I don't understand why you can't quit, just get out of it. And I also don't see how you can stop Giles from carving me up whenever he feels like it.'

'I have a certain influence.'

'What influence?'

'I'm his wife.'

I rolled on my side like a wounded animal. I felt physically sick.

'No, no, no,' she said, reaching over quickly and holding my shoulder. 'Edward, please listen — don't jump to conclusions, just hear me out. I was forced to marry Giles, I had no choice; you can't believe that I would choose to do it. I told you he's a psychopath, but like all psychopaths he's got a veneer of normality.'

I really didn't want to listen to any of it, there didn't seem any excuse she could offer for being Giles Kingston's wife.

'Giles was insanely driven by knowing for certain that he couldn't have me, and any thought of not being able to get what he wants fills him with violent fears about his own inadequacy.'

'I don't want to hear about your marital difficulties,' I said. It was cheap and I regretted it later, but right at that moment I felt everything, including myself, to be cheapened, easily bought.

'Do you think I wanted to marry him? You only seem prepared to credit me with some intelligence when it suits you. Listen, I had no choice. I had no choice!' She paused. What could I say?

She interpreted my silence as an attempt to sidetrack.

'I don't care, you're all the same to different degrees — Julian's father, Giles, you — nothing is acceptable unless it's on your own terms. Everything must be exactly as you want it, if it's not then kill it quick, stone dead, that's the way it is, isn't it?'

I got up and pulled my trousers on and sat on the sofa. She didn't bother about her clothes but remained sitting on the floor, leaning back on her arms, legs stretched straight on the floor, and looking into the fire.

'I'm sorry,' I said after a while. 'It's just a bit hard, that's all.'

'Everything's hard,' she said, 'but things are always less hard on others than they are on me. That's not self-pity, it's just a fact.'

'Go on,' I said.

'Is there any point?'

'Yes. And you can start by explaining why Giles has kept it a secret.'

'The sole reason for that is Hugo. You don't think Hugo would countenance anybody else having a claim on the Kingston fortune by allowing Giles to marry, do you? However much Giles may fear his own inadequacies, he fears Hugo much more. Hugo is no less a psychopath than Giles but he knows the meaning and the value of control, which Giles doesn't. Without Hugo doing his thinking for him, Giles couldn't exist and he knows it. And if Hugo ever found out that Giles was married then he most certainly would not exist; Hugo would have him killed along with myself.'

'But how did Giles get you to marry him?'

'By threatening to kill Julian if I didn't, it was as simple as that. Of course I didn't believe him at first; as I said they always have an advantage because you don't believe anybody could be capable of it. At first he offered me money to support Julian, he opened a bank account in Julian's name with a large deposit, but I wouldn't touch it — I will never touch it. Finally he said that he had a sure-fire way of proving to me that he was able to carry out his threat to kill Julian and to get away with it. He said that Hugo and he were going to arrange to murder their father. I thought he was mad, of course, but I also thought it was all talk, just a bluff. I had just placed Julian in his school and he loved it and was happy there. Everything I earned went into making him happy. It was three years ago, when Giles, knowing I would be up here visiting Julian, 'phoned me and told me to meet him in Crewe on a particular evening. He said that if I wanted to help my son and my job I must not fail to come. I went, but only to tell him that he could keep his job and that I was going to go to the police if he kept making threats. We met in an Indian restaurant and he told me that he was there, in Crewe, to complete the arrangements for his father's murder which would take place that night aboard a train. I still thought he was bluffing but his father's death was all over the news the following day as Giles promised it would be. He told me that if I went to the police van Pallandt had orders to kill Julian and make it look like an accident. The same thing would happen to me if I didn't give in and marry him. I knew now that he wasn't bluffing, that he was capable of murder. I couldn't take the risk for Julian's sake so I married Giles Kingston.'

'Does Hugo know you met Giles on the night of their father's murder? Does he know you know they had him killed?'

'Oh no, or I most certainly would be dead by now. Giles told me, by way of a boast, that they could kill their father without the police being able to trace it to them, however suspicious they might be. Van Pallandt, as you probably know, is not averse to killing people, but they couldn't use him. If something went wrong, or if van Pallandt was identified as being on the train that night, then he could be traced to them. But van Pallandt had friends in the killing trade and was instructed, without being told why specifically, to provide Giles with a number which would enable him to hire a contract killer from overseas. Giles handled the rest, there were no names, no faces, just monies deposited in Swiss accounts. The killer turned up in Crewe, as was arranged by 'phone, was given a photograph of his victim whom he knew would be on the train and that was it.'

'Who gave him the photograph? Giles?'

'Yes, after he left me; though the killer only saw the hand that passed it to him, in an envelope. Like I said, there were no names and no faces.'

'Except yours! Augusta, you must realise the danger you're in. No matter how obsessed Giles is with you there's got to come a time when he realises that he is never entirely safe while you live. He was taking an incredible risk meeting you in Crewe, making you a witness. Why did he do it?'

'Because he had to take the risk to get what he wanted, to convince me. Timing was everything; to make me believe he was capable of murder he had to tell me before, not after it happened. Laying claim to arranging his father's death afterwards was never going to be as convincing as telling me everything on the night it was going to happen.'

'So the only people who know are the Kingstons and you, and very probably van Pallandt and — '

'And now you. I've endangered your life by telling you, but no one will ever find out you know. I had to tell you to make you understand that the things I've done were not because — '

'It's all right, I wasn't exactly free from danger anyway, was I? But what about the police? Surely after the Kingstons' father's death the police must have realised that in spite of it looking like an accident or suicide, the only people to benefit from his death were his sons — they must have had their suspicions.'

'Of course, but suspicions are not proof. Hugo had a cast-iron alibi, he actually arranged to be seen at a public dinner in London that night. He had taken no part in the arrangements for his father's killing and the only person who could implicate him was Giles, and Giles couldn't do that without implicating himself. From Hugo's point of view it was foolproof. Giles wasn't quite so invulnerable, he made the arrangements, but after all van Pallandt was his own hired thug, he wasn't going to go to the police, and the "hit man", whoever he was, didn't know the name of his employer.'

'And Giles' whereabouts that night? How was he able to satisfy the police?'

'Somebody provided a sworn statement that Giles was in his apartment drinking all night.'

'Who?'

'George Mischel MP. Would the police have any reason to doubt the word of an MP?'

'I take your point — but then Mischel must have his suspicions too?'

'Well maybe, but Giles told him that the night his father died he was with some older married woman — Giles has a penchant for middle aged bodies, Mischel knew that because they live in the same mansion block. Giles said that the police would naturally want to question him, but that it would be very embarrassing both for him and the married lady in question if it came out. Mischel most likely believed him, but it doesn't really matter. Like van Pallandt, he knows which side his bread is buttered on.'

'God, so he really wasn't taking any risk by your knowing

he was in Crewe that night. Even if you went to the police it would be your word against an MP's.'

'Yes, and Giles would have killed Julian as he said.'

'Well I can't see how his alibi is any less foolproof than Hugo's.'

'It isn't foolproof, precisely because he gave an alibi.'

'I don't understand?'

'Giles is rash; he doesn't think things out in advance like Hugo, he just acts. He's like a spoilt child who can't wait for what he wants. He has to act, to get it immediately. For a start he arranged to meet me in a restaurant — '

'You mean he took the chance of being recognised?'

'No, there was not much chance of that. It was dark, the waiter didn't see his face because he had it in a book. And even if the waiter had seen him, would the waiter have any reason to remember him days, weeks, months later? Do you remember the face of the last waiter who served you? It's even more unlikely the other way round, when you serve hundreds of people a week.'

'True.'

'Anyway, the police weren't going to walk into that particular restaurant in Crewe and say "was this man here on such and such a night" — he was safe there.'

'So?'

'So although he knew it didn't matter particularly whether the waiter saw him or not if he had to be in Crewe to hand over the envelope, better in a dark restaurant than walking the streets. He still, however, took precautions, hence the head in the book. He didn't want to take it from his face when the waiter came with the bill. He assumed that I would pay, but I had left my purse in my car. He slipped a credit card on the plate, disappeared outside, got me to tell the waiter he was going to be sick and didn't want to throw up in the restaurant. I asked the waiter if I could take the credit slip outside for him to sign. He thought he was being so cautious, so clever. He signed the slip outside, I gave it to the waiter and gave Giles back his card outside —'

'And then what happened?'

'Nothing happened, we parted — but I had only given

him his card back, I had unconsciously crumpled up the receipt and put it in my pocket —'

'And you still have it?! Proof that he was in Crewe, date, place and signature!'

'Yes, and he had told the police he was with George Mischel that night, all night. I have proof that he lied to them, as did Mischel, that he was in the same city as his father on the night he died. I didn't consciously keep it — it was only afterwards when I was clearing out my pockets that I realised what I had.' She laughed. 'And Giles was being so cautious, so clever, he didn't want to put down his book, open his wallet and pay by cash — that would have required both hands, whereas he could feel for a card with one hand and remain incognito — Hugo would never have been so careless.'

'Augusta, you've got to give it to the police.'

'I can't, don't you understand? That's my insurance policy, I told Giles I had it —'

'You what?!'

'Or rather I told him, which is true, that a solicitor has instructions to send an envelope that contains both the receipt and a letter to the police in the event of either my death or, God forbid, Julian's death. If I go to the police, van Pallandt has orders to kill us. If we get killed the solicitor has orders to send the letter — it's a stalemate. Now do you understand why I am Mrs Giles Kingston?'

I moved from the sofa and held her to me tightly.

'I'm sorry for being so stupid, for doubting you,' I said.

'Don't worry about me,' she said, 'you understand that the receipt means Giles won't harm me, and I'll make sure he doesn't harm you. I'll tell him I've added a rider to my instructions to the unnamed lawyer, to send it if anything happens to you. It means we're safe.'

'It also means that you will never be free of him.'

'I told you they can't be beaten.'

'They've got to be beaten, not just beaten but completely wiped out. There's got to be a way.'

'There isn't.'

'And what are they really up to at Tubelis Research, apart from trying to bleed it dry which I already know? Why have they got you playing up to Pelham?'

She told me of their plans to steal the formula and the vast profits they would make by selling it to unscrupulous foreign manufacturers who could mass produce it without any of the stringent trials and safety checks Tubelis were facing. She told me about van Pallandt's role, how the contacts had been lined up by him. She laughed her way through her night in the laboratory with the ridiculous Pelham, her would-be-lover, and his dashing between Formula A and Formula B in an orgiastic state stimulated by his own vain sense of self-importance. Her job was almost done; she had got Pelham to show her what it was they needed to steal, or rather copy — Formula B.

'All I'm supposed to do now is to go down to the labs late next Wednesday night with the security guard, who is a Kingston's man, point out Formula B, and he will take the plans and replace them in the morning after they've copied them. That evening van Pallandt will be winging his way round the world and the Kingstons will be many millions of pounds richer by the end of the week.'

'We could, of course, stop them now you've told me what they're going to do. We could get Campion to sack the guard and remove Formula B to a safe place.'

'Yes, you could do that,' she said casually, as if it didn't matter.

'But then, of course, they will wonder how we found out, and you are the only person who would be in the position to give us that information. Hugo's revenge at losing all that money would be final.'

'That's right, you can either save Tubelis or save me, but you can't save both.'

I walked round the room. I looked at her stretched out on the floor and knew it would be impossible for me to abandon her to the wrath of H Desborough Kingston. Nor could I contemplate betraying the trust placed in me by the brittle Gordon Campion, who was trying to scramble out of the pit of an attempted suicide. We sat without saying anything for a long while. I had to make an impossible decision and she knew it. The sky began to lighten on a cold grey Sunday morning.

'I'm going to bed,' I said, 'I'm tired.'

'Have you decided what you are going to do?' she asked. 'Let Hugo make his millions by selling the research.'

'I shouldn't have told you, should I? I shouldn't have put you in a position to have to choose, but I felt that if I didn't tell you I would be deceiving you, that they would steal it anyway. I had to give you the opportunity to stop them if you wanted to. And you still can, I'm prepared to ride out Hugo's storm, to take my chances.'

'You wouldn't survive the week,' I said. 'After we get some sleep I want you to drive me back to London.'

'But what about van Pallandt? I'll have to make my deal with Giles first before — '

'There'll be no deals with Giles, and I'll take my chances with van Pallandt. Nobody is to know we've been together this weekend.' I looked her in the eyes and with a face that was expressionless and a voice that was cold said, 'And in future I would ask you to stay out of my life. I've given you yours by making the choice I have. I've had a lot of hours to think about how I shall feel about myself when the coming week is over, having betrayed Campion and all my colleagues at work. Tubelis will go under and the Kingstons will get what they want as you predicted. Then I want to make a clean break. I'll 'phone Giles when I get back and tell him that I quit. I don't want to be drawn into any further involvement with the Kingstons, either through you or anybody else. I just want to stay alive. I will stay on doing the work at Tubelis 'till it's complete. It wouldn't be fair to let somebody else come at this late stage. After which I shall resign and go away and try and pick up the pieces. As I said, I've had a lot of time to think, and this seems the only way out.'

'And you've had a lot of time to think about other things too. Caroline's her name isn't it?'

'Yes I've thought about her too. Like I said, I've got no option but to stay alive and pick up the pieces as best I can.'

'I understand,' she said. 'I don't see why you need even to leave your job. It's not your fault that the Kingstons are too ruthless and too strong. To the world it would be just another takeover, or just another company going under. Who's to know?'

'I would,' I said, and went upstairs to bed alone.

We drove back to London that afternoon. I don't know if Augusta had slept after I had gone upstairs but I suspected that she hadn't; she looked drawn. We drove back in silence. When we got to the centre of London I said: 'Drop me off anywhere. I don't think it would be wise to take me to my flat, someone might be watching and we can't risk being seen together.'

She pulled over to the kerb.

I got out and watched her drive away, knowing that to her, life was to be lived in the shadow of that great glass house that was the City headquarters of Kingston & Kingston Financial Services Limited; and that the shadow would be cast as far as a little boy playing rugby in the Yorkshire Dales.

I got in a cab and went straight to Alison Lester's house. Dave opened the door.

'Edward,' he said, looking me up and down. 'For God's sake, you look terrible, you look like you haven't slept for a week — you're wearing the same clothes you had on when you left here.'

'Dave, would it be a terrible imposition if I stayed here tonight?'

'Of course not, but you'll have to shave, you'll frighten the children wandering around like that.'

That evening I went round to Gordon Campion's house, talked to him for about an hour and went back to the Lesters' where I slept heavily. First thing the next morning I bought myself a suitcase, two new suits, several shirts, underwear, socks, ties, the lot. On the Monday night I asked Howard if I could sleep at his place. Sunday night I slept at Danny's, Wednesday at Bernard Wright's. In each case I neither left with whoever I happened to be staying with next nor explained where and why I was going. People asked but I was evasive. Neither did I go to Tubelis Research when I needed to be there. I stayed in my office in 8 Baker Street until it was time to go to someone else's house. I would vary my point of exit from the building, sometimes leaving by the front door, sometimes by the exit in the partners' car park. I was behaving in a bizarre fashion and people were starting to talk. On Thursday morning Caroline, who had not spoken to me since finding Augusta in my flat, could contain herself no longer.

'All right, what's going on?' she said, bursting into my office.

'What do you mean, "going on"?' I replied.

'You know what I mean, living out of a suitcase in other people's houses without so much as a "by your leave", not going to Tubelis Research when you're supposed to be there, sitting in your office avoiding people, and then creeping round the partners' car park in the evenings, sometimes waiting for an hour down there before you finally leave —'

'I don't creep round the partners' car park every evening, only some evenings, other evenings I creep round the front exit for a while before I leave.'

'People think that you've flipped, that you're having some kind of a breakdown or something.'

'And you don't?' I said.

'No,' she said, 'you're too bloody self-centred to have a breakdown. Only people with consciences are good enough to have breakdowns and you don't have a conscience.'

'Oh,' I said, smiling.

'But just in case you are having one,' she continued, 'I want to make sure it's not on account of — well — on account of our — our — '

'Breakdown,' I said, still smiling.

'Why have you got that idiotic grin on your face? I know what it is, people know we've split up — they don't know why, but they know we have — you're doing this to embarrass me, aren't you? You're trying to make me feel guilty? It would be just your style to do that. I hear you've asked Tom Harris in Personnel if you can stay at his place tonight.'

'Yes, but there's a bit of a problem there, he's not sure yet whether his wife's sister may be coming down from Walton-on-the-Naze and if she does it's out I'm afraid. Could I sleep at your place tonight, it would save a lot of problems?'

'You've got a bloody cheek,' she said.

'I mean on the sofa, of course.'

'You bet your life of course! You wouldn't be sleeping anywhere else in my flat, unless it was the bath.'

'Then I can stay?'

'I didn't say that.'

'But can I?'

'Only if you tell me what you're up to.'

'Thank you,' I said. 'Are we friends?'

'No we're not,' she said and then changed her tone completely. 'You hurt me very much, Edward.'

'I know,' I said. 'And you must believe me when I say that it was the last thing in the world I wanted to do, to hurt you.'

'Then you did sleep with that Augusta woman that night?'

'Not that night, no, but another night. Can I still sleep on your sofa? I'm in trouble, Caroline.'

She looked down at the floor, her straight blonde hair falling over half her face.

'Yes, if you're in trouble,' she said.

I didn't offer any explanations to Caroline. I made arrangements to get round to her place as late as possible, just before the time I knew she would be going to bed. I arrived, made up a bed on the sofa and went to sleep. I stayed in her flat for a full week and then one morning I 'phoned Giles Kingston.

'Well, this is a surprise,' he said.

'You probably know by now that I haven't been to Tubelis for some time.'

'I did hear rumours,' he said, obviously pleased with himself.

'Nor, as you probably know also, have I been at my flat. This is just to let you know that you win, your pal van Pallandt is very persuasive, so you can call him off — you might tell him also that wearing a balaclava may improve his looks but you can still tell it's him by the way he behaves.'

'I'm pleased to hear you've come round to our way of thinking. Is that all you wish to say?'

'No,' I said, 'I want you to arrange for me to meet your brother this afternoon.'

'My brother! What on earth for?'

'I want some of the action. I want to, as they say in spy novels, "come across". If Tubelis goes to the wall I haven't got much of a future here. I've got some useful information via Campion that he might be interested in buying. It's something he ought to know about, but it'll cost.'

'My brother rarely sees anyone,' he said. 'He does most of his business through me.'

'No disrespect, Giles,' I said, 'but I'm still a little wary of you at the moment, besides I want to go to number one if I'm going to negotiate terms. You must have realised by now that I'm not as much of a pushover as Dai or Harry and the rest of your playmates. I'm better than anything they can offer.' I put the 'phone down. Sometime later I got a call from Miss Muxloe to say that Hugo would see me at four o'clock that afternoon. I knew their curiosity would get the better of them.

When the time came to keep the appointment I got a cab. All the way to the City I felt myself getting hot, my chest, my neck and face were burning up, and my breath was short. Once inside Kingston & Kingston there would be no turning back; my own and other people's lives would be in the balance.

For the rest of my life I shall not forget the approach to that building. The rain was falling heavily and the cold wind that swept the whole area made it fall uniformly, suspended in little pockets that edged and collided with each other. Cold as the wind was, I was still burning up.

I seemed to be going up forever in the lift. I felt as though I was in my coffin on a big conveyor belt that was taking me to the Last Judgement. Hugo had the whole top floor of the building to himself. When I got out of the lift I was immediately in a large room with a single desk in it with Miss Muxloe sitting behind it. She ushered me through to an even larger room. It was enormous. She closed the door behind me. The room was so big I didn't immediately pick out Hugo Kingston sitting in one of the many armchairs.

'You're punctual, Mr Cartwright. I value that.'

'I hope you value the information I've got for you,' I said.

'I believe you have gleaned something via your association with Gordon Campion that you think will be of interest to

197

me, though I very much doubt you have anything to tell
me that I don't already know.'

I started to shuffle about nervously, he hadn't offered me
a chair.

'You appear to be somewhat agitated, Mr Cartwright?'

'Well, I must confess I am just a bit on edge — Mr
Kingston, could you tell me where your brother and van
Pallandt are right now?'

'Yes, I can tell you precisely where they are right now,'
he chuckled through that tight gummy mouth of his, clearly
enjoying my discomfort. 'I can usually tell you where most
of my employees are most of the time.'

'But not all of the time,' I said cryptically.

'I don't follow,' he said.

'Never mind,' I said, 'it's just that I'd feel a whole lot better
if I knew that they weren't hanging about on this floor.'

'Nobody "hangs about", as you put it, on this floor. My
brother and Mr van Pallandt are at this very moment
meeting in my brother's office.'

'Thank God for that,' I said. 'I've had the feeling all week
that van Pallandt's been following me about.'

'That's quite impossible,' he said. 'For the last week and
a half Mr van Pallandt has been flying round the world
finalising several business ventures for my company. He
only got back yesterday morning, so he couldn't have been
following you, could he?'

'Good,' I thought. So it's done.

'I hope he made a lot of money for you,' I said.

'Someone like you could never hope to even imagine the
money he has made for me. But time is also money, as
they say, and my time is valuable. What is it you wanted
to tell me?'

He was right about time being valuable, for me it was
critical. I had to get out of there before the end of normal
office hours.

'It'll cost you,' I said.

He looked at me as though I was some kind of little toy,
an amusement which was beginning to lose its appeal. He
had become so familiar with greedy young men they no
longer gave him the same entertainment value.

'How much?' he asked.

'Everything,' I said.

His face brightened up, maybe I was entertainment value after all. 'Everything?'

'Did you know your brother was married, Mr Kingston?'

'Married?' he said, screwing his eyes up tightly. 'I'm afraid you're very much mistaken.'

'You should be afraid, but I'm not mistaken. I have a copy of the marriage certificate here.' I passed it to him. 'You will see that I have blanked out the name of the lady in question, but it's real enough.'

'It can't be my brother that this refers to, it must be another Giles Kingston. He would never be foolish as to risk — ' he stopped.

'Getting killed?' I said. 'Losing his brother's affection? Which amounts to much the same thing. Have you banked all the money you made as a result of Mr van Pallandt's trip?' I threw this in, hoping to sell him a dummy.

'Of course,' he shouted, taking the bait. 'What's that got to do with this? I want to know the name of this woman that you claim is married to my brother!'

'You'd better ask him that,' I said, and walked towards the door. 'Oh and by the way, will you tell Giles when he gets here that I now have the credit card receipt.'

'Credit card receipt?'

'From the card he used in Crewe on the night you and he arranged to have your father murdered.'

Hugo looked stunned, there was no way he understood what I meant by the credit card receipt but that was as nothing to his incomprehension as to how I knew about his father.

'I almost forgot,' I said, with my hand on the door. 'The copies of the project formula you've had van Pallandt flog off for you. It's a dud I'm afraid; anybody using it won't even get to first base. You're going to have a lot of unhappy drug pirates on your hands, Hugo.'

I opened the door and left.

'Miss Muxloe,' I said, 'will you do me a favour? When Giles arrives in there, will you put your ear to the door and tell me what went on next time you see me?'

'I most certainly will not!' she bellowed.

'You ought to, you might hear them talking about how they arranged the murder of their father.'

Her eyes widened to the size of tennis balls. 'Never know' I thought 'she might just eavesdrop, no harm in trying to drum up extra witnesses for the prosecution'. I was now racing against time. I couldn't know what hour Hugo would set for our meeting, I wasn't sure he'd set one at all. I was unlucky that the time he chose was four o'clock, I had wanted it to be earlier. When I got outside the building, Howard was waiting with my car as I had arranged as soon as Hugo had nominated a time. Howard was not fully briefed with regard to what I was up to but he knew I was going after the Kingstons. I had 'phoned him from Campion's house the night I got back from Yorkshire and gave him advance notice that I might behave somewhat oddly in the coming two weeks — 'How will I notice?' he had said. I asked him to trust me. He did, as he had done from the very beginning at Stoy's, though it must have been difficult to shield me over those weeks when I appeared not to be doing my job. I needed to avoid going to Tubelis to convince Giles that I had been scared off, and to allow van Pallandt sufficient time to sell off as many bogus project plans as possible.

'Everything going OK?' he asked, getting out of the driver's seat and letting me in.

'So far, but I'm pushed for time, see you Monday — I hope.' I was on my way as I spoke.

I fought my way through the Friday evening traffic as best I could. At one point I was stopped at a set of lights beside a taxi. I glanced to my right as I waited for the lights to change, and in one of those chance occurrences, of no great import at the time, that return often in the coming years, I saw Dai in the taxi. His eyes were fixed on nothing, I could tell they saw nothing that was external; they looked inward to those dark recesses of the memory. He looked sick and his face had passed the point of mere despair. I automatically signalled to him but the lights changed, he did not see, and he disappeared with the taxi.

I drove into the Tubelis car park and took the lift to the

finance department. I flung open the door of Augusta's office. There were two or three other people with her; one was Pelham but I didn't notice who the others were. I grabbed her hand and ran her down the corridor to the lift.

'What are you doing?' she said out of breath in the lift. 'Where are we going?'

'First to the offices of that solicitor who holds the envelope with Giles' signature from Crewe, and please, please don't tell me his offices are miles from here —'

'They are,' she said, 'but I'm not going to tell you — '

'And then we're going to get Julian.'

'Julian?'

'I've just told Hugo, and Giles will know all about it by now.'

'Oh God.' All the blood drained from her face.

'Now for God's sake give me the solicitor's address. I want that envelope in the hands of the police who investigated Old Kingston's death.' By now we were in the car. 'I rang the detective concerned this week and told him that both Giles and Mischel had lied and I could prove it. I didn't mention your name just yet.'

'Why?! Why?!' she screamed. 'He'll kill Julian!'

'The address,' I shouted.

She gave it to me and I drove as fast as I could. It was now coming up to half past five. I thought of all the people that would still be working in Stoy's and I prayed that this solicitor loved his work as much. When we got there it was ten past six and he was gone. There was only a cleaner in the foyer of the building.

'Mr Adams,' he said, 'No, no, — he left about half-five.'

'Do you know his home address?' I asked Augusta.

'No,' she said, still in shock.

I asked the cleaner but I knew it would be a waste of time. I was starting to panic a bit myself. I knew Giles would dispatch van Pallandt as soon as he heard about the card receipt from Hugo. I pinned my hopes on a delay caused by the inevitable fracas that would take place when Hugo confronted Giles about his secret marriage. Hugo would also want to know what I meant about the receipt, as well as having to ponder on my claim that he had taken a bogus formula. I was gambling on van Pallandt's going after Augusta first, Giles would have wanted her out of the way first because she was a witness — Julian, being pure revenge, could wait. Just as we were going out the door the cleaner said, 'they sometimes all go for a drink round the corner on a Friday.'

We dashed into the pub and dragged an aggrieved Mr Adams back to his office.

'Couldn't it wait 'till Monday?' he said.

'If you don't get it quick we may not be here Monday,' I shouted.

He dug out the envelope and we, minus Mr Adams who grumbled his way back to the pub, were on our way to Scotland Yard. I left it for the detective concerned.

'Right, that should get them round to Giles straight away, which will mean van Pallandt will be cut off from his commandant, unable to get orders when he can't locate you. He'll come after you first because you're a potential witness, van Pallandt will go to Tubelis and won't find you, then he'll go to your — '

'But everybody in Tubelis knows I'm going to Yorkshire to see Julian this weekend!'

'Oh God,' I cried.

We were by now speeding up the M40.

'Why are you doing this to me?' she said.

'I'm not doing it to you, I'm doing it for you — and for Julian and Campion and Dai and the man in Sunderland whose face was cut up, and all the others who will never be free until the Kingstons are put away.'

'Where are we going, this isn't the quickest route to the North?'

'We're going to Kidlington Airport in the other side of Oxford. I've got a friend who has a private plane. I've arranged for him to fly us to the nearest airport to Julian's school. We'll get there before van Pallandt, he'll almost certainly drive there, he'll need a car for what he's got in mind, he needs to be mobile to kill cleanly.'

She let out an agonising cry.

'I'm sorry, I didn't mean to — ' I kept driving.

I was right, however; as it turned out van Pallandt did travel by car.

A terrible thought, a ghastly, so, so obvious thought hit me with a smash on my forehead. Why had I been so stupid? Why had I assumed that they would have to necessarily get hold of Augusta first because she was the witness? They could equally decide that all they had to do was to kidnap the boy, a far easier task; and Augusta would never go anywhere near the police, but come running to Julian and to them whenever they wished. The more I thought about it the more this seemed the most likely action on their part. I cursed myself, I was not attuned to thinking about this kind of dirty business; Giles had a head start on me there as well. That was precisely what he had done, in the midst of the most violent of arguments with Hugo he had dispatched van Pallandt post haste to 'get the boy'. I kept my thoughts to myself, I knew he would be well ahead of us by now. 'The 'plane will take care of that,' I thought.

'Sorry, Edward, there's just no way I can take her up, the pre-flight safety check shows there's something not right with the...'

My friend's words tailed off into a technical explanation that I didn't care to hear. I not only cursed myself again but I felt cursed. I tried to hire another plane but there wasn't one available. We had no other choice but to get into the car and drive.

'They are going to kill my son.' She said it so matter-of-factly as though she were commenting on the weather, it was the thin tones of shock that she couldn't help but use.

'No, nobody is going to hurt him, we'll get there before them.' I knew I didn't sound as if I was convinced of it, but I tried hard to.

As we were still driving through the country roads of Northamptonshire, van Pallandt was pulling into the service station on the other side of Leeds. He was feeling hungry; van Pallandt often felt hungry, but his appetite always seemed more voracious when he was doing the work he loved best. He noticed a camping wagon with a Dutch number plate on it pull into the bay behind him. They had passed and re-passed one another all the way up the motorway. 'From home', van Pallandt thought nostalgically; van Pallandt was prone to nostalgia. He greeted his fellow countryman, he was on a camping tour of England and Scotland, van Pallandt learned as they chatted over coffee. 'There's nothing like talking one's native language again after you've been deprived of the opportunity for so long,' he thought. 'Just talking becomes a pleasure.' But there was to be little time for pleasures of the conversational kind, other pleasures awaited him. He wished his fellow countryman a pleasant holiday and got on with his business.

Van Pallandt had arrived at his destination several hours before us. It was very late when we drove through the gates but there were a lot of signs of activity. There were more lights on than were normal and when we entered through the door the staff were milling about in earnest consternation. One of the boys had gone missing — the look on the headmaster's face as he approached us was an unnecessary confirmation of what we already knew.

The night passed by in the slow torture of Augusta's face, and the long morning wracked its way to an interminable afternoon. No news.

'I must go back to London,' she said; her first words in many hours. 'They will get in touch with me there.'

I was putting on my coat and searching its pockets for the car keys when a policeman walked in through the door with his arm around Julian's shoulders.

'We found him tied up in the boot of a parked car in a country road just outside Moorbeck,' the policeman said.

There was something else the police were yet to find off that country road outside Moorbeck; the body of van Pallandt. He was driving through Moorbeck just before dawn. The lights on the car behind him were on high beam and it was aggravating him. The lights were yellow and he was annoyed to think that somebody from across the Channel should be so inconsiderate; that he associated with the British. Julian, at this stage, was tied up on the floor in the back. After he passed through Moorbeck he decided that it was a good time to report back to Giles, who would be waiting. He slowed down, let the car behind pass and pulled into the side of the road. He bundled Julian into the boot, left the boot slightly open — 'We don't want any accidents just yet' he thought — and walked back to Moorbeck to the public telephone. He was disturbed not to find Giles on the number they always used for this sort of occasion. He was not to know that both Giles and George Mischel had been taken in for questioning. He ambled back down the road to his car. Van Pallandt was so used to abusing people physically and fatally that, unlike a first-timer whose nerves are ajangle, he knew that there was no real reason to ever rush things. He took his time at everything, even carving people up. He noticed a camper parked by the road, on the same side of the road but some distance form his own car. It hadn't been there on his walk to the village. He recognised the vehicle of his compatriot in the services cafe. 'Must have come through when I was on the 'phone,' he thought. All the lights were out and van Pallandt walked past. He got no more than ten yards when he dropped to the ground, dead. His body was rolled down a steep embankment. The camper drove off at a moderate speed. Monsieur Chastaret, now Rudi Martens, also enjoyed doing things leisurely. Giles, in the heat of the moment, with Hugo pressing him for answers, had forgotten that they had put a contract on van Pallandt to be carried out at the killer's convenience as soon after van Pallandt returned as possible. That night was convenient for Monsieur Chastaret.

I said my goodbyes to Augusta.

'You may have Giles, but there is still Hugo; he is untouchable.'

'That very much depends on what Giles tells the police; but I doubt very much if there is anywhere in the world right now where Hugo is untouchable. You see he sold, for many millions of pounds, a formula that could not do the job it was supposed to.'

'But that can't be,' she said. 'I gave the security guard Formula B. I know it was the same.'

'How do you know? You're not a scientist.'

'No, but Pelham is.'

'You mean Pelham was with you the night you identified the plans!?'

'I thought the original arrangements were going to be as I told you, but unbeknown to me Hugo was not satisfied with that. You're right, I'm not a scientist, there was just an element of uncertainty. He was going to make it foolproof. He had bought, either by money or by threats, Pelham. You know how successful they are at persuading people. Pelham verified that it was unquestionably Formula B that he handed to the guard.'

'Well, you see, I must have learned a thing or two from your erstwhile brother-in-law H Desborough. I think people trying to kill you sharpens the wits, even mine. I suspected that Hugo must have contemplated buying Pelham too at some point; I mean, it made sense to go straight to the horse's mouth and he certainly couldn't buy Gordon. Be that as it may, Gordon and I did a little buying of our own. We bought back the security guard for a lot more money than Hugo was paying him just to play postman. Gordon worked for three days from the time I left you, drawing up another Formula B, very similar in detail but with sufficient difference to make it not worth all the money van Pallandt's clients were prepared to pay for it.'

'You lied to me that morning in my cottage, didn't you? You never intended to leave the field to the Kingstons, did you?'

'No, but I almost slipped up very badly with the most important thing of all, didn't I? I thought I had worked out the timing of everything.'

'You couldn't have predicted that your friend's 'plane would be grounded.'

'There are a lot of things I find difficult to predict.'

'After I dropped you off in London, where did you go? You couldn't have gone back to your flat, it would have been too dangerous.'

'I still haven't been back to my flat. I've lived out of a suitcase for nearly two weeks with friends from Stoy's.'

'With Caroline?'

'Mostly,' I said.

'She's forgiven you, then?'

'No, but she didn't drive a stake through my heart while I slept.'

'I'm glad things have worked out for you, Edward. I'm glad there are no more victims, I've seen too many victims.'

'There will always be victims,' I said. 'It's in the blood.'

When I got back to London, I discovered that not only was Giles in custody, but that Hugo had disappeared. Without Hugo to think for him, Giles would damn himself in the eyes of the police. He was a liar but he was neither a consistent nor a clever one. Augusta told her story both to the police and to a jury. The kidnapping of Julian by van Pallandt, Giles' henchman, was sufficient to confirm its truth. Giles, in desperation, tried to shift all the blame onto Hugo, but it did not convince the jury. He was convicted of both attempted kidnapping and murder. I called in on Gordon before going back to my flat to thank him for the courage he had mustered when he was at his weakest.

'I feel my spirit coming back, for all sorts of things,' he said.

'I'm only interested in your entrepreneurial spirit,' I said jokingly. 'Let's see how your spirit is when it's lock-up time. Watch Howard, he's merciless, his invoices travel faster than the speed of light.'

'I've got Tubelis back, and my self-respect.'

'You'll get a lot of things back if you just give it time, and you won't just get things back,' I said, 'you'll get more. If I were you I'd look to a number of companies that you will soon be in a position to buy. Might be a good move.'

'Such as?' he said.

'Such as the subsidiaries of Kingston & Kingston Financial Services Limited, I hear they're pretty rocky. I'd give your old pal Alison Lester a ring in Corporate Finance, I'm sure she'll be able to help you. Give my regards to Eva.'

'I will,' he said. 'You know, Edward, she's a good sort. She may have been silly but a lot of that was my fault too. I don't blame her any more, she was more a victim than anything else.'

There was that word again, victim. I wished it would go away.

I went back to my flat craving sleep and the peace that

unconsciousness would bring. I was more exhausted than I ever hope to be again. I slept for hours and when I woke I eventually sifted through the accumulation of junk mail and bills until I came upon the first of a few real letters.

It was dated on that long day Augusta and I waited for news of Julian. I didn't recognise the hand. Phrases leapt out at me but I had to keep on reading to try and believe what my eyes were seeing. My eyes saw what my mind could not accept. Words, phrases; there was no real meaning in any of them, their only connection being disbelief.

'his best friend.......we are still trying to under-stand........cleverest at school of all our......doing so well.......his lovable......

And then his words of those years came back: 'I'll tell you why, I'm lovable that's why. As a child I could be as naughty as I liked and get away with it because a goodly dollop of lovableness was in my chromosomes.'

That was the essence of Dai's belief in the way the world should see him, and how it should treat him. The letter was from Dai's mother, telling that me he had died in a tragic accident. She could not write 'overdose of heroin'. Gordon Campion had tried to take his own life and was now, he said, 'getting his spirit back'. Who would give Dai Bunch his spirit back? How did he ever lose it in the first place?

I attended his funeral in Bargoed on a drizzling, valleys day. I was the only one of his university friends there, there were no work colleagues. One or two school friends who had stayed in Bargoed were there, the rest were family.

Celia would meet Ross McGregor again in a wine bar two years later, and they would marry and probably talk about 'fate', and she would have her children and not think much about her nursing days.

I put my wreath on his grave and found myself saying audibly, 'Better luck next time, Bach'. What did I mean by that? Words again; they just slip out and that's an end to it.

In his parents' house after the burial I heard his father say to someone in his thick Hungarian accent, as he pointed out of the window: 'Look at that. You don't buy something like that if you're not doing well; you don't own one of those unless you work hard. That must have been it, he was working too hard; the pressures, they get these young boys to work too hard these days — they should have more fun like we used to when we were young.'

I looked out of the window and saw Dai's midnight blue Morgan standing in the rain.

A few days later I was offered the financial directorship of Tubelis Research. I turned it down, though only after a lot of soul searching. My future at Stoy's seemed too promising to accept even that opportunity. But it brought Dai to my mind again.

———

Caroline was looking at me, demanding eye-contact, and waiting for me to answer. 'Please tell me that was real at least?' was the question she had asked. But that wasn't really a question, it was an order to answer in the affirmative.

'Caroline, I'm too tired to do any more sparring tonight. Too tired to talk round things.'

'How do you mean?'

'If we're going to talk, let's talk about the present, what we are now, how we feel now. You seem to want something from me that I can't give. Maybe if you came straight out and told me what you want I could give it.'

'Well,' she said, putting her hand on my arm, 'that's just the problem. I really don't know, but I'll try a few things on you, OK?'

'Ready,' I said.

'Do you think I should marry Stephen? And please don't give me an "if you want to" answer.'

'No,' I said.

'Why?'

'Because I don't think he's got enough "fun" in him to make you happy.'

'Do you think you have enough "fun" in you to make me happy?' she said.

'Yes,' I said, remembering the bitter words that had been

exchanged after she had demanded the truth about my relationship with Augusta. I had explained to her about the time she found us together in my flat, that I was being set up, but I also felt compelled to tell the truth about that night in Augusta's cottage.

'Ah, but there you are, sometimes what you call "fun" scares me. But you expect to be matched equally all the time, and for someone like me who likes to do things in the ordinary normal ways a lot of the time, perhaps even most of the time, it can be a bit scary. It very often makes me feel that I'm not doing my bit, not keeping up, not entertaining you in the way that you want.'

'That's not your fault, it's mine,' I said. 'I want change too much — people, places, things. I get restless too often and you, perhaps, don't get restless often enough.'

'Do you think we could ever go back to the way we were?'

'We could, but I think it would be a mistake.'

'So do I,' she said. 'Can I get you another drink?'

'No I don't think so, thanks — perhaps after work tomorrow.'

'Look forward to it,' she said, pretending to be polite but businesslike, and shaking my hand with equal mocking formality.

'Don't look forward too much. I'll be in a foul mood after the first batch of queries from Louise. I gave her a brown-paper-bag job to do at the end of last week with one of the juniors. The bank statements only turned up this morning. Still, she asked for an awkward job.'

'You asked for the same three years ago, I remember.'

'And look where I ended up,' I said.

'You're off on an overseas trip very shortly, aren't you?'

'Yes, and then I'm going to take my winter holiday.'

'Skiing?' she asked. 'Switzerland? Austria?'

'No, in front of a fire in the Yorkshire Dales. I've got a feeling I shall spend all my winter breaks there from now on. There's something about that particular fire that will always draw me back to it.'

'And you're the one that's supposed to crave change. See you at Stoy's tomorrow.'

'Yes, see you at Stoy's.'